"*Love in All the Wrong Places* is a really good novel."

—Robert B. Parker

"With wit, pathos, searing psychological perceptiveness, and a crystalline prose style, Frank Devlin takes the femme fatale where she has never gone before—into the dark, lonely shadows of the human heart. The characters in *Love in All the Wrong Places* display a convincing humanity wrestling with their loves and failures at love while also negotiating the messy, odd, ironic, and sometimes brutally hilarious realities of American murder. Meanwhile, the story capers along with a deceptive briskness, to the point that the reader often has to stop just to savor the brilliance of a particular turn of phrase or insight. Books this smart should always be this entertaining. A savvy little gem."

—David Corbett, author of *Done for a Dime*

"Devlin writes a mean sentence and has the sensitivity to make you care about even his most unlovable characters . . . beautifully presented." —*Kirkus Reviews*

"Pick up this smart and stylish novel. Enjoy the sleek prose, suspenseful storytelling, and witty repartee."

—Eddie Muller, author of *The Distance* and *Shadow Boxer*

"Enthralling." —*Midwest Book Review*

Love
in All the
Wrong Places

Frank Devlin

JOVE BOOKS, NEW YORK

THE BERKLEY PUBLISHING GROUP
Published by the Penguin Group
Penguin Group (USA) Inc.
375 Hudson Street, New York, New York 10014, USA

Penguin Group (Canada), 90 Eglinton Avenue East, Suite 700, Toronto, Ontario M4P 2Y3, Canada
(a division of Pearson Penguin Canada Inc.)
Penguin Books Ltd., 80 Strand, London WC2R 0RL, England
Penguin Group Ireland, 25 St. Stephen's Green, Dublin 2, Ireland (a divison of Penguin Books Ltd.)
Penguin Group (Australia), 250 Camberwell Road, Camberwell, Victoria 3124, Australia
(a division of Pearson Australia Group Pty. Ltd.)
Penguin Books India Pvt. Ltd., 11 Community Centre, Panchsheel Park, New Delhi—110 017, India
Penguin Group (NZ), Cnr. Airborne and Rosedale Roads, Albany, Auckland 1310, New Zealand
(a division of Pearson New Zealand Ltd.)
Penguin Books (South Africa) (Pty.) Ltd., 24 Sturdee Avenue, Rosebank, Johannesburg 2196,
South Africa

Penguin Books Ltd., Registered Offices: 80 Strand, London WC2R 0RL, England

This is a work of fiction. Names, characters, places, and incidents either are the product of the author's imagination or are used fictitiously, and any resemblance to actual persons, living or dead, business establishments, events, or locales is entirely coincidental.

Lines from "A Drunken Man's Praise of Sobriety" by W. B. Yeats reprinted with the permission of Scribner, an imprint of Simon & Schuster Adult Publishing Group, from *The Collected Works of W. B. Yeats, Volume I: The Poems, Revised*, edited by Richard J. Finneran. Copyright © 1940 by Georgie Yeats; copyright renewed © 1968 by Bertha Georgie Yeats, Michael Butler Yeats, and Anne Yeats.

LOVE IN ALL THE WRONG PLACES

A Jove Book / published by arrangement with the author

PRINTING HISTORY
G. P. Putnam's Sons hardcover edition / August 2004
Jove mass market edition / September 2005

Copyright © 2004 by Tim Farrington.
Cover design by George Long.
Cover photos by Getty/Photographer's Choice (Couple Kissing) Chad Ehlers; Getty/Stone+ (Naked Woman) Matthias Clarner.
Interior text design by Meighan Cavanaugh.

ISBN: 0-515-13954-8

JOVE®
Jove Books are published by The Berkley Publishing Group,
a division of Penguin Group (USA) Inc.,
375 Hudson Street, New York, New York 10014.
JOVE is a registered trademark of Penguin Group (USA) Inc.
The "J" design is a trademark belonging to Penguin Group (USA) Inc.

PRINTED IN THE UNITED STATES OF AMERICA

10 9 8 7 6 5 4 3 2 1

Acknowledgments

Heartfelt thanks to the marvelous Leona Nevler, my editor, for her friendship and the fineness and savvy of her shaping efforts. A special thanks to Elinor Lipman for her deft reading, sweet appreciation, and encouragement of the shaky work-in-progress, to Kate Johnson for sharing the journey, and to Andrea Marks for laughing at all the right places. Laurie Horowitz remains a true friend and welcome fount of healing hilarity. I owe an ongoing debt of gratitude to Linda Chester, of Linda Chester and Associates, for her unflagging support and kindness, and thank God, as ever, for Laurie Fox, my agent, friend, and finest comrade in arms.

O mind your feet, O mind your feet,
Keep dancing like a wave,
And under every dancer
A dead man in his grave.

—W. B. YEATS

1

H E LOOKED SO BEAUTIFUL as he came into the bar that for a moment Helen was sorry he was going to die. She didn't even know his name yet, but she'd known for almost a week that he was the one. Their eyes had met on the previous Monday, once, and then twice. A slow night, her trolling night. She'd fingered her empty bottle and he alertly bought her a beer. As the bartender put the drink down, he'd moved from the end of the bar to sit beside her. Modestly, tentatively, even a little fearfully, she thought. But he was easily encouraged. He had soft brown eyes, like a koala bear, and a sweet, eager face. She'd wanted to touch his perfect rounded ears, to run her finger along the razored edge of his fresh corporate haircut. Instead, they chatted about the relative merits of domestic versus imported beer. He had strong opinions about beer, which struck Helen as ridiculous. But that was what you got in bars.

He was just past the age of getting carded, maybe thirty, his black hair receding slightly, combed and moussed to delay the inevitable. He was tired from work—he did something with mutual funds—but he'd perked up at her attention. He talked about cars, and then the Giants, more ridiculous opinions; and finally, just when she was about to give up on him, about fishing, which he really loved. He lit up describing a Montana trout rising to some bug he'd tied himself and she had watched his face and thought, Maybe you will love me, too.

She'd checked her do in the mirror behind the bar: every freshly platinum hair in place. A simple cut, short, with a hint of a Jean Harlow wave. She liked her blond phases. She liked her blue-eyed phases. She looked like Miss Iowa with laugh lines, a corn-belt beauty queen dressed to kill in the glittery, breast-hugging silver blouse she only wore as a blonde, a taut black skirt that showed off her fine long legs, and black stiletto heels pitched at what she liked to think of as a fuck-me angle. Her earrings were understated gold hoops, the real thing, her eyes were deftly lined and shadowed with a breath of blue, and she smelled of L'Air du Temps. She was overdressed for this bar, but there was no sense wasting time.

The kid had talked on, more fishing, going with what had drawn the best response. A simple soul. She'd nodded, caressing him with her eyes and letting him think for half an hour that this was his lucky night before she'd drained the Rolling Rock in a way that would have made her mother cringe and plunked the bottle down. He'd already been reaching for his car keys, but she'd shaken her head and given him a smile, and told him she came in on Fridays, maybe she would see him then.

Now it was Friday and here he was. Dressed in crisp gray slacks and a black silk shirt opened one button too far. He spotted her the second he came in, but he played it cool. She hated that, the false survey of the rest of the bar crowd, the pretense of a second recognition. The pretense of surprise. Even his too-broad delight was pretense by the time he got around to displaying it for her benefit. He'd have done better to have just come in and frankly looked for her. Done better to be vulnerable. But still, he'd do.

Maybe you *will* love me, she thought as he crossed the floor toward her. He was still hedging his bets, ready to veer toward another stool if she didn't broadcast welcome. She tossed her shiny hair, gave him a perfect smile, and thought again, Maybe you'll love *me*.

His name was Henry and his Marina apartment was modest but neat, a bachelor pad without much ambition or personality. A single shelf of books, Dean Koontz and Stephen King in bargain-bin hardbacks, some utopian best seller about the future of the Internet, a family Bible, touchingly discordant, and computer manuals. The furniture was newish and nondescript, and none of it quite blended. She had the impression he had bought it piecemeal at separate clearance sales. The living room's only item with any character was an exquisite old mirror in a lavish Queen Anne frame, blackened with age. His grandmother's, Henry explained sheepishly. He seemed to think the piece was a flaw in the tapestry somehow, an item unbecoming to the hip man-about-town, but it endeared him to Helen. She liked a man with his grandmother's mirror on the wall.

The refrigerator smelled of stale fish and was filled with Chinese takeout boxes and German microbrews. Helen accepted something in a green bottle with an unpronounceable name. Henry assured her it was sublime.

"I'm not looking for sublimity in my beer," Helen said.

Henry laughed uncertainly. He was going to go on about the damn beer, she saw, how he'd discovered it in a charming little *Bierhaus* in the Black Forest or something, and to head him off she set her bottle down on the coffee table and stepped closer. He stopped talking instantly. She stretched out her hand and ran her index finger from the base of his throat to the place where he'd left his shirt unbuttoned. His chest was wonderfully smooth, a little weak but warm and taut. She felt his breath quicken.

"Skin hunger," she said.

"What?"

"Skin hunger. We're all starved for simple touch. It makes us come alive." He'd drawn his abdomen tight beneath her fingertip, sucking in the beginnings of a belly. A man with rigid ideas about what it was to be a man. She swirled her finger gently, a soothing circle below his heart, and met his sweet koala's eyes.

"Relax," she told him. *"Relax."*

"You're . . . so beautiful," he murmured. "I can't believe . . ."

His voice trailed off. Helen felt the first searing touch of compassion. Of tenderness, that dangerous thing.

"That someone like me would want to sleep with a schmuck like you?"

He smiled ruefully, chagrined to hear it said so baldly, but nodded. Bravely, she thought. He was real suddenly, made real for a moment by her touch, by the rise of his skin to her finger's tip. She traced a line back up to the center of his chest, found his heart with the flat of her hand, and felt it leap. She could see the two of them in his grandmother's mirror. They looked incongruous together, a platinum-blond panther and a Labrador retriever in a black silk shirt. He was so earnest, so well-meaning, so hopeful in his canine good-will. And so utterly futile, playing it so badly by the numbers. She felt another pang of dizzying compassion.

"I'm going to tell you a secret, Henry," she said. "I don't think it will do you any good. But I hope it does."

"I'm listening," he said. He really did have the sweetest eyes.

"Two secrets, actually. Three. Hell, Henry: I'm going to tell you as many secrets as you can stand."

"I'm listening," he asserted again, meaning it.

She almost kissed him then and there. Instead, she buttoned his third button for him. Henry's face fell a little. Buttons going in the wrong direction. A simple man.

"First secret," she said. "Everybody knows you've got a chest, Henry. But only a few people want to see it."

He swallowed gamely and nodded.

"Are you up for this?"

"Go," he said.

"Okay. Second secret: You're not a schmuck." Henry smiled his uncertain smile. "Seriously, you're not. You try too hard, I think. You're in the grip of silly ideas and you may lack imagination. But you're a sweet man. A good man."

"I like that secret." Henry smiled.

"I've got more."

"Do they get better?"

"They get more dangerous."

"Then maybe I'll quit while I'm ahead."

You're not ahead, she thought. But she held her tongue and waited. Henry, buoyed by the banter, met her eyes with what probably passed for boldness in his usual circles. Helen gazed back impassively, conscious of her own eyes hooded into cool blue by the lenses, of her hair shining like a knife. Henry's jaunty look wavered, and his eyes fell away. Noticing the bottle she had set on the coffee table, he hastened to slip a coaster under it. And suddenly she wasn't sorry anymore that he was going to die.

While he saved the surface of his coffee table, Helen crossed the living room and stood before the broad window that looked down onto Chestnut Street. She would be out there soon, back into that night, torn free from all pretense. The thought was comforting. She wondered if that made her evil.

Behind her, Henry bustled quietly. He slipped a CD into his expensive system, and the relentless strains of *Bolero* began to swell. He turned off the overhead light, and clicked the three-way lamp to its dimmest setting. They were going to do this by the numbers after all, without leaving rings on the furniture. When he finally crossed to stand behind her and put his hands on her bare shoulders, his fingers were cool from holding the beer. Helen closed her eyes, hoping that his hands would warm up before they really got into it.

"One more secret?" she suggested, without turning.

"Why not?" Henry agreed, burying his nose in the bend of her neck.

"It's not about sex, Henry."

"Of course it's not," he said, humoring her, comfortable now with things in motion. He turned her by the shoulders and kissed her, competently enough, a warm meeting of lips, and then a deftly probing tongue. His hands slid down to her elbows, thrillingly, and then to her breasts. She murmured involuntarily.

"So what's the secret?" he smiled.

"That was the secret, Henry."

"Ah!" he said, and kissed her again, gently, to show that he understood it was not about sex.

"You smell so wonderful," he breathed into her hair. "You smell like—"

"Jasmine and gardenia, with peppery rose, on a bed of sandalwood and iris," Helen said. "Could we get on with this?"

His bedroom was the only room in the apartment with a coherent decor. No grandmother's mirror here; it was definitely about sex. The bed was king-sized, with a vermilion velvet spread, flanked by Cupid lamps with red shades. The walls were some sort of gaudy crimson that turned blood-red when Henry dimmed the overhead light. A clicker kicked the stereo on: Chopin in a dreamily passionate mode. Helen had the impression that Henry had bought copies for each room of *Classical Music for Seduction* from the 800 number on a TV commercial. *Bolero* was still thrumming in the living room, an uneasy background dissonance. She briefly considered fine-tuning his technique, then decided there was no point.

There was art on the walls, unlikely Georgia O'Keeffe prints, a giant purple petunia, a pelvic-looking bone beneath a blue sky, and, over the bed's massive mahogany headboard, a frankly vaginal lily. The sliding wardrobe closet was mirrored from floor to ceiling, which had the odd effect of making the room seem at once enormous, crowded, and claustrophobic. There was a mirror on the ceiling above the bed, too, glowing with the breathed-on embers of the room's lit reds like a window into a circle of hell. There was a big-screen TV, mercifully blank.

Henry was waiting as if he'd opened Tutankhamen's tomb for her. Helen said, "I sense a theme here."

"It's my little retreat," Henry demurred.

"Not exactly a trout stream, is it?"

He laughed, brought up gratifyingly short; she thought for a moment that there was hope. She reached to gently touch his cheek, and he turned his face into her hand and closed his eyes like a child.

"Who taught you to fish?" she asked.

"My grandfather," he conceded. He didn't want to mingle his passions.

She waited. Henry opened his eyes at last and gave her a sheepish look. "He had this summer cabin east of Billings," he said. "It was like a religion with him. My father hated it, the whole fishing thing. Said What's the point of standing around freezing your ass off in a stream to catch something with no meat on it? But I'd spend two weeks up there every July." He smiled, remembering. "God, my grandmother could cook those trout."

"It doesn't have to be about eating," Helen said. He gave her a sharp, almost hopeful look. "It doesn't even have to be about catching."

He considered that for longer than seemed necessary. She wondered whether he was making another clumsy point—*See, I'm taking you seriously*—then decided, no, he really was a little slow. She liked that. She pictured him on one of his trout streams, mulling the speedy world at his leisure, dropping a dry fly in a quiet spot. Comfortable with the pace.

At last his eyes came back to hers. Her hand was still on his shoulder and he brought his own right hand up to touch her cheek in turn, tentatively, gently, even a little wonderingly, as if seeing her for the first time. She moved her own hand to trace his cheekbone again, holding his gaze. They stood like that for a moment, mirroring each other. The Chopin was too loud and the room was too red and there was that damned *Bolero* pounding away in the other room and a second clicker on the table by the bed, no doubt the TV, preloaded with a tastefully erotic video. If she pushed him too hard, he'd take a stuffed and mounted trout out of the closet and put it on the wall. But for the moment, for just this moment, it was right.

Henry's free hand drifted to her hip. Seeking nothing, a light, fond touch. She swayed a little, meeting the pressure; his hips answered spontaneously and for a moment, somehow, they were dancing. To Chopin's andante, or maybe it was the Ravel. It didn't matter. She leaned into him. Henry's nose found her forehead at the hairline and she heard him breathe her in with a sort of sigh.

Don't tell me again how good I smell, she thought, just before he said, "You smell wonderful."

"Jasmine," she said dryly. "And gardenia."

To her surprise, Henry caught the tone at once and shook his head at himself, chagrined. "Right. Of course."

"With peppery rose—"

"Right. On a bed of sandalwood and iris."

"At least you pay attention."

"You scare me," he said ruefully. "I don't know why."

The vulnerability touched her. She reached for his hair with her free hand, bent his head to hers, and kissed him. It caught Henry off guard, and he floundered for a moment. She kissed him more deeply, caressing his tongue with hers, softly probing. Their hips had drifted out of contact and she took his belt and drew him against her, pivoting to bring her thigh up into his crotch. She could feel his surprise rippling through the places where they touched, an instinctive flinch, like the jolt of a hooked fish as the line went taut. He actually tried to pull away, to regain control, but she kept her mouth pressed to his. Insisting, tenderly, holding him by the hair until suddenly something in him yielded and he was kissing her back. Surrendered to it, as she was surrendered to it. His tongue came alive in her mouth and she was conscious of his hands on her bare shoulders, warm now, and hungering. She let his energy swell to meet hers, let the pulse of him move through her in rising waves until she couldn't tell where he began and she left off, as if they were chambers of the same heart, joined by the surge between them. And then she broke it off and stepped back.

Henry looked at her dazedly, panting a little, his hair standing out at the side, still crumpled into the shape of her fist. She reached out to smooth it.

"I'm scared, too, Henry," she said gently. "Don't you see? That's just the way it is. If you're not scared, you don't know what's going on."

He laughed nervously and shook his head as if to clear it. Helen held her breath, feeling the moment alive between them, delicate as a fresh-laid egg, warm and real and palpable. Feeling the still unshattered possibility, and the fragility of it. Be real, she thought. Please. Please please please. Don't bullshit me. Just take the chance.

But Henry said reassuringly, "You're safe with me, sweetie. I promise. You really are."

"I suppose I am," Helen said, and she felt the sadness rise in her, the weird liquidity of grief, viscous amid the shards.

He was back in his comfort zone after that, and it began to get tedious. They made out standing there, necking like two high school kids in a corridor between classes. Henry was a competent, earnest kisser, with a busy tongue and a lot of hand action. Freshly fortified against the demons of vulnerability, he was even a little aggressive, cupping her breasts fiercely and massaging her ass with an almost comic passion. The moment had passed, Helen thought; the egg was dropped. Assured of sex, Henry appeared to be content to just get on with it in workmanlike fashion. And she wondered, as she always did, if what she had glimpsed was a lie, if she had made it up because she wanted so much to see it, however fleetingly. But it didn't really matter anymore. The wheels of the same old thing were in motion, and it was just a matter now of rolling through.

Before they got into the bed, she sent him out into the living room to turn off the *Bolero*. Henry seemed surprised, and even a little put out by the request. Perhaps he found her unappreciative; perhaps he just didn't like the brief delay. But he complied. While he was out of the room, Helen turned off the Chopin.

"Could you close the front drapes, too?" she called, in the sudden, delicious silence.

"What for?" he asked, more grudging in his voice. The touch of pique made it easier, somehow.

"It's a signal to my jealous boyfriend. He's out front, waiting to come in here and kill you."

"Ha-ha," Henry said, clearly deciding to humor her, and Helen heard the clickety-slide of the curtains closing.

She kicked off her heels and slid out of her dress, letting it drop in a silken heap at her feet. She'd worn the smooth blue spaghetti-strap number precisely because it was so easy to get out of. And to put back on. She was wearing no underwear. She never did. She loved good underwear too much to wear it for some urgent idiot who wanted nothing but to get past it. Good underwear was for second dates, and she hadn't had a second date in years.

She could hear Henry rummaging in the refrigerator. Wasted effort, but he couldn't know that yet. Helen lay down on the bed and looked up at herself in the obscene sweep of the ceiling mirror. The red glow of the lamps made the tanning-salon gold of her flawless skin seem a little muddy, she noted with a critical eye, but on the whole, she'd held up well: the legs still firm, long and shapely, shaved smooth for tonight; the flat belly framed by the gently prominent points of her hips; the high breasts so round and full that men invariably asked at some point whether they were real, apparently under the impression that she'd take the crudeness as a compliment. She always marveled at the sight of herself, as at a beautiful stranger. Because the weariness didn't show. Her body, somehow, was still eager, still seeking. Her body still hoped, and longed, and hungered. It was her soul that felt so tired.

Henry came into the bedroom with two fresh beers. Businesslike now, even a little brisk, prepared for the challenges of the next round of what he no doubt still thought of as a seduction in progress. His face lit up at the sight of her lying there naked, a look of pure naïve delight as obvious as the wagging of a puppy's tail. Mission accomplished, that bright gawk declared; it was all over but the fucking. He hurriedly found two coasters and set the beers on the bedside table.

"For afterward." He smiled, apparently in the grip of the notion that it was his suavity that had accomplished this miracle. He'd go to his grave without ever knowing he should have stuck to fishing. Because all Helen could think now, as he turned the Chopin back on, was, Damn, his hands are going to be cold again. He was so pleased with himself, so utterly and imperviously pleased, that she wasn't sorry at all anymore that he was going to die.

2

SFPD INSPECTOR ROSE BURKE gave herself a last critical look in the bathroom mirror and frowned at the threads of gray that ran through her silken black hair like spiderweb cracks from a bullet hole. It was as if certain spots on her head were aging faster than others. Maybe it all began in her brain, she thought. There were parts of her brain that were way, way too old. She had to start thinking younger thoughts.

"I'm thinking about coloring my hair," she called to Seamus, who was knotting his tie in the bedroom.

Her husband just grunted and tightened the knot at his Adam's apple. Putting on the cyanic blue PsiberSystems tie was the worst moment of every morning now. Worse than donning the damned corporate blue pants, which Seamus insisted on calling slacks, to register his self-contempt; worse than the inevitable search for a clean shirt, worse than the perpetually missing cuff links. Sometimes, on a good day, Seamus would start making chimpanzee noises, a primate protest against being leashed. Or he would grab the tie and yank it upward, his tongue lolling and his eyes askew, as if he were dangling from a hangman's noose. Rose always found this rueful goof on his corporate uniform heartening. But Seamus hadn't done anything remotely silly in quite a while. It was scary, actually, how resigned he'd been lately. How dutiful and how grim.

"I'm thinking chartreuse," she said as she came out of the bathroom, to see whether he'd been listening.

"Uh-huh," Seamus murmured, peering morosely into the mirror. He'd already popped the buttons off his brand-new button-down shirt, Rose noted. She could see the ragged bits of thread where the buttons had been and the empty slits on the collar. Seamus's little statement. He'd started out in a T-shirt and jeans as the resident tech genius in a software start-up with a clever angle, working eighteen-hour days for five years for pizza and coffee and 750,000 shares of stock initially valued at seven cents a share. 4Real.com had gone public the year before, and the stock had gotten as high as thirteen before the bottom fell out. On the brink of going under the previous April, the company had been bought out by PsiberSystems, Inc. It had seemed like a godsend at the time, but Seamus felt trapped in a salary again. Trapped in a suit, trapped in an office—even, Rose sometimes feared, trapped in his marriage. Seamus was not a man who responded well to confinement. He'd had his 4Real stock certificates made into savagely ironic memo pads, and she couldn't even leave him a note telling him she'd gone out for a jog without rubbing salt in the wound. Their grocery lists these days were written on paper that had briefly been worth 9.75 million dollars.

I'm going to tell him, Rose thought. Today is the day. I'm going to tell him. But not until we've both had some coffee.

"Or magenta," she said.

Seamus finally registered incomprehension and glanced at her. "What?"

"My hair. I'm thinking of coloring it. Something bright and young and foolish."

"I love your hair, Rosie."

"The gray's getting out of hand."

"What gray?" Seamus said, charmingly enough. But then she realized that it might be true, that maybe he really hadn't noticed it. There was so much he hadn't been noticing lately.

She offered tentatively, "I'm afraid it might be because I'm having old thoughts."

Seamus, who had already moved on, blinked. "What?"

"The gray. Like, maybe it's rooted in certain thoughts. Tired thoughts. Sad thoughts. Cynical thoughts. I mean, what if those thoughts are in certain spots in my *brain*, see, and they affect—"

"That's ridiculous," Seamus said. "First of all, *what* gray? And second of all, that's not how the brain works."

"Maybe I have an unusual brain."

Her husband shook his head indulgently and turned to rummage through his top drawer, no doubt looking for his cuff links. In the past, he would have taken the opportunity to laugh and tell her that she certainly *did* have an unusual brain, and that's why he loved her. Or, better still, he would have picked up on the gray thoughts themselves. Rose wondered how long she could keep thinking of Seamus's preoccupation as just a phase. When did the creeping mediocrity in their intimacy stop being the symptom of a passing disappointment and become the new reality? It felt like they were close to some point of no return; the rut might already have become the road. But she didn't want to go there yet. It was just another prematurely aged thought, sifting out of her head like ash from a neglected hearth.

"Shit," Seamus exclaimed, still pawing through the dresser drawer. "Where the hell are my cuff links?"

"I think I saw them out on the coffee table."

Seamus muttered another expletive and hurried out. Rose shook her head. She took her shoulder holster from its hook in the closet and shrugged it on, settling the strap next to her left breast, then moved to the bedside table. She opened the drawer and pushed aside her needlepoint work-in-progress, a perpetually unfinished version of the Irish Blessing, all Celtic hearts and flowers. Seamus's mother had given her the kit as a Christmas present some time back, apparently expecting to see it warming up the wall in their kitchen within weeks. She asked about it every time she came to visit. But after a year and a half, Rose had only MAY THE ROAD RISE TO MEET YOU, MAY THE WIND BE AL-WAYS AT YO— done, in leprechaun green letters. She hated needlepoint, and she only worked on the damned thing when she was too mad at Seamus to read in bed but not mad enough to go sleep on the couch.

Beneath the needlepoint was her gun. A black Smith & Wesson 9mm semiautomatic pistol, a serious weapon for which she took a lot of teasing on the job. But she'd have taken more shit, Rose knew, if she carried something dainty.

She took the Smith & Wesson out of the drawer and checked it. Safety on, chamber empty. She drew a twelve-bullet clip from the special pocket in her purse and slipped it into the magazine, conscious of the weird comfort of the metallic *cha-chunk* as the clip clicked home. What was it Jack had used to say, taking his own elephant killer of a Colt .45 out of his locker before their shift began? "Ahhh. Breakfast." Rose could still see him breathing in the oil smell as if it were bacon and eggs. Every workday morning for the five years they'd been partners, until the night he'd taken the gun home with him.

"Got 'em!" Seamus called from the living room, as if she'd been hanging on a hook waiting for word on the cuff-link search. Rose holstered the 9mm and found her blue jacket. There'd be the usual bulge beneath her arm, and the usual jokes at work about Amazons and lopsided tits. She felt a little wave of pure weariness. The smell of coffee began to waft in from the kitchen, which was heartening. But coffee suddenly didn't seem like enough. Maybe it was the thought of Jack, sneaking in like one of those gray hairs. Maybe it was those damned cuff links. In any case, she just didn't have the heart to try for a real conversation with Seamus this morning after all.

Tonight, Rose thought. I'll tell him tonight.

He always have-a da girls in there," the old Italian lady said. "Lotsa girls. All a da time, da girls."

"'Girls,'" Rose repeated uneasily. "You mean, like, little girls?"

Mrs. Saltimbocca shrugged. "Little. Big. He's-a not so picky."

"How old were the girls?"

"Your age, Fragolina. Da younga girls."

Rose laughed. "I'm thirty-six, Mrs. Saltimbocca."

"And I'm-a sixty-seven," Mrs. Saltimbocca replied aggressively. "Who's-a counting? You're a baby, *una bambina.* What's a couple a gray hairs?"

Ouch, Rose thought. She could see only a four-inch-wide vertical section of Mrs. Saltimbocca, as much as the chained apartment door, grudgingly opened, allowed, but the sample was enough to establish that the woman was enormous. She appeared to be wearing a large purple tent, and slippers with rodents' heads. Not cute rodents, like bunnies: mean, toothy rodents. Rabid squirrels, Rose thought. The old woman was wearing rabid squirrels on her feet.

"Do you know who any of these women were?" Rose asked. "The ones who came and went?"

"I don' know none a dem, honey. I don' wanna know. He

brings-a his cookies home, he turns his music up. It's-a not my business. I turn-a my music up, too."

Her gesture took in the ceiling, and Rose became aware of the sound emanating from the upstairs apartment—classical piano music, something irritating and relentless, the notes muffled by the ceiling to a dull ache.

"That's his music?"

"It's-a been playin' since Friday night. It's-a why I called da cops."

"The same music?"

"Same-a damn song."

Rose said carefully, "Did Mr. Pelletier have any, um, female visitors Friday night? Have you noticed anybody unusual coming or going at all this weekend?"

The old woman fixed her with a surprisingly penetrating look. "He's-a dead, no?"

"Yeah," Rose conceded. "He's dead."

Mrs. Saltimbocca crossed herself.

"Do you have any idea who might have killed him?" Rose asked, figuring she might as well cut to the chase.

The old woman gave a big Italian shrug. "Who's-a say? Is God. *La volontà divina.*"

"God?"

"You don' live like-a dat," Mrs. Saltimbocca said ominously, and put one fat finger alongside her enormous nose. "That's-a all I gotta say. It's-a God's hand." She crossed herself again and closed the door.

U p the stairs in apartment B, Joshua was still in the bedroom waiting for the photographer to finish up. The dim red space looked crammed with people, but that was just the multiplying effect of the mirrors. The piano music Rose had heard from downstairs was blaring from the all-too-excellent stereo's speakers like a car alarm. Her partner and the medical examiner stood to one side of the bed, squinting a little at the din, frankly impatient with the photographer, a kid in a black turtleneck and jeans who apparently had artistic aspirations. The windowless room's air was heavy with rot. Old blood, bad meat. And something else, an incongruous hint of freshness. Murphy's Oil Soap, Rose realized with a start. Someone had recently cleaned the hardwood floor.

"For Christ's sake, Perry, it's not for the goddamned cover of *Vogue*," Joshua snapped at the photographer, as Rose came in.

"If it was for the cover of *Vogue*, there'd be a way nicer ass involved," Perry said, unfazed, tilting his head and pointedly closing one eye to compose his next shot. Joshua shook his head, banged a cigarette out of a battered pack, and stabbed it between his lips. He wouldn't light it, Rose knew. He would just let it hang there, like a promise to himself. If things got really tough, he'd start chewing on it.

"What's the story?" Rose asked Chester Sparks, the assistant medical examiner, raising her voice to compete with the stereo.

"He's dead," Chester said laconically. "We'll know more when Ansel Adams here is finished."

"Do we really need this music?"

"It was on when I got here," the uniformed cop offered from the door, a little defensively.

"Chopin," said Chester, who liked to know everything. "Sonata in B-Flat Minor."

"Noted," Rose said, poking the stereo's Off button with her pen. The abrupt silence seemed to make the room smell worse.

"Anything from the neighbor lady?" Joshua asked Rose, at a mercifully normal pitch, his soft North Carolina drawl lending the question an incongruous folksy note.

She shrugged. "The guy liked the fräuleins, apparently. A lot of female traffic in general, but nothing particular from this weekend."

"Nothing at all?"

"The music's been on since Friday night." Rose met her partner's clear blue eyes. "She thinks God killed him."

Joshua smiled ruefully. "God or his maid. This place is cleaner than a new toothbrush."

Perry finally settled on an angle and composed his shot. He focused twice, and then a third time, probably just to piss Joshua off; and then the big flash went off and the mirrored walls and ceiling exploded into light, as if the room had dissolved into a supernova. The black stains on the bed's rumpled sheet flared into shocking crimson. In the stark-white instant, all Rose could see was the body that lay amid the blood, a young man, naked, sprawled facedown like something dropped carelessly from a height. The kid was weirdly lonely-looking, with one arm flung sideways, blindly outstretched, groping toward an empty embrace. A pietà without the Virgin Mary, Rose thought. Some mother's son, his journey finished.

The flash faded, and her eyes swam with green and orange dots. Joshua stuck the cigarette behind his ear and he and the AME shouldered past the photographer to the bedside.

"One more," Perry protested.

"Bite me," Joshua said. "Can we get some real light in here?"

The uniformed cop at the door spun the rheostat knob for the overhead, and the lamps' red glow yielded to unforgiving electric daylight. The bed was a gory mess, except for a single pillow, plumped and placed with apparent care, that cushioned the dead man's head. An oddly tender touch, Rose thought. The rest of the bedclothes had been kicked into a sexual tangle near the foot of the bed.

Chester, gloved, was already turning the body over with a deft, practiced gentleness. The dead kid's arms flopped as he moved, one hand falling to the pillow, open and empty in an eerie appeal.

Perry, shunted aside, glanced at Rose, apparently in search of support for his art.

"I'd quit while I was ahead, Perry," she said. "I don't think Joshua's had his coffee yet. He could get testy."

"I've got a job to do here, too."

"And you've done it, sweetheart."

Perry hesitated petulantly, then set his jaw, clipped his lens cap on, and left in a huff. Rose turned to the AME. "Whatcha got, Chester?"

"One to the heart," he said. "A sharp, slim knife. Upward thrust, well placed, right in under the ribs. Probably happened right here in the bed. The lividity indicates he just fell on his face and lay there."

"Killed in action?" Joshua suggested, one eyebrow arching.

Chester shrugged. "Maybe. They certainly didn't have a cigarette afterward."

"How long has he been dead?" Rose asked.

"The rigor's passed. The guy's room temperature. Somewhere between twenty-four hours and three days. Any more than that and he'd be bloating by now."

"Fits with the music," Joshua said. "Friday night."

"A bad date," Rose agreed.

The three of them stood for a moment contemplating the corpse, which lay on its back now, the arms and legs flaccid in a swastika of surprise. The kid's dead eyes stared vacantly, a look of pure incomprehension. Flopped like that, splayed and shocked, he looked like a cartoon character who had run into an invisible wall.

He was older than Rose had thought at first. More like thirty. An earnest face, a small-town face, the face of a kid who had helped old ladies across streets; and a smooth, fit body, just starting to lose the effortless tautness of youth, the hint of an emerging beer belly highlighted now with blood dried to the color of a rotten apple. She wanted to look away, but every surface in the room seemed mirrored.

"Nice round hole," Joshua noted.

"He twisted it once it was in," Chester said. "A half-turn at least."

"He?" Rose repeated dubiously.

"Or a lady wrestler. It's a clean move. It would take some serious hand strength."

She frowned. "The neighbor said the guy liked girls."

"If it was Olive Oyl, she's got Popeye's forearms."

"Rosie could put a hole like that in a guy," Joshua said stoutly.

The AME laughed and glanced at Rose. "Are you confessing?"

"Joshua just thinks I'm Superwoman, since I beat him at arm wrestling."

"Just that once," Joshua demurred.

Chester looked at the gaping hole in the young man's chest and shook his head.

"I suppose it could have been a chick," he conceded. "Two hands on the knife, maybe? And catching him off guard. But I'll tell you one thing: whoever it is, they didn't make a lot of small talk. One jab, boom. With authority. No hesitation marks, no defensive wounds. It wasn't a squabble that got out of hand. This thing was over fast."

The bedroom's single-minded décor, the total commitment to seduction, had produced a paradoxically Zenlike environment. A search of the simple space went fast and yielded nothing. Joshua was right: The apartment was very, very clean. The forensics techs were going through the motions, but it was plain that the place had been thoroughly wiped. The bathroom, way too tidy for a bachelor's, reeked of Lysol; the shower sparkled, and the toilet had been cleaned. In the living room, away from the faintly putrid air that dominated the bedroom, Rose could smell lemon-scented furniture polish. Here, too, the hardwood floor was bright and redolent of wood soap. The flat surfaces were dust-free and the antique mirror shone. Even the coat closet, its floor stacked neatly with tackle boxes, fly-fishing rods, and several display cases full of hand-tied flies and lures, appeared to have been straightened.

The tiny kitchen was also impeccable, though there wasn't much to it: a refrigerator full of German beer, a few square feet of well-wiped counter space, and a two-burner stove and half-oven. There were two plates and a cereal bowl in the dish rack, and the plastic silverware drainer held three clean spoons, a fork, a pair of lacquered chopsticks, and a gleaming L.L. Bean trout fillet knife with a reinforced varnished rosewood handle and a four-inch blade of tapered Scandinavian stainless steel. Rose and Joshua exchanged an amused look before bagging the fish knife carefully. It wasn't often you found your murder weapon mixed in with the clean silverware.

There were also four empty beer bottles in the drainer; they'd actually been washed. A fifth bottle sat on the coffee table. It was the only thing in the apartment that seemed out of place.

"Maybe the cleaning lady came in over the weekend and didn't notice the body," Joshua said.

"Maybe our gal's a pro," Rose said.

"I wonder if she does windows. I've been looking for a housecleaner."

Rose noted that she and Joshua were on the same wavelength, as usual. Despite Chester's take, her gut said the killer was a woman.

"She's good with floors and bathrooms," she conceded. "I'm not sure you'd be happy with the way she makes the bed."

"Nobody's perfect," Joshua said.

Rose squatted beside the beer bottle on the coffee table.

It had already been dusted for prints, she noted. Nada. Of course. She pulled on a latex glove and picked up the bottle, which left a pale ring on the otherwise flawless cherrywood surface. There was a coaster six inches away from where the bottle had been. A little still life of heedlessness, Rose mused. Or of spite.

"So he picks up a girl and brings her home, his usual Friday night," she said. "He plays his piano music and plies her with expensive beer and eventually coaxes her into the hall of mirrors back there. Business as usual."

"Then she sticks him with a fish knife," Joshua said. "Oops."

"Sticks him very, very effectively. And cleans up afterward."

"Not exactly a crime of passion, you're saying."

"Who brings a knife to bed on the first date?"

"I'm betting it was his knife. Maybe Romeo needs help to get laid."

Rose put the beer bottle back on its ring and straightened. "So it's a date rape that backfires? He tries to force the issue, but she disarms him somehow and kills him?"

Joshua smiled. "It's a nice feminist theory."

"One stab? No hesitation marks, no wild flailing, no defensive wounds?"

"Beginner's luck."

"She twisted the knife."

"So the girl has issues." Joshua shrugged. "Who doesn't? I'd twist the fucking knife too, if some guy tried to pull that shit on me."

"Misdemeanor murder, you're saying. Justifiable homicide."

"Not even that. Self-defense."

Rose looked at the antique mirror on the living room wall. The surface was pocked with black age spots, but the reflection was true. Almost certainly the killer had glanced into this mirror, too, at some point, and seen herself looking back. Rose's skin puckered briefly into goose bumps. It seemed like a weird intimacy.

She caught a fleeting whiff of Windex. Like everything else, the mirror's surface had been shined, as if to ensure that no incriminating afterimage lingered.

"So why the cleanup?" she persisted. "Why not just dial nine-one-one and tell the truth?"

"Maybe she didn't want to take a chance on not being believed. Maybe she had doubts about the gentle compassion of our justice system's treatment of rape victims. Maybe she didn't want to see her face on page one of the fucking *Chronicle* and have everybody in the Bay Area opining about her sex life for the next few months."

"Maybe she should have thought about that before she got in bed with the asshole."

"Maybe she didn't want to let one bad moment in bed with an asshole ruin her entire life."

Rose had a sudden, vivid image of the body on the bed. It wasn't something that went away: those eyes staring forever at nowhere. Brown eyes, eyes that had once been soft and warm, hard now, and cold. She shook her head, partly at Joshua's theory, partly just to rattle the image away.

On one of the well-dusted shelves over the stereo, an old snapshot in a frame showed the kid, much younger, with an old man. The two of them, decked out in baggy fishing clothes and floppy hats, were holding up a string of fish. Laughing. Above them, framed by crisp pines, the sky was blue and lovely.

"You're a sweet guy, Joshua," she said. "A southern gentleman of the old school. But our gal ain't no magnolia blossom."

They spent the rest of the morning knocking on doors up and down Chestnut Street. There were plenty of stories attesting to Henry Pelletier's active social life, but no one seemed to have seen anything in particular the previous Friday night. A number of neighbors in good locations weren't home, and Rose noted the addresses for later.

Pelletier's briefcase, parked neatly beside the coat rack like a homework assignment he hadn't gotten to, yielded his work address, and after lunch Rose and Joshua drove into the financial district and took the elevator up a shiny skyscraper on Sacramento Street near Battery to the twelfth-floor offices of Earthwise Investors, Inc. Henry Pelletier's absence on a Monday hadn't caused much fuss yet; apparently he often took a day to recover from his weekends. The shock throughout the office at his death was real, though. No one had seen anything like this coming. The guy was well liked, despite his assiduous bachelor lifestyle, which everyone seemed a little amused by, as by the exploits of an ambitious younger sibling. Pelletier had handled a number of important portfolios for the socially responsible investment firm, and there was no hint of financial troubles or dubious transactions. Several of the women in the office had dated him and had no real complaints, other than the guy's utter inability to commit to anything deeper than a boozy weekend in the mirrored bedroom. No one had ever seen him use drugs, and all the breakups and letdowns seemed to have happened genially enough.

A nice guy, the consensus seemed to run. A three-date guy. A man who got his job done, paid his bills on time, and devoted his plentiful disposable income to the pursuit of relationships stamped clearly with an expiration date. Not bad in bed, but nothing to write home about. Certainly he had never forced himself on anyone, and no one had ever seen him handle anything more deadly than a cheese knife.

Pelletier's last office fling had been a weekend in Carmel with a CPA named Betsy Barber, some three weeks before. Betsy's office, like Betsy herself, was tiny but plush, and had a view of the bay and walls hung with yards of Egyptian tapestries. She was a zaftig henna redhead squeezed into a pricey leather skirt that left little of her sturdy thighs to the imagination, and sheer black hose. Her black ankle boots cocked her at an angle of almost military efficiency, and the pearl buttons of her blue silk blouse strained against the firm counterangles of her breasts. She seemed pleased to be cast as the widow in the tragedy, and sobbed copiously. Rose barely kept herself from rolling her eyes as Joshua played the southern gallant and offered his handkerchief. Betsy accepted it gratefully, blew her nose, and raised her red-rimmed eyes to meet Joshua's. Her mascara had already run, Rose noted unsympathetically. Betsy looked like a raccoon with big blue tits.

"Poor Henry," Betsy said, her voice quavering. "He was such a *decent* guy."

"I know this is a terrible shock," Joshua allowed. He paused delicately. "I'm sorry for what may seem like a crude question at this point, but do you have any idea who, uh . . ."

Betsy held his gaze bravely. "Yes?"

"Well—"

"Who he dated after you," Rose supplied impatiently.

Betsy's lower lip trembled, and then she began to cry again. Josh gave Rose a chastising look, and she shrugged.

"I'm sorry," Betsy sobbed. "I'm just terribly upset. I've been working through some abandonment issues lately anyway, and now *this*—"

"Of course," Joshua said. He seemed prepared to offer further comfort, but Rose gave him an eyebrow and tilted her head toward the door: Enough, already. Joshua nodded reluctantly. He glanced back at Betsy, who was blowing her nose again. His handkerchief, clearly, was a goner. Joshua cut his losses and laid a card on the desktop.

"Ms. Barber, if there is anything, anything else you can think of that might help us figure out who did this terrible thing, I hope you won't hesitate to give us a call."

Betsy's wet lashes fluttered. "Of course."

"I'm sorry for your loss."

"Thank you, Detective, um—"

"Inspector. Inspector Joshua Falkner. It's on the card."

"Of course," Betsy said. "Thank you, Inspector. You've been very . . . sensitive."

Rose was already two steps down the hall. Joshua hurried after her. It was almost five o'clock by now; Betsy Barber had been the last interview at Earthwise Investors, Inc., and by tacit agreement they headed straight for the elevator. They were silent on the way down, both tired, both conscious of the fruitlessness of the series of interrogations. The elevator car had mirrored walls, and Rose noted that she looked like shit in all sixteen versions of herself. What a day it had been for mirrors.

"Don't think I don't know what you're thinking," Joshua said.

Rose laid on the drawl. "Oh, Ms. Barber, if you can think of anything, *anything* I could possibly do with your breasts, please don't hesitate to call."

He laughed. "I *knew* you were thinking that."

"That's because you're so . . . sensitive."

The elevator opened and they crossed the marbled lobby floor and exited the heavy gold doors onto Sacramento Street. The sidewalk was crowded as the downtown offices unloaded. They found a niche out of the traffic, against the building's black stone façade, and pondered their next move.

"There's a decent Irish pub around the corner here," Joshua said. "How about we grab a beer or two and some bangers and mash, then catch the after-work crowd along Chestnut Street? Some of those missing neighbors must be home by now."

Rose hesitated. It was the first time in the six months they had been working together that Joshua had proposed that they have a drink together or extend their shift, and she didn't want to just blow him off. But she wanted to get home in time to catch Seamus before he drank six beers watching CNN and sank into a mood. She said reluctantly, "We should get back to the office and generate some paperwork on this thing."

"What's to write, at this point? The guy's name is Henry. He's dead. I like Betsy for it, frankly."

Rose laughed. "You're just looking for an excuse to reinterview."

"You've got to admit, there's something suspicious about those boobs."

"And you're just the man to get to the bottom of it."

Joshua shrugged modestly and lit a cigarette. Loose, but attentive; he was still waiting for an answer. Rose had a sudden urge to snag one of his Marlboro reds and light it up herself. She hadn't smoked since she'd worked with Jack. She hadn't had a beer with any of the several perfectly good partners she'd had since then either. There were a lot of things that hadn't happened since she'd worked with Jack, Rose knew. But that was the kind of thought that gave a woman gray hair.

"I really should get home and make a decent dinner for my husband," she said apologetically. "It's sort of an occasion."

"Ah!" Joshua said at once, appropriately supportive. "Of course. Anniversary?"

"Not exactly." He looked quizzical at her tone, which even to her own ear had a note of ruefulness. Rose added, trying to brighten it up, "An announcement."

Her partner nodded benignly, waiting for the other shoe to drop, ready to be pleased for her. Rose realized that she had gotten herself out on a limb.

"Can I bum one of those cigarettes from you?" she asked.

Joshua laughed in surprise. "You're kidding, right?"

"If only I were."

Bemused, he produced the box and flipped open the top. "I had no idea."

"I've been off 'em for over a year. It comes out under stress." Rose plucked a Marlboro and slipped it between her lips. Joshua hastened to fire his lighter and she bent over the flame, then straightened and let the smoke out in a long thin stream.

"Okay, I'm fucked," she said. "I'll probably buy a carton now on the way home."

"It's a stressful announcement?" Joshua prompted casually.

She glanced at him, surprised by the deft probe to the heart of the matter. Though she probably shouldn't have been surprised. She'd seen her partner do it often enough with suspects: lulling them with the drawl and a seemingly clueless southern nonchalance, then quietly nailing them.

"It's complicated," she said.

"So I gather."

"It's just . . . Oh, fuck it. I'm pregnant, goddammit. I'm fucking pregnant."

Joshua cocked one eyebrow and let it ride for a beat, then offered, "Uh, congratulations?" which was perfect because it let them laugh.

"Well, of course, congratulations," Rose conceded sheepishly, struck by how relieved she felt, how strangely unburdened, simply to have aired out the ambivalence a little. "It's just—you know, *complicated*. It's not like this is planned or anything. Seamus has got a lot on his plate right now. I have no idea how he's going to take it."

"Oh, come on. He loves you, right?"

You silly child, she thought. Married people can't talk to unmarried people about love. Same word, different planets. But she said, "Of course he loves me."

"Then he'll be fine. He'll be happy."

It confirmed her sense that she'd probably already said

too much. But it was kind of Joshua to be so thoroughly obtuse. The formalities had to be observed, in any case.

"Yeah," she said. "He'll be happy. It's just going to be—well, you know—"

"Complicated."

Rose laughed. "Exactly."

Joshua ground his cigarette out beneath his toe. "Well, okay, then, how about this: Forget the damned beer and forget the damned neighbors. You get yourself home right away and cook that guy a good dinner and thrill him with your news, and I'll mosey back to the office and make some paper on this case and call it quits for tonight."

"Oh, no, Joshua, you don't have to—"

"It's no big deal. Tomorrow's another day, and Henry Pelletier is not going to get any less dead. Think of it as an early baby shower gift."

Rose considered the offer. It would actually help a lot. She still had some shopping to do if she was going to make Seamus a properly festive meal. And she wanted to buy a wine that said something. Like: Can you handle this? Like: Honey, I'm scared to death.

"I'd owe you," she said tentatively. "Big time."

"You could stop telling people about beating me at arm wrestling, for starters. Chester's lost all respect for me."

Rose laughed, wondering why it was so hard for her to accept help. But it always was. Her cigarette had burned away and she felt a flash of regret that she'd managed to smoke so little of it. She was going to relapse after all, apparently.

She spent way too long picking out a wine that said the right thing, floundering through subtlety into absurdity and finally incoherence before she settled at last on a medium-priced Sonoma County Chardonnay with a pretty label. She hurried home with both arms full of groceries and the wine in a skinny little paper bag, but when she got there the house was empty. Rose already had the chicken in the oven before she noticed the flashing light on the message machine. It was Seamus, still at work. The fucking network for the latest fucking job needed some kind of fucking something-or-other finished by Tuesday morning, and he was stuck for the duration. Seamus's voice had that locked-in tone she'd come to recognize as his work voice lately: bitter and hard and trying to be funny about it all, but, increasingly, not funny.

She finished chopping the tomatoes on pure momentum, then gave up, left the salad unfinished, and started eating the vegetables out of the bowl with her fingers. She opened the bottle of wine and poured herself a glass. It was fruity and crisp, with a touch of oaken smoke, and it said unmistakably that she had spent eighteen dollars to drink alone. She wished now that she'd had that beer with Joshua.

When the chicken finished baking, she just turned the heat off and left the bird sitting in the oven. She had decided to leave it there until Seamus noticed. It would be interesting, she thought, to see how long that took. She refilled her wineglass and carried it into the bedroom, where she climbed under the covers and started working on the Irish Blessing needlepoint.

She worked until after midnight, making furious progress, and was up to AND UNTIL WE MEET AG— when she finally began to feel like she could sleep. She put the needlepoint back in the drawer on top of her gun and clicked off the lamp. The images of the day ran through her mind, as they always did: the body on the bed, echoing like a scream in a nightmare through mirrors in every direction; the huge old Italian woman in her garish purple gown; and the incongruous gallantry of Joshua grinding her cigarette butt under his foot. Betsy's round little knees, and the fish knife in the dish drainer. Seamus's face, his look too distant and too cool. Jack was in the mix, as he so often was. But oddly enough, the image that wouldn't go away was the single beer bottle sitting on the coffee table in Henry Pelletier's living room, and the starkness of the ring it left, six inches from that coaster. It was a ridiculous thing to fixate on, Rose thought, in light of the bloody mess in the bedroom. But it had struck her, somehow. It seemed like such a mean little thing to do.

3

'M NOT A MONSTER, Helen thought. Monsters don't do the dishes. Monsters don't clean the tub. Monsters don't try so hard to try to make a decent life with their one true love. But she felt like a monster sometimes when she started to get bored.

The thing was, it was always the same with Jimmy. He was as predictable as a charcoal grill. You laid the coals, you spritzed a little lighter fluid, soaking the lumps with anticipation, and you struck the spark. The blaze was a miracle. But it was always the same miracle.

Helen studied the ceiling over his shoulder as he thrust away. It was the same pattern it had been the night before, and the night before that, the same spiderweb of cracks in the plaster, radiating from some forgotten flaw, the same tilted light fixture with the same dead bulb. She should have been grateful, she knew, for Jimmy's perfect reliability. You could set your watch by his love for her. She'd already come twice; he always made sure of that. He was good with his hands and tongue, and devoted to her pleasure. First things first, he liked to say. And even when he moved on to what he clearly thought of as *his* turn, Jimmy was a thoughtful lover. She loved the feel of him between her thighs, the certainty of his desire, his gasping hunger in her ear, and the hunger of his hands. But he never met her eyes anymore.

Sometimes she watched. She waited. Jimmy pumped and moaned and gnawed at her gently; he whispered her name in passion, and he stroked her hair. He was gratifyingly voracious and he wanted her and her alone, but his eyes were fiercely closed. And when, once in a long while, his eyelids flickered open briefly and met her gaze, they both were embarrassed. Like cockroaches, shocked back into the shadows by a sudden light. Like Adam and Eve, naked in the sight of God.

Jimmy's groans deepened into urgency and the rhythm of his hips went almost frantic, then faltered deliciously. His head rocked, the blond mop of hair heaving back and then forward over his eyes; a drop of sweat from his forehead hit her lip and Helen tasted the sweet sizzle of salt. He thrust with his hips, one last time, as if he wanted to go right through her, his pubic ridge slamming into hers, bone on bone. Helen thought, involuntarily, of the knife, of the sickening wet thud it made, plunging into Henry's chest, and the thought finally closed her eyes. She dug her fingernails into Jimmy's back and clung to him as he came. She could feel the surge of him inside her, the closest thing to love she knew, the liquid heat that filled her as he emptied.

She made him breakfast as she always did, bacon ritually charred until it nearly crumbled, eggs cooked through until the yolks were pale yellow memories, and grits spilling a lake of butter. Jimmy's mother had taught her to make grits as if she were passing on the key to the universe. In eastern North Carolina, a woman who couldn't make grits was a sad, sad thing and Helen was constantly surprised even now by how deeply Jimmy held to the standards of his Martin County childhood, the hardscrabble certainties and absurdities of the bleak peanut, pine, and tobacco country between the Tar and Roanoke rivers. He'd taken her there only once, shyly and with his tongue firmly in his cheek, prepared to mock everything with her, but Helen had seen the way Jimmy lit up driving through the peanut fields along U.S. 64 and the odd but genuine pride he'd taken in Miss Camellia, the World's Largest Ceramic Guernsey Cow. She'd heard the way his accent came back strong, slurping sliders by the peck to jukebox rockabilly and country blues in the Sunny Side Oyster Bar in Williamston, where they had no plates, only paper placemats, and where black men in green aprons stood in the sawdust behind the counter, shucking oysters as fast as the rowdy crowd could down them and knocking the shells aside. It was what made Jimmy so endearingly solid, of course. He knew in his bones that there were absolutes, fundamental things beyond questioning. Like Wonder Bread for his sandwiches, pure fluffy American certainty with the substance of a cloud and the surety of stone.

"What are you going to do today?" Jimmy asked as he gathered himself to leave for work.

Helen shrugged. "The usual."

Jimmy nodded, accepting that. It hadn't been a real question, and she knew he didn't really want to know. Her superfluous complexities, the emotional intricacy of her days, the baffling little meanings she pursued only frustrated him. He was still in that window of tolerant indulgence that always followed what Helen knew he thought of as her safe return to his loving arms. Jimmy really was that simple. He believed "the usual" meant something good. For days, sometimes weeks, he would be like this, protective and gentle and making the effort to be attentive. He would make love instead of fucking her. He would act genuinely grateful to have her around. But inevitably, Jimmy's armor and obliviousness came back. Helen could already see it starting to happen in the little things. The small hardenings, the almost imperceptible settling into a complacent male stupor. It was like watching barnacles form. She said, "The usual," and he didn't rock the boat by questioning it, and the usual drifted inexorably into waters he would never know, sinking beneath the weight of her growing desperation. Until the next time she went under. They called them "crises." There was the usual, and then there was a crisis. Helen wondered if someone had to die for Jimmy to pay attention. If someone really had to die for Jimmy to be tender.

He kissed her good-bye, a palpable degree more perfunctory than he'd been the day before, and clumped down the stairs, his tool belt slung over his shoulder. Helen watched him as he went, seeing the slight limp, the hitch in his easy feline swagger. Jimmy liked to say the limp kept him humble, but she knew he hated it. He was working on a construction job in Burlingame these days, a bank building going up. The money was good again, and she supposed that she should be glad. But the love was so much sharper when they were poor and scrambling. And it was better still—the best, somehow—when they were flat-out scared.

Turn, Helen thought, as Jimmy got to his truck. Turn and wave. Blow a kiss. But Jimmy dropped his tool belt in the truck bed and clambered into the cab without looking back; he turned the Chevy's engine over, lit a cigarette, and was off.

If only you knew, she thought. You'd pay attention then. And she turned to go back inside.

Rose and Joshua began knocking on doors along Chestnut Street at seven-thirty the next morning, catching the last of Henry Pelletier's startled neighbors in bathrobes and sweatpants, cranking their espresso machines. The word had spread by now, and everyone knew there'd been a murder on the street. But no one had noticed anything out of the ordinary the previous Friday night. It made sense, actually. Chestnut was only a block away from the Lombard bars, and the weekend party traffic was vigorous.

The last address on the list was the building directly across the street from Pelletier's apartment. Another duplex, with a barred entrance gate swathed in anemic bougainvillea. The downstairs tenants were a mild gay couple in complementary robes of blue and Kelly green silk, breakfasting on oat-bran muffins with no butter and fresh-squeezed orange juice. They didn't seem overly perturbed to learn that Henry Pelletier's Friday-night action had gone sour—the risks of rampant heterosexuality, their attitude seemed to imply. The two of them had been away for the weekend, in any case, visiting one of the partners' parents. Family values all the way.

The upstairs tenant, "A. Powell" on the mailbox, didn't appear to be home. Joshua knocked twice and rang the bell, and would have turned away, but Rose lingered stubbornly.

"There was a morning paper inside the entry gate," she noted.

Joshua shrugged. "He picks it up after work. We'll catch him tonight."

"Someone's here. I can feel it."

Her partner laughed. "Feminine intuition, Rosie?"

"Call me crazy," Rose said, and rapped on the door again.

Joshua decided to humor her and settled in. "So how'd the announcement go?" he asked conversationally, as they waited.

She glanced at him quizzically. "The announcement?"

"To your husband." He laughed, as Rose continued to look blank. "You know—the B-A-B-Y?"

"Oh! Of course. Right. That." Rose realized that she was tempted to lie, to tell Joshua it had gone wonderfully, that Seamus had been delighted. But lying seemed even sadder, somehow, than the sad truth. "It never happened. Seamus had to work late, and I'd conked out by the time he got home."

"I guess it's not the kind of thing you break to someone over breakfast."

He was way too all over it, Rose thought. It was a little unnerving. She actually felt foolish for having confided in him the day before, for having been so desperate for someone to share her predicament that she'd exposed herself to the embarrassment of good-hearted follow-up questions with no good answers. Seamus had dragged in at three in the morning and crawled from the bed again at seven cursing the day computers had been invented. Rose had found herself bored, unsympathetic, and even snappish, which really wasn't fair. It wasn't her husband's fault she didn't have the guts to hold his nose to their little grindstone of incipient reality. Nor was it Joshua's fault she didn't have a bright little headline of marital joy to report. But she was feeling vaguely querulous toward both men. With all men, maybe. With humanity. She shrugged and banged again on the door, by way of changing the subject, then leaned on the bell.

Sure enough, a moment later, the door's several locks rattled. Rose gave Joshua an I-told-you-so smile. The door opened a cautious eight inches and a face peered out, frankly indignant. A. Powell was dressed for a white-collar job, a balding, harmless-looking little man with a blunt nose like a turtle's beak.

"Can't a guy even take a crap in peace?"

"Sorry to disturb you, sir. We're with the San Francisco Police." Rose held up her badge. "We just need to ask you a few questions."

Powell looked uneasy. "I'm disputing that ticket."

"It's not about the ticket, sir," Joshua assured him. "We only need a moment."

"Well, I'm afraid I don't have a moment this morning. I'm running late."

He went to close the door, but Rose inserted her foot deftly. "*About* that ticket, Mr. Powell—"

The turtle features registered alarm. "I thought you said this wasn't about that."

"It can be about whatever you want it to be," Rose told him, deadpan.

Powell took this in by degrees, a bad chess player, his face showing every calculation. Joshua, playing soft, drawled reassuringly, "Just a couple of questions, sir. Really. We won't be but a minute."

The man did the math for a moment more, then sighed resignedly and opened the door another three inches. He had some kind of berry jam on his badly knotted tie, Rose noted, and his fly was unzipped. She had a maternal urge to tidy the poor schmo up. But it was too late for her to be nice to him.

"So—?" Powell conceded, addressing Joshua now.

"Do you know your neighbor across the street, Henry Pelletier?" Powell looked scrupulously blank. "Thirtyish white male?" Joshua prompted. "Black-haired, professional. The upstairs apartment, straight across."

"I've seen him around, I suppose." Powell gave an elaborate shrug. "I know very few of my neighbors, to speak to. It's not exactly a small town here."

"Were you aware that Mr. Pelletier was killed in his apartment Friday night?"

"No!" Powell seemed genuinely shocked. His eyes flickered briefly, off to the left, retrieving some image and reconciling it with the new fact. "No, my God, I had no idea . . . *Really?*"

"Were you home on Friday night?"

"I was in and out," Powell allowed vaguely.

"Well, obviously, we'd like to know if you might have seen anything that would help our investigation. While you were in."

"I keep my drapes closed most of the time." Powell was still processing something. Joshua waited pointedly, and after a moment Powell's eyes came back into focus. "These apartments are like fishbowls with the damned things open."

"So you didn't see anything," Rose insisted.

He gave her an uneasy glance, then addressed Joshua again. "Not a thing. Zero. Nada. Zilch. I'm sorry."

"No problem," said Joshua, who had apparently decided the guy was just a nervous Nellie with outstanding traffic violations. "It was worth a shot." He reached for a card. "If you can think of anything else—"

"Are you an astronomer, Mr. Powell?" Rose asked.

Joshua, ready to move on, gave her a bemused look, like, Okay, Sherlock, what*ever.* He obviously considered it a unique way to beat a dead horse. Powell drew himself up. "I beg your pardon?"

"Are you some sort of amateur astronomer?"

"No," Powell said warily.

"Because I couldn't help wondering what you do with your telescope."

She actually felt bad for the guy, his face fell so. Joshua peered over Powell's shoulder and noted the tripod set up in front of the apartment's white leather couch. The scope was level, pointed straight across the street. There was even a camera attached.

Joshua laughed.

"Wow, it really *is* like a fishbowl in there, isn't it?" he marveled, then added cheerfully, "Mr. Powell, I'm afraid you're going to be late for work."

"And for God's sake, zip your fly," Rose said.

They spent most of the ride downtown convincing their new star witness that he was not a loathsome man, which was tricky, because he was. But Powell had collapsed into himself and required propping. They stopped at a Starbucks and bought him a mocha cappuccino and a raspberry danish that matched the smear on his tie. They promised to write a note to his boss at work, explaining his absence in the service of civic duty. They nodded at his twisted rationalizations and smiled at his nervous jokes and ignored the appalling way he smacked his lips and spewed crumbs as he devoured his pastry. By the time they had him settled in Interrogation Room 2, Joshua and Rose had pretty much convinced Alfred Powell that he was a fascinating guy with a unique take on human nature.

"Hell, you're practically an anthropologist," Joshua told him. They'd given Powell the comfortable chair, the one with padded armrests. Joshua sat on the table near him at a nonconfrontational angle, letting his feet dangle and emanating casual bonhomie. Rose, feeling her own bonhomie to be overtaxed, sat at the far end of the table, trying not to say anything vicious. She had dropped off the film from Powell's camera at the lab on the way in and was counting the minutes until she could get out of the room and pick up the prints. She just hoped Alfred Powell was a better photographer than he was a human being.

Powell shrugged modestly and slurped his cappuccino. He'd ordered a tall decaf but Rose had gotten him a Vente, full strength, to encourage reckless confidences.

"I'm just a people-watcher, really," he demurred. "What was it Aristotle said? The proper study of mankind is man, eh?"

"Those Greeks had their shit together," Joshua agreed. Rose shot him a poisonous glance. Her partner was having way too good a time. He gave her a wink. "So, Mr. Powell, about your study of Henry Pelletier—"

"I always thought of him as Bud."

"'Bud'?"

"Well, you know, I never knew the guy's name. I just called him Bud." Joshua looked blank. "You know, *Urban Cowboy,* the John Travolta character? Looking for love in all the wrong places?"

"Bud," Joshua said. "Got it."

"It was pathetic, really," Powell confided. "The obvious desperation, you know, the emptiness of it. I mean, the guy had a new woman in there twice a week! What the hell does that say about his self-esteem?"

"That it needed shoring?" Joshua ventured.

"Exactly," Powell exclaimed, pleased, as by a bright student. "*Exactly.* I mean, the turnover was *incredible.* Sometimes two or three different ones in the course of a weekend." His watery blue gaze drifted briefly, apparently reviewing highlights of Henry Pelletier's futile search for self-esteem. "Hot ones, too! I remember this one brunette—"

"Maybe we could focus on Friday night, Freddie," Joshua said. "You don't mind if I call you Freddie, do you?"

"I prefer Alfred."

"Of course." They looked at each other for a moment. Powell appeared to be in no hurry. Joshua prompted, gently, "So, about Friday night—?"

"Right, right," Powell said. "Well, to tell you the truth, they closed the curtains before they really got into anything."

He seemed bizarrely aggrieved by this, as if the curtain closing had been a personal affront. Joshua and Rose exchanged a glance, and Rose rolled her eyes. Joshua, striving for an even tone, said, "'They' being Henry Pelletier and his, uh, female companion?"

"Yeah. A platinum blonde. But not cheap, you know? Very stylish."

"You got a good look at this woman?"

"Oh yeah."

"Could you describe her?"

"Hot," Powell said. "Definitely hot."

"Uh-huh."

"I mean, like, nine-point-seven. At least."

"Nine point seven?" Rose said.

"On a scale of ten. Maybe nine-eight."

"Right," Joshua said. He slipped a Marlboro red out of the box and stuck it between his lips. "Listen, Freddie—"

"Alfred."

"Whatever. I'm going to have to ask you to be a little more specific."

Powell looked a little lost, as if he couldn't imagine being any more specific. "Well, okay, sure . . . Let's see. Great body."

"Uh-huh," Joshua said, beginning to chew on the cigarette.

"Great legs. Great face—"

"Great," Rose said. "We'll just put out an APB and start arresting Barbie dolls."

"Think of it as the Miss America pageant, Freddie," Joshua coaxed. "They're all beautiful. But we need to know what Miss Nebraska looks like."

"Miss Nebraska?"

"Joshua, could I speak with you outside for a moment?" Rose said.

Her partner hesitated, clearly frustrated by what was starting to look like a waste of heroic rapport, then nodded resignedly and hopped off the table.

"Sit tight, Freddie," he said. "We'll be right back. Think features. Think age, height, weight, eye color. Think distinguishing characteristics."

"I'm really feeling weird about missing work like this. You're gonna write that note for my boss, right?"

"Yeah, yeah," Joshua assured him, before following Rose out into the hallway.

"Don't say it," he said, as soon as the door had shut behind them.

"I don't have to. Picture this guy on the witness stand, being cross-examined by a half-decent defense attorney."

"He's a little vague," Joshua conceded.

"He's got nothing. He couldn't pick our gal out of a lineup to save his life. His brain doesn't register anything above the nipples."

"He said she had a great face."

"All he saw was a Playmate of the Week. It's a generic ID by a sick fuck and it won't hold up. And anyway, she was clearly wearing a wig—"

"Why don't I get the sketch artist in here?" Joshua suggested placatingly. "And I'll run through some mug shots with him. Meanwhile, just take a breather. Go check with the lab. Those photos must be ready by now."

"If there's one good photo, just one, that guy doesn't get any more cappuccino." Rose took a breath. "And if there isn't, I say we flush him entirely. Christ, all that shit about Aristotle and the proper study of mankind."

"The line's from Pope, actually," Joshua said. "'*Know then thyself, presume not God to scan . . .*'"

"I don't know how you can stand to be in the same room with that pervert, much less swap quotes with him."

Joshua shook his head wearily and stuck the chewed-up cigarette back in his mouth.

"We can't all afford to be on a high horse, Rosie," he said, turning back to Interrogation Room 2. "You go get those pictures and we can both be done with the son of a bitch."

Jimmy swung the hammer, and the nails disappeared. Two hits per nail, the twenty-two-ounce Vaughan singing in its arc, the sixteen-pennies popping into the creamy pine.

Pa-*poom*. Pa-*poom*. Movin' on down the line. He loved
framing; it was simple, wholesome work and the results
showed right away. You banged a bunch of boards together,
and pretty soon you had walls where there'd just been a pal-
let of two-by-fours. It was fast and clean and nobody
fucked with you. Just that simple thing, a nail to drive, pa-
poom. He could even endure the asshole foreman on a day
like this, when it all felt right.

As he worked, he thought of Helen, as he always did.
Helen wasn't like framing; Helen was like nothing else in
the world. She was most like the music box he'd taken apart
when he was eleven to see how the hell it played that song.
He hadn't been able to put it back together, and his old man
had whipped him good for it. But he had learned something, making that unfixable mess of the flimsy golden
gears and rods. He'd learned not to fuck with miracles. Helen was a music box with a song like an angel's song,
haunting and ethereal, a melody he had never heard and
could only wonder at. There had already been way too
many people in her life ready to take her apart—the psy-
chiatrists and the therapists, the doctors and teachers, the
well-meaning preppie boyfriends, and that asshole father
of hers, all of them just fucking with her, trying to fix her
into something they could control, something they could
use. But you couldn't control a fucking miracle, and it was
a crime against God to try. Jimmy was glad he'd known
enough by the time he met Helen just to let that precious
music play.

He remembered the first time he'd seen her, in a bar-
room near the university, one of those joints just off the
main drag where the wilder students and the locals mixed a
little uneasily. Dressed like a cross between a southern
sorority girl and a Richmond hooker in tight designer jeans,
a red silk blouse tied off beneath her breasts to leave her
midriff bare, and a pair of heeled sandals with a dizzying
tilt, she'd been standing toward the student end of the bar

with a couple of football-player types, crew-cut assholes, big and buff and not entirely bright. The football players were doing their loud best to impress her, posturing like bulls, flexing and braying, to no avail. Helen was drinking vodka martinis as if they were Kool-Aid and smoking skinny menthol Virginia Slims that were so long they looked like straws. She blew three smoke rings on every exhalation—perfect circles, uncannily coherent. She was obviously bored out of her mind, but she was deep in her phase of trying to piss her father off by dating idiots and losers.

One of the linebackers kept putting his beefy hand on her butt in a proprietary way, and Helen kept swatting it away as if it were a deerfly and blowing the occasional smoke ring in his face to try to back him off. Jimmy watched the comedy for a while, nursing his Bud, a sense of violation beginning to rumble in him like water coming to a boil. Helen was more beautiful than any woman he had ever seen, untouchably beautiful, like someone in a movie where every close-up was shot through a lens smeared with Vaseline. Her hair was straight and shoulder-length then, a golden bottle-blond, and her eyes were as green as a stormy sea. She had an angel's face and a queen's demeanor and something of a child's innocence despite the slutty outfit and the bad company she was keeping. She was awesome, a miracle, and no one could touch her, Jimmy thought. No one should, ever. Certainly not some fuckhead choking on his own pectorals.

The linebacker kept groping, and finally Jimmy couldn't stand it anymore. He went over and told the football player that it didn't seem like the lady wanted his hand on her ass and maybe he should leave her alone. The guy grinned knowingly at his buddy and said, "Fuck off, redneck," cocky with bulk on his side. Rather than let the two of them get any more prepared, Jimmy broke the first guy's nose with the heel of his hand, one quick thrust, then kneed him in the groin. As he crumpled, Jimmy ducked the first punch from the guy's friend, hit him with a beer bottle across the forehead, and kicked his legs out from under him. The second guy hit the floor hard and Jimmy kicked him in the stomach, then picked up another beer bottle and looked at the little group of the football players' friends down the bar.

"Anybody else?" he asked.

None of the other guys moved. On the floor, the first two were trying to get it back together, and Jimmy kicked the bigger one in the balls, not hard enough to jeopardize future generations, but enough to crumple him again.

"You'll have to excuse me, ma'am," he told Helen, who had followed the fracas impassively, her eyebrows lifted slightly, without moving from her spot at the bar. "I just can't abide seeing a woman getting pawed at like that."

"How very southern," she said. Her voice sounded like honey to him, smooth and slow and amused. "But I think you may have overreacted a little."

"I'm working on that," he conceded.

The football players were still trying to get up. Their friends moved over to help them, making a wide circle around Jimmy, who kept a cold eye on them.

"Jimmy, if you kill any of them boys, I swear to God I'm gonna call the cops this time," the bartender said. "It's fuckin' bad for business, man."

"I'll pay for the beer I hit him with," Jimmy told him.

"No, I've got it," Helen said. Jimmy gave her a startled glance and she smiled back and that was pretty much that. She really was the most beautiful thing he had ever seen and he would already have done anything for her by then.

Pa-*poom*. Pa-*poom*. The hammer rose and fell; the sections came together and the walls went up, like the bones, the hard truth of the building. The foreman drifted by, checking Jimmy's work, and Jimmy eyed him back until the asshole wavered and walked on. Jimmy shook his head in amusement, set another nail, and swung. Pa-*poom*. Someday it would be that motherfucker's head under the hammer, if he didn't watch out. But today was such a lovely day. Today everything was easy, and clean, and simple.

"Got a minute, Rosie?" Sandi Thanh called from her open office as Rose hurried by on her way to the stairs.

Rose hesitated, but there was really no question of not having a minute for her boss. Lieutenant Alexandra Thanh ran the Homicide Investigations section of the Personal Crimes Division, with nobody above her but captains, chiefs, commissioners, and the mayor. Once you got to a certain point in the hierarchy, everyone had a minute for you. Rose grabbed one side of the office doorway to secure her patience. "Sure."

"A real minute," Sandi said dryly, and Rose laughed, caught. She released the doorjamb and stepped into the office.

"What's up?" she asked.

"How's it going with your witness?"

Rose shook her head, wondering, as she often did, how Sandi Thanh managed to keep abreast of everything that was happening in her domain. The Buddha radar, some of the other homicide inspectors called it, not entirely happily. There did seem to be a mystical quality to Thanh's attunement at times, though Rose knew for a fact that her lieutenant was a Presbyterian. But even a Presbyterian could be telepathic. Rose wasn't even tempted to bluff or exaggerate Alfred Powell's subliminal virtues. The only way to deal with Sandi was straight up. "Not so great. He's a clueless pervert, a self-justifying scumbag, and probably a liar."

"Does it still look like a woman did it? The date?"

"Yeah. But that's all it looks like, at this point. This guy couldn't eliminate a well-shaped mannequin from a lineup, and he'll be useless on the stand. But we're hoping he's a good photographer."

"If only out of sick self-interest."

Rose laughed. "Exactly."

"When will the pictures be ready?"

"I was just on my way down there now."

"Good. Let me know right away what you've got."

"Sure." Rose turned to go.

"Rosie?"

She paused. "Yeah?"

"Joshua thinks this was probably self-defense. The guy's own knife. A date rape."

Rose said impatiently, "Joshua is way too nice a guy sometimes. You don't clean the entire apartment and touch up your lipstick after you kill a rapist in self-defense. This feels like a murder to me."

"I'm just wondering about the allocation of our resources. Dick Burke is hollering for help on that Japanese tourist thing."

So that's what this was about, Rose thought. A Japanese tourist had gotten shot for his video camera and some traveler's checks in his Powell Street hotel room the week before, and the case was making unfortunate waves in the Tokyo newspapers. No doubt there was some downward pressure to solve the thing quickly. She said, "You want me to back-burner Pelletier and pitch in on the Chamber of Commerce pick of the month? Is that what you're saying?"

Thanh sighed, a rare break in her normally unruffled mask of serenity. She had a flawless, heart-shaped face the color of dark honey, slow almond eyes of depthless black, and a tidy, supple body that filled her smart power suits in a way that had moved some of the cruder male detectives to nickname her Lieutenant Thong. At the age of forty-seven she still looked twenty-five, in that ageless Asian way. But Rose knew the smooth surface was deceptive. Sandi Thanh had a fourth-degree karate black belt and fire in her belly. You didn't get to the top of the Homicide Section without some steel. "I'm saying that here in the real world with only twenty-four hours in every day and not enough inspectors to start with and a budget that doesn't cover the amount of crime-scene tape we use, much less our overtime, that you can go to a lot of trouble to ruin some woman's life because she stuck a rapist with his own fish knife, or you can spend your time helping to find the killer in a case with a real victim." And, as Rose stubbornly said nothing: "I'm between a rock and a hard place on this one, Rosie. They want all hands on deck."

Rose recognized the tone of the appeal: girl to girl. There was no denying the camaraderie of being the only two women in Homicide. Her menstrual cycle had been synched with Sandi Thanh's for a year and a half, a fact they hadn't shared with the male detectives.

Rose said, just as frankly, "If I work with Dick Burke, it won't help find that tourist's killer. Dick won't let me do anything meaningful. It'll just be weeks of me being called No-Dick Burke and tracing traveler's check numbers and telling him and his asshole partner Fratello to get their own damn coffee, and in the end I'll have an open file on Pelletier and Burke'll get promoted to sergeant for solving the case of the year."

"It sucks, I know," Thanh said. "But think about it, Rosie. And talk to Joshua. The deputy mayor's got me on speed-dial three times a day."

The photo-lab tech started grinning the moment Rose came in the door. A bad sign, she thought, her heart sinking. It was not a justice-will-be-served grin. It was lewd and it was male and she'd had enough of both for today.

"No comments, please," she said. "I am just . . . not . . . in the mood."

"Just the facts, ma'am," the tech agreed mock-grimly, doing a Joe Friday. Apparently the photos spoke for themselves. He gave her the manila envelope, and she signed the chain-of-evidence receipt. The tech was still grinning knowingly, like someone who'd heard a juicy story about her in a bar, and Rose kept him fixed in a don't-fuck-with-me glare until she was out the door.

Safely in the hallway, she opened the envelope at once. Only thirty-one of the thirty-six frames of 35mm film had been exposed; no doubt the early closing of the curtains had disappointed Alfred Powell. The prints were all time-stamped and dated, apparently accurately, which was convenient but not ultimately important; it was too easy to manipulate such things for a time stamp to stand up in court.

The first photo, dated Friday night at 10:35:17 P.M., was badly out of focus, but it still took Rose's breath away: a man and a woman, presumably Henry Pelletier and his killer date, standing in the living room of Pelletier's apartment with their backs to the camera and bottled beers in their hands. Small talk, the arrival. The woman was all that Powell had said and more, a stunning platinum blonde in a blue silk georgette dress that showed tawny shoulders held erect like a runway model's, an alluring stretch of willowy back, and lithe, shapely legs. Her self-possession, bordering on regal, was obvious from the body language even in the unfocused image. She was way out of Pelletier's league, Rose thought. He looked like a high school kid beside her, like a happy rabbit in a python's cage.

A rapid series of shots from the same angle followed, each with a tighter focus, until Powell had zoomed in, incomprehensibly, on the woman's shoulder blades, which were exquisite but not necessarily edifying. It wasn't like she had a tattoo or something. Rose leafed through half a dozen similar prints, her frustration sharpening. It was just her luck to get a pervert witness with a shoulder-blade fetish.

The shoulder-blade sequence gave way at last to several blurry long shots, the images almost haphazard as Pelletier and his date briefly went their separate ways in the living room and Powell zoomed back and struggled to reframe: a section of the coffee table and the couch, the north wall with its antique mirror, Henry Pelletier's tight little butt as he bent to tidy something, and, in print ten, a dusty patch of floor with an elegant high-heeled foot striding through it. The toenails, in perfect focus, were flawless, painted a dazzling cranberry. Their suspect wore Stuart Weitzman, Rose noted, two-hundred-dollar crisscrossed evening sandals of black peau de soie on a lethal stiletto.

Print number eleven, time-stamped 10:39:37 P.M., was the most tantalizing image yet, as Powell finally began to pick up his target again. The woman had crossed to the window and stood looking out into the night, directly at the camera, though clearly unaware of it. The focus was hasty and, with her body in silhouette, the woman's features were a blur, but the shot had promise. Rose flipped eagerly to the next photo and found that Powell had zoomed in on his subject's chest.

It explained the lavish attention to the shoulder blades, at least, Rose thought ruefully: Powell had been waiting for the woman to turn around. A breast man, all the way.

She flipped through the remaining prints: breasts, breasts, cleavage, and breasts. There was nothing the least bit erotic about the shots; they were like a word you said over and over until it lost its meaning.

By print twenty-four, Henry Pelletier had joined the woman in front of the window and turned her around, and there were half a dozen shots of her lovely back as she stood there in his arms. Pelletier's features were plainly visible over the woman's shoulder, except for the shots in which he was nibbling on her neck.

Note for the case file, Rose thought: From 10:41:07 to 10:43:16 P.M. on the night in question, the victim had his hand on the suspect's ass.

The last two photos, numbered thirty and thirty-one, were of Pelletier alone, his black silk shirt unbuttoned to the waist, his hands raised to draw the drapes together. Print thirty was a bit blurry and the body language was odd; Pelletier, looking straight out into the camera's eye, seemed almost to be shrugging, as if to say, "What can you do?" But number thirty-one was, ironically, a hauntingly perfect shot, with every feature etched in profile and both hands on the drapes, and so it had a certain poignancy. The peepshow curtain was falling. It was 11:02:43 P.M. on the last Friday night of Henry Pelletier's romantic run, and Alfred Powell's bit of futile voyeurism was the last time anyone but his killer would see the guy alive.

*B*ack in Interrogation Room 2, Powell's cappuccino cup was empty. He was sitting in the same chair, jittering one foot as if he had to go to the bathroom, which he probably did. The table was strewn with open mug-shot books. Joshua, looking bored with the company he was keeping, had chewed through his second cigarette and was pulling a fresh one out of the pack as Rose came in. He arched one eyebrow hopefully, and she handed him the photos without comment. Joshua flipped through them quickly and shook his head.

"Ah, Freddie," he said sadly. "Freddie, Freddie, Freddie. What a disappointment you've turned out to be."

"It seems that the proper study of mankind is breasts," Rose said.

"Can I see them?" Powell asked hopefully.

Rose ignored him. "What do you make of print number thirty?" she asked Joshua.

Her partner flipped back and studied the photo briefly, then met Rose's gaze. "He's mugging for the camera?"

"It sure looks like it to me." She turned to their witness. "Mr. Powell, was Henry Pelletier aware that you were in the habit of documenting his love life?"

"Ummm . . . I don't know?"

"What do you mean, you don't know?"

He hesitated. "Well, which is worse? If he knew, or if he didn't know?"

Joshua laughed. "It's all the same to Pelletier at this point, Freddie."

"I meant, worse for *me.*"

"We know what you meant, Mr. Powell," Rose said.

They found the photos in a bottom file drawer in Henry Pelletier's apartment, in a manila folder labeled "Accounts Payable." Apparently he and Alfred Powell had had what Powell called their "little understanding" for quite some time, as the pictures went back several years. The archive pretty much covered the varieties of human sexual behavior possible in a living room, with the entire spectrum of female types. The cumulative effect was a little dizzying, and Rose understood the vertigo: Only one woman had killed Henry Pelletier; but here were dozens more who should have.

It appeared, she noted in passing, that Betsy Barber's breasts were real.

"Sandi wants us to give Dick Burke a hand on that Japanese tourist thing," she said to Joshua, who to his credit looked as sickened as she felt.

"Yeah," he said. He hesitated, then offered, "You've got to admit, it would be nice to be trying to solve a crime with an innocent victim, Rosie."

"I suppose it would."

"I mean, look, we catch this woman and it's not just going to be her on trial. It's going to be the women in these pictures and every woman who ever got sweet-talked into bed by a slick loser who came on too strong. It's going to be victims of date rape and exploitation on parade, Little Red Riding Hood on trial for killing the wolf. Our gal's not a murderer. She's a fucking folk hero."

"Do you really believe it's all that simple? That mean old Pelletier seduced her? A woman like that?"

"What the hell else would a woman like that be *doing* with a guy like him?"

"She's lonely," Rose said without hesitation, surprising herself. "And starved for love. She saw something in him, something special, a possibility."

"So why did she kill him?"

"Because he disappointed her."

Joshua laughed nervously and shook his head. "If women were really like that, Rosie, no man would live a second."

Rose said nothing. It had been way too long a day. She was looking at the pale ring on the coffee table, where the beer bottle had been, and thinking, for some reason, about Jack and how fascinated he had always been with the extraordinarily high suicide rate among police officers. There were only two reasons a cop ate his gun, Jack used to say. One, he wasn't a cop anymore, he was burned out, and couldn't think of anything else to do. But Jack had been a cop right up to the end. Which left the second reason, which was what Jack used to call *the unaccomplished task*. She hadn't understood it at the time, but she was starting to catch a glimpse now and then, at the end of a day like this, of what Jack had meant. It got to you, in the long run, the accumulation of loose ends, the things you'd missed and the things you hadn't pursued. The things you flat out couldn't catch up with and the things there just hadn't been time or energy for. The things left undone. They just kept piling up, like dirty laundry.

"I suppose we should talk to Dick Burke in the morning," she said resignedly. "He'll give us nothing but shit-work to do, I guarantee it."

"I hate working with that guy," Joshua agreed, but she could tell he was relieved. His heart hadn't been in this one from the start. They gathered up the photos, put the folder in a bag and tagged it, and turned off the lights as they left. Outside the apartment, they paused to reseal the crime-scene tape, but it felt empty to Rose, just going by the book now. They weren't coming back. There'd be a new, more urgent case to work on by the time they were done with the Japanese tourist, and then another, and this one would fade away into the statistics. For all the right reasons, and some of the wrong ones, someone had gotten away with murder.

4

THE LAUNDRY WAS ALREADY piling up again, but Helen let
it go, along with the breakfast dishes in the sink, the
vacuuming, and the shower curtain with its dappling of
incipient green. Her mother never would have done that,
she knew, feeling both the stab of guilt and the sense of lib-
erating free fall that always came with the thought. Cora
Rainey would have died before she let a trace of mold
bloom on the shower curtain or a single dish rest beyond its
moment in the sink.

Had died, literally, before she did. Helen remembered
coming home from her last day of junior high school, the
day Travis Gurnham had kissed her in the hallway and
promised to call over the summer. She'd walked into the
house to the usual roar of the vacuum cleaner and found
her mother lying on the living-room floor beside the top-
pled machine, looking up at a skein of cobweb on the chan-

delier. That must have been maddening to poor Cora, to be *hors de combat,* a casualty of the war on disorder.

She had been gasping for air, her mouth opening and closing like a beached fish's, as if she'd finally realized there was no oxygen in the house, that there hadn't been for years. Helen had knelt beside her and taken her hand and kissed it. She'd felt strangely serene. Her mother's helpless eyes were wild with supplication, begging silently in her dying as they had urged and prodded in her life: *Do something! DO SOMETHING!* But Helen had done nothing: hadn't called 911 or plunged into heroic CPR or screamed for the neighbors, or even turned off the vacuum cleaner. She'd just sat there, holding Cora's hand, her beautiful, neglected pianist's hand, emptied of dust rags and sponges, stilled at last, feeling the dry scrape of her mother's skin. She wanted to tell her mother that she'd waited for this day, that she'd watched Cora polish and scrub and shine the surface of their lives until it had rubbed thin, into transparency. That she could stop laboring now and feel, if only for this single moment, the love that was supposed to have been the reason for all that goddamned cleaning.

The terror slowly settled out of Cora's gray-green eyes; the starkness of accusation faded and something like acceptance began to dawn. Her body relaxed and her breath began to ease and slow. Her mother might, truly, have been relieved, Helen thought: Cora might even have been glad, at last, to be so thwarted, to have nothing left to do but love and die.

She held her mother's hand, meeting her gaze as defeat passed into peace, and peace, into mystery. The vacuum roared on, the sound track of her childhood, useless now, white noise merely, and even weirdly soothing, like surf or rain on a roof. And still her mother gazed up at her, tender and unblinking, from a stillness so deep it was impossible to say when it emptied finally into vacancy. When it had, Helen reached over and yanked the vacuum cleaner's cord.

The plug popped out of the wall socket and silence settled on them, unmoving and vast, as if time itself had stopped.

Her father came home from work that night a little late, baffled by a house without its cooking smells and inclined to be irritated by the failure of routine. He found them there in the twilit living room with the lamps still off. Helen remembered it as the single time she'd ever loved him wholly, that instant torn from his impenetrable banality. Parker Rainey had clicked on the overhead light and taken in the scene with a glance, his swift lawyer's mind grasping at once that the thing was beyond appeal. He'd taken a single faltering step and stopped, unnerved by the surprise of death if not by grief. And then her father had fallen to his knees for once in his life and wept.

Helen drove through the Presidio to the Marina Safeway that afternoon to shop for things she could just as easily have bought in the Richmond neighborhood where she and Jimmy lived. But the produce section and the wine aisle at the Marina Safeway were as good as any singles hot spot, and she had to get out of the house, with its burglar bars on the windows and the leaden ocean dampness puddled on the hardwood floors and Jimmy's pit bull, Bubbles, barking the day away in the foggy backyard, chewing at the chain-link fence and looking for something innocent to kill.

She wandered the supermarket's aisles perfunctorily, pushing a cart she didn't really need, her freshly pecan hair soft with the smell of Clairol aloe, chamomile, and ginseng. She'd gone for a Winona Ryder look, perky and simple, layered short with slightly ragged pixie bangs and a fringed neckline. It made her look seventeen, another reason to fish here rather than in a bar, where bartenders remembered women they'd carded way too well. She was dressed down in loose jeans with a hole in one knee, beat-up Adidas running shoes, and a tan corduroy shirt of Jimmy's falling open over a white tank top. Her nipples showed, but only when she wanted them to, and her eyes were nutmeg brown.

There was a candidate down the wine aisle, a hunky ad-agency type in a beige turtleneck with a diamond stud in his left ear, mulling the reds in the expensive end of the French section. He met her eyes with an impassive poise, investing nothing; she pushed her cart past him without slowing, plucked a cheap California Merlot from the shelf farther down, and moved on.

In the produce section, there were three more, a gay accountant planted in front of the designer salad dressings; a literate financial-district wonk, probably bisexual, his loud tie loosened, lingering conspicuously near the asparagus; and, amid the melons, a cocky thirty-something in bicycle tights with red and yellow racing stripes and a Nittany Lions sweatshirt. The financial-district wonk eyed Helen frankly as she rolled by. Definitely bisexual. She pushed her cart on to the fruit section, where the Penn State alum was hefting two cantaloupes at chest level like somebody from a *Saturday Night Live* skit doing bad supermarket come-ons.

"I can never tell what's ripe," the guy confided artlessly. He had a bleached crew cut, a tasteful Nautilus-tuned physique, defined but not excessive, and a salon tan.

"It's an art form," Helen conceded.

"I thump and I sniff and I shake, but I just can't tell." His hazel gaze was pure innocence, but it flickered as a lithe brunette in a sports bra and spandex pants cruised by, snagging his attention briefly. Helen waited until his eyes came back to her and said, "Maybe it would help to just check one melon at a time."

The guy laughed appreciatively, not even bothering to be sheepish. She could see that she had surprised him, which was easy enough for her. But this guy liked surprise, even at his own expense. There was even a touch of respect in his manner, suddenly. Taking her more seriously. He set the smaller cantaloupe down at once, without grudging, and said, "Point taken. My name's Mike, by the way."

"What a nice name," Helen said noncommittally, and he laughed again. Two for two, she thought. Most guys would already have crumpled and retreated, if they'd even noticed that they'd been zinged.

"So about this cantaloupe—" he persisted.

She took it out of his hand and sniffed the spot where the stem had been. It smelled like cardboard. The fruit was almost comically hard, like a duckpin bowling ball.

"Those are very striking earrings," Mike offered.

"Oh, these old things," Helen said, pleased. The earrings were the only real thing she was wearing today. She'd affixed twenty-four-karat white-gold wires to two of Henry Pelletier's trout flies, laboriously delicate concoctions of fine silver tinsel and yellow floss, with black and blue strips of peacock tail feathers for the wings.

"Those hooks look dangerous," Mike noted. "They could catch on something."

"Isn't that the point of hooks?" she said.

He met her eyes, a sharp, startled look, as if he wasn't sure he'd heard her right. Helen gazed back impassively, her turn to look guileless, and after a moment Mike smiled.

"I suppose that it is," he conceded.

Beside them, the produce misters blossomed suddenly, a fine chill spray accompanied by a jaunty snatch of Gene Kelly.

"*I'm SING-ing in the rain, just SING-ing in the rain—*"

They both took half a step away to stay dry. Helen felt her nipples stiffening against the tank top at the onrush of cooler air. She closed Jimmy's corduroy shirt over her breasts, but she knew that Mike had noticed.

The music faded and the brief weather of the misters cleared. They stood looking at each other for a moment more, and then Helen dropped Mike's cantaloupe back into his hand and smiled.

"This is nowhere near ripe," she said. "Not even close."

"That's okay. I'm a patient man."

"Are you?"

Mike fondled the melon frankly and grinned. "It's one of my best qualities."

"Well, I'd give it a couple of weeks, at least." She almost laughed at his look of dismay. It was heartening, somehow, to know he wasn't as patient as he thought.

"That long?" Mike asked, a trifle plaintively.

"Some things just can't be hurried," Helen told him. She left him with a trace of a smile and wheeled her cart away, neither fast nor slow, the barbs buried in the feathered earrings tickling her neck, her heart racing deliciously. She knew his eyes were on her as she went, that he watched her until she was out of sight, and even after Helen turned the corner toward the checkout aisle, she could feel the thread of his attention, like tapered filament, pulling taut where it disappeared beneath the surface.

Jimmy was working late again; the Burlingame job, to his great delight, was paying a lot of overtime and he loved working under the lights. Helen had some leftover lasagna and tried to watch TV, but in the end, as she had known she would, she went out. It scared her that the restlessness was back already. It scared her that her eyes were already starting to hold other eyes an instant too long, that her gaze was turning sticky with the question. That her heart already ached, that her skin had begun to hunger again so soon. Love wasn't supposed to be like this. Love was supposed to last longer than a Level 2 hair colorant. But love had never been what it was supposed to be.

She took the Geary bus downtown, skimmed the

Tenderloin, and found a harmless yuppie bar south of Market. The place was alive with the after-work crowd, market analysts and brokers in loosened ties, women with briefcases, in crisp suits and sneakers, and dot-commers in name-brand jeans and crocodile-logo polo shirts with beepers in the pockets. An irritating surfeit of hanging plants and shrubbery in urns dominated the décor, in an apparent effort to disguise the fact that the bar had been a burrito joint six months before, but the new owners hadn't bothered to paint over the murals, and scenes of idyllic Mexican village life peeked through the foliage: children at play, salt-of-the-earth men laboring beneath huge sombreros, women in bright red dresses happily hauling water, and overloaded burros with patient, placid faces.

Helen ordered a vodka tonic and took a seat at the end of the bar near the bathroom, well out of the action. It seemed like a night to just watch the scene. She was dressed for mediocrity, if not invisibility, in a frosted blond wig that looked as though she'd spent the last year trying to get her hair right, and a midlevel secretary's outfit straight off the rack at Target. Several men approached anyway, but she fended them off with ease. A little disdain up front worked wonders; in a target-rich environment like this, no one had time for an hourly-wage girl with an attitude.

The last candidate, a square, red-faced buffoon in a loud tie, doomed to middle management, was the most persistent. He actually tried to move her purse off the stool beside her and sit down.

"That seat is taken," Helen told him, before he could slide his ass into place.

He signaled the bartender anyway, in jovial okay-I'm-game fashion. "I've got a fresh drink coming at you, honey, that says it's not."

She took her purse off the bar where he had set it and placed it firmly in the center of the seat again. "Taken."

The guy's watery blue eyes lost focus for a moment; he blinked twice, then touched his helmet of immobilized black hair as if resecuring a hat after a gust of wind, and said, "Well, fuck you, too."

"Not in your lifetime," Helen said. The guy moved off shaking his head and rolling his eyes for the crowd, as if he'd discovered, almost too late, that she had a sexually transmitted disease. Helen watched him touch base with his loser friends at a table beneath one of the more extravagant ferns, jerking his thumb toward her, putting his spin on the incident like a cat licking itself after a fall, pretending he had meant to do it that way. The loser friends all laughed sympathetically. They had to; he'd taken one for the team.

The bartender showed up with the new vodka tonic, looking a little uncertain in light of developments.

"Is this on Asshole's tab?" Helen asked. The barkeep, a pretty young blonde who looked like she was probably a dancer in real life, nodded, perhaps a little conspiratorially, and Helen picked the drink up and tilted it toward the rapt table of men in mock acknowledgment. The losers all hooted and the asshole fretted for a moment, floundering for a foothold on what pride required, then actually started back toward her, apparently intending to claim the vodka tonic as his own. Helen gave him a smile and dumped the drink in the spill tray. The guy stopped in his tracks.

The losers laughed. Team spirit only went so far. Helen turned back to the bar.

"The next one's on me," the bartender said.

After that, the room pretty much had the picture, and Helen was left to herself. That suited her on this particular night. She preferred to pick her own moments, and in any case her sense was that Cantaloupe Guy from the Safeway would do for the next real thing. But it was always interesting to watch the mating dance. The tilt of the bar toward young professionals gave it a distinctly mixed flavor:

unbuttonings among the yuppies happened fast, when they happened, but the prelims had an air of résumés being exchanged.

The asshole, she noted, recovered quickly from the fiasco with her; within five minutes he was chatting up two women midbar and shouting, "Hey, beautiful!" at the bartender to secure more drinks. He paid by holding out a twenty and then pulling it back when the bartender reached for it, repeating this process several times before flipping the bill in the general direction of the poor woman's breasts. The bartender kept a professional smile frozen on her face, but she looked like she was ready to call the bouncer. The two women the guy was hitting on also looked finished with him, but apparently neither had the wherewithal to dislodge him.

Helen watched the payment process repeat itself a second, and then a third, time; on the last round, the guy actually flicked the bartender's breasts with the twenty before pulling it back when she reached for it.

Helen realized that she was thinking of picking up the asshole and killing him just for the satisfaction of it. It wasn't usually her thing, that kind of public service.

"Bad apples," a quiet voice said from beside her.

Helen glanced to her left. A middle-aged man had taken the seat next to her, so quietly that she hadn't noticed him. It gave her a moment's uneasiness. She didn't like to be taken off guard.

"Excuse me?" she said.

He nodded toward the asshole. "It's guys like him who give men a bad name. Makes it sort of embarrassing to have a Y chromosome."

"Actually, I was just thinking about killing him."

"I could do it for you, if you like."

Helen turned back to her drink. "Thanks, but I already have a boyfriend to kill people for me."

The guy was silent for a moment, and she thought he'd

taken the hint, but after a moment he said, "You look beautiful in this light."

Helen smiled, a little relieved. "Now that's a line, if I ever heard one."

He shrugged. "It's all lines, at this point. No way around it."

This was true, and she liked truth. Helen said, "I'm not looking for lines."

"What are you looking for?"

She looked at him closely for the first time. He was solid, not fat but not a gym rat either, a forty-year-old at some peace with his body, dressed mildly enough in khakis and an open-necked blue shirt. A good, if bland, face, without predatory qualities. Balding slightly, but no comb-over. No gold jewelry, no ring. Blue eyes, steady and amused. Helen said, "Simple perfect love will do."

The guy laughed. "God help you."

"Yeah. But He seems to be letting nature take its course."

"I'd settle for some genuine affection and oral sex, personally."

"Sounds like we're both aiming too high," Helen said, and he laughed, which she liked. She took out a cigarette, and the guy deftly produced a gold Zippo. Very gold, with an inscription. She breathed in the flame and blew the smoke toward the mirror. The guy set the lighter on the bar, inscription side up. Harvard '79.

"You look beautiful in this light," he said.

"You already said that."

"It just gets truer."

"Alcohol tends to have that effect."

"No, it's a fundamental aesthetic. Beauty is truth, truth beauty; that is all ye know on earth, and all ye need to know."

Helen smiled. "Now, *that's* a line."

"No, it's Keats."

He had a nice quality of confident self-possession. She

realized she was tempted, and wondered why. If he drove a Japanese car, perhaps she could begin to believe.

She persisted, "In context, it's a line."

He shrugged. "It passes for my soul. I was raised Westchester County agnostic, and our family values ran more to getting into a good college and supporting the New York City Ballet. Hopeless romanticism wasn't on the agenda. Reading Keats amounted to getting a tattoo." He sipped his bourbon and water and met her eyes. "In context."

Or a Chevy Cavalier, Helen thought. Something domestic. Something that got good gas mileage. "And now?" she asked.

He shrugged. "I terrified my family for fifteen minutes by writing free verse as an undergrad, then fulfilled the family dream, basically. Harvard MBA, good marriage, competent civilized divorce. I've added a little weekend cocaine, and I support the San Francisco Symphony. Keats is still my only vice."

"And the cocaine."

"No. The coke's just secular humanist maintenance."

Helen laughed and thought, What the hell. Roll the dice. "You got a car?"

"What?"

"A car," Helen repeated patiently. "A motor vehicle."

He came up with a set of keys as quickly as he'd found the lighter. The key ring had a Mercedes logo the size of a beer coaster.

Oh well, Helen thought. She realized that it hurt. He'd had her going, for a moment there.

"An S500," he specified, gratuitously. "But I'm going to upgrade soon."

"How Keatsian," she said.

5

"THAT CAN'T BE GOOD for the upholstery," Joshua said.

Rose grunted a perfunctory acknowledgment. It was not yet dawn, too early for black humor, and it didn't help that they had been up past midnight the night before, crunching American Express check numbers for the greater glory of Dick Burke. The Mercedes in front of them had apparently been stalled in the rinse cycle of the automated car wash with its windows wide open for most of the night, and was filled with water to the tops of the doors, like a mobile luxury hot tub with a steering wheel. The occupant, a white male, looked strangely tranquil, buckled into the driver's seat, aside from the fact that his neck was broken.

"You've got to be impressed with the way that car holds water," Joshua persisted. "German construction, man, you can't beat it."

"Why don't you go find us some coffee, Joshua, if you can't just get on with this?"

"Touchy this morning, aren't we?"

"I hate getting my feet wet," Rose said. "Especially before sunrise."

"Don't open that door, then. This thing is a waterfall waiting to happen." Joshua dipped a tentative finger into the water beside the corpse. "Jeezus, it's still warm. This is going to totally fuck up the time of death."

"No rigor."

"So what? The guy's been in a fucking Jacuzzi all night."

"I'm betting forensics doesn't come up with anything from the car either. Unless our killer left a rubber duckie."

"Looks like a wash, evidence-wise," Joshua agreed, straight-faced, and Rose finally relented into a smile.

"God, there must be some coffee around here somewhere," she said.

Chester Sparks, the AME, showed up a few minutes later, as did Perry, the young photographer, who seemed sexually rumpled and reeked of uncigarettish smoke. He looked like he hadn't been to sleep yet. Between Joshua and Chester teasing Perry, and the necessity of making every single obvious joke about their murder victim's undignified situation, it made for a tiresome fifteen minutes or so while the in situ photos were snapped and Chester made his preliminary examination of the corpse.

Joshua and Rose did scissors-paper-rock for who opened the car door, and Joshua won. They set up a screen to filter the flood, then Joshua, Chester, and Perry all retreated to high ground while Rose grasped the driver's-side door handle of the Mercedes. She tried to lean over and keep clear, but the door stuck and she finally had to just set her feet and yank.

The door blew open, and the water duly deluged. Rose danced back from the wave as well as she could, trying not to think of the likelihood that the dead man's bowels and bladder had released, as often happened in traumatic death. It was bad enough to get soaked to the knees by a Mercedesful of corpse bathwater without considering it as semi-sewage.

The flood subsided at last, and they all stepped back up to the dripping car. The filter screen was remarkably clear; no doubt anything that floated in the car had washed out during the free flow of the night's ongoing rinse cycle. The body slumped against the seat belt, looking pathetically bedraggled now without the support of the water. Draining the car had aged their victim fifteen years. A decent-looking guy, presubmersion.

"His fly is open," Joshua noted. "Maybe he's some kind of car-wash pervert."

Chester laughed. "Industrial-detergent sex gone bad. I've seen it a million times." He made a brief inspection of the body, then pronounced, "Clean break of the cervical spine. Cause of death, failure to keep his head on straight."

"Maybe it's some kind of weird new dating fad," Rose said. "A blow job in the tunnel of love. Maybe a little kinky, the seat belt still on. But it got too rough, and the partner panicked and bolted."

Joshua shook his head. "Not with the windows down. Any high school kid knows you have to close the windows before having oral sex in an automatic car wash."

Perry shot more photos from every angle, somewhat hastily and without his usual attention to artistic considerations, then took off, probably back to bed. Chester took a quick liver-temperature reading and confirmed what Joshua and Rose had already assumed, that the body temperature was relatively high and that it meant little in determining the actual time of death. According to the car-wash employee who had discovered the body in the drowned car when he came to open up at around five in the morning, the place had been unattended since about ten P.M. the night before. The dead man's wallet was gone, which was practically the only thing about the crime that had made any sense at all so far.

"A carjacking?" Joshua suggested.

Chester laughed. "With a finicky perp, right? 'Gimme your car, buddy, but for Christ's sake, it's filthy. Let's run it through the car wash first.'"

"Maybe it was an accident," Rose said. "I mean, say the guy decides to take a midnight ride through the car wash, he's drunk or something and forgets to roll up the windows—"

"And to zip his fly?" Joshua demurred. "Not to mention the missing wallet."

"The car-wash guy might have lifted the wallet, postmortem."

"It was underwater. That kid doesn't strike me as the type to pickpocket a drowned corpse. Besides, the car didn't go all the way through the cycle. Somebody hit the Stop button, Rosie."

"I don't think the car wash did this," Chester agreed. "The water pressure wouldn't be enough, no way, and even if he'd gotten smacked by a brush, I don't think the break would be that clean. I'll be a lot more sure of it once I do the autopsy, but I'd have to say early indications are somebody twisted this poor guy's neck about a hundred and eighty degrees too far and sent him on his little joy ride to screw up the crime scene." He shook his head, looking at the Mercedes. "If so, I have to say, it's a pretty nifty technique."

"I don't know," Joshua said. "I don't think they went for the deluxe wax job."

"We're not going to get shit out of this car, that's for sure," Rose said. "We've just got to hope for a witness."

Witnesses were not immediately forthcoming. The car wash was set back from the street, between two stores that had closed at nine the night before, and no residential windows had a view. The car-wash employee who had found the body that morning had seen nothing, knew nothing, and didn't want to know anything. He was fretting about the lost business, as a stream of commuter sedans slowed near the yellow caution tape strung across the Geary Street entrance, gaped, and drove on. But he agreed that for the car to have stopped in the middle of the cycle, someone would have had to hit the emergency Stop button. Rose had the control panel fingerprinted, but she didn't think it likely they'd get anything there. She also set the Crime Scene Unit team loose on the car, improbable though it was that any evidence had survived the hours of submersion and flushing.

The registration in the Mercedes's wonderfully watertight glove compartment indicated that their victim was probably one Dexter Haskell, resident of a Gough Street condo near Japantown. It didn't look promising, Rose thought. They would do the legwork, of course. But she knew that with no witnesses, no physical evidence, a dubious time of death, and an apparent robbery motive indicating a spontaneous killer unknown to the victim, it looked bad for solving the murder. Meanwhile, her cell phone had rung three times while she'd been standing there, two calls from Dick Burke trying to get her back on his tourist-killer case, and one from Sandi Thanh, also trying to get Rose and Joshua back on the tourist case, and asking frankly leading questions about whether it looked like an accident or suicide. It was a murder all right, Rose had to tell her lieutenant, and a mean one at that. But it wasn't a charttopper; it was just another dead body in San Francisco.

Rose stood by the car for a long moment, hoping for a lightning bolt. On an impulse, she fished the dead man's cell phone from his pocket. Miraculously, it was still functional. German cars and Japanese phones. She hit redial, a technique that often opened unexpected doors, and got someone breathy named Brunella. A 900 number. Brunella seemed an unlikely candidate for the crime, as she was somewhere near Chicago and seemed preoccupied with other activities.

Rose put the cell phone back in the man's soggy pocket and went for another cup of coffee from the overworked brewing machine in the car wash's dank office, painfully conscious that she was already grasping for straws, less than an hour into the investigation. If Haskell's wife or girlfriend hadn't recently taken out a million-dollar auto-insurance policy with a special clause covering car-wash incidents, or if some junkie didn't walk into the bank tomorrow and try to cash out Haskell's MasterCard, this one was probably staying on the board in red letters. Rose hated that. It ruined her fucking day.

6

H ELEN STUDIED HERSELF in the mirror, trying to decide
who she was going to be. Her mother's eyes looked
back, those limpid, depthless, maddeningly mild eyes,
transparent quicksilver tinged with green. It still unnerved
her sometimes, to glimpse her mother in these gaps between personas, in the little moment of naked possibility
before the next identity jelled. Her skin, washed free of
makeup, was her mother's milky, faintly freckled skin; her
hair was her mother's hair, wet from the shower now, the recent pecan rinsed away from the base of anonymous dun,
which Cora had cheerfully called "dishwater blond" and
colored a modest russet. Helen's features were her mother's
regular features, plain and unemphatically elegant, the kind
that wouldn't draw a second look without enhancement. It
was a face that could be what you made of it. Cora Rainey
had used that gift of mutability to fit in. She'd disappeared

into her domestic life like a chameleon, blending into the
drapes and the wallpaper and the understated pattern of
the living room couch. A waste of talent, Helen thought.
She used the same gift to stand out, to break free, to leave
the tired features of everyone she'd ever been behind, playing with looks the way you might play with combinations
on a lock, waiting for the click that told her she'd finally
made a face someone could love. Somewhere in that parade
of people in the mirror was the person she was supposed to
be. It was just a matter of finding her.

And so she got to work again. She put on one of
Jimmy's old work shirts and cranked up Neko Case's *Furnace Room Lullaby* on the CD player. The rubber gloves
and bleach were laid out neatly by the sink, along with the
comb, brush, and hairpick, the aluminum foil, and two
packages of dye. She'd found Mike lingering near the Safeway's melons again and she'd made this date as the same
old pert brunette, but it was time to warm that pecan up
with some good Malaysian Cherry.

Jimmy knew at once. He always knew instantly, and he
was always surprised. Helen wondered how his brain
worked, that he could still be surprised so deeply. But it
wasn't feigned. There was no faking anything for Jimmy.
Helen saw the dismay in his face the moment he came into
the kitchen, and the hurt in the way he turned to the refrigerator and wrenched open a Bud. He flipped the bottle top
onto the counter, struggling to be casual, but it ricocheted
off the toaster with a kind of violence before it rattled to a
stop.

"So—" he said. "What's his name?"

"Mike," Helen conceded. The great thing about Jimmy
was that he didn't waste time.

"Mike," Jimmy repeated. And in a bitter singsong, "Mike,
Mike, Mike."

"It's just a bike ride, Jimmy."

"Yeah, right." He took a savage pull of the beer. He was frankly sullen, like a dog that had been kicked for no reason, and Helen felt a stab of guilt, which she promptly resented. Jimmy had had his chances, God knew. It wasn't her fault that he only knew one trick.

"We've always said we could see other people," she said. "We've always said we weren't tied down."

"*You've* always said it, you mean."

Helen let it go. It was true enough. They stood for a moment in silence. Bubbles was barking furiously at something in the backyard, a cat or a squirrel or a seagull; it didn't matter. The damned dog was always barking at something. Helen turned to pick up her belly pack and strapped it on, then gathered up her urban bicyclist's necessities, her sweatshirt and her helmet, the water bottle and the little can of Mace.

She felt Jimmy's eyes on her as she readied herself. He was watching her as he hadn't watched her in weeks, hurt into alertness at last, studying her as if she were the other person in a knife fight. The rage in his silence was almost palpable; she could hear it in the shallowness of his breathing, a low pant like the muted rhythm of flames behind a closed furnace door. She felt deliciously naked in the new biking outfit, the black spandex sheathing her like a cool caress, like oil on a blade. She felt taut and free and dangerous.

"What time are you going to be back?" Jimmy demanded as she gathered up the last of her things, his voice strained, as if the words had forced their way through a rubber seal.

Helen hesitated, then hated herself for the hesitation, for the fear in it. "I don't know," she said. She could hear the rattle of the fence out back as the pit bull slammed against it. How stupid did an animal have to be to keep attacking a chain-link fence?

"I'll kill the son of a bitch, if he lays a hand on you," Jimmy said, feeling her waver. "I'll kill you both, if you fuck him. I swear to God, I will."

"Always the southern gentleman," Helen said. And, coldly, because she had to, "Don't wait up, Jimmy."

His nostrils flared, but he didn't move. Helen knew how dangerous that stillness was. But she made herself turn toward the door, walking normally, steeling herself to not flinch as she passed him, because if she flinched, she was his forever in her fear.

She got to the windmill in Golden Gate Park five minutes early, but Mike was already there, straddling his fifteen-speed Peugeot by the flower beds on the rise above the ocean, clad in yet another blue Penn State sweatshirt, sleeveless this time, and silver bike pants that left nothing to the imagination. He looked suspiciously posed as Helen rolled up, his chiseled features rapt, gazing out to sea with one foot cocked on a pedal and the other planted firmly in a way that showed every muscle of his lean leg. Framed by masses of scintillating red tulips, with his fine arms puckered into goose bumps and the breeze ruffling his short bright hair, he might have been the August cover for a yuppie health magazine. But Helen decided to give him the benefit of the doubt. The poor guy couldn't help that he was beautiful, that he looked like Keats with a bleached crew cut, gazing soulfully at the Pacific. The sea was navy blue, flecked with whitecaps; the sky was cloudless but she could see the fog bank on the horizon, a leaden mass like an ugly premonition.

When she stopped beside him and he smiled at her, his gaze was genuinely serene. She loved that, that he'd really been looking at the ocean.

"You're beautiful," she said, because she didn't have forever.

Mike laughed delightedly, perfectly, pleased but not puffed up.

"So are you," he said. "Is that red in your hair new, or it is just the sunlight?"

"It's new," Helen said.

Mike said he had forgotten something, a music tape he wanted her to hear, and they stopped briefly at his shabby little apartment across the street from the Richmond Safeway on the way past Ocean Beach. Helen stood just inside the front door, making a point of not touching anything, while Mike rummaged through a shoe box full of cassettes. He lived like a college kid, all garage-sale furniture and boards on blocks for shelves.

As Helen stood there, a beautiful Siamese cat wandered up and rubbed itself against her leg. She stooped to scratch behind its ears and flip over the silver name tag, which read "Agatha," wondering yet again what she was doing with Jimmy and his dog. She was not a pit bull person. She was a cat person.

Mike surfaced with two portable cassette players with headphones and twin copies of a tape he'd apparently mixed especially for their date, and they went back down the stairs to their bikes. Mike clipped one player to Helen's waist and slipped the headphones over her ears, then set up the other cassette player for himself.

"Ready?" he asked, as they stood poised on their bicycles side by side, and Helen nodded, feeling oddly, marvelously, like a child in good hands. Mike reached over and punched the Play buttons, first on her machine, then on his own, and Madonna kicked in, the opening notes of "Like a Prayer" surprisingly rich through the tiny headphones. Mike gave Helen a questioning thumb's-up to make sure the music was playing. She smiled and held her own thumb up in reply, and they leaned over their handlebars and started up the long hill toward the Cliff House listening to the same music.

For the forty-five minutes of the tape's A side, it was pure magic. Helen had half expected some kind of macho endurance test, but Mike took the hill languidly, tightroping the white line ahead of her in second gear, impervious to the car and bus traffic, his perfect gluteal muscles working easily. As they reached the Cliff House, Madonna gave way to some classic Carole King, "Where You Lead, I Will Follow," which might have struck Helen as presumptuous had she not been enjoying Mike's ass so much. As it was, she found herself singing along.

They snaked through the S-curve above the sea and the view opened up to their left: the cormorants and pelicans coming and going on Seal Rock, the afternoon sunlight glittering on the Pacific, a Nissan freighter riding low toward the Golden Gate, on its way in from Japan. The day was balmy enough for them to break a gentle sweat on the climb, and when they crested the hill above Louie's Diner and turned through the parking lot toward Land's End, the breeze off the ocean was deliciously cooling.

Mike took the trail easily, too, riding slowly enough to savor the summer-brown Marin headlands across the water and, as they rounded the corner, the glimpses of the bridge on the switchbacks. It felt like wilderness now, nothing but sea and rocks below them and the scrubby oaks and stunted cypresses above. Mike's tape played on in Helen's ears, U2 in an expansive visionary vein, the Supremes, and George Michael, post-Wham. It was unexpectedly intimate and even more unexpectedly moving, to be held so firmly in the embrace of the songs Mike had chosen: the wit and bite in the lyrics, the ironies and the passion, the lilt and drive of the music seemed to be his, for her. It was like being sung to.

The fog was seeping landward but it seemed unreal and far away, a false heaviness discoloring the border between a sea full of sunlight and the robin's-egg blue of the flawless sky. Beyond the first half-mile of well-traveled tourist views, the trail was deserted. As they rounded a corner and came into sight of the Golden Gate again, Mike glanced back over his shoulder and said something, but Helen couldn't make out the words over the music in her ears. It didn't matter. They had forever to enjoy the moment and they had the moment all to themselves.

It can't last, Helen told herself. It was a soap bubble; it was a dream just before the alarm buzzed. She'd wake in a moment with morning breath and bad hair, and it would be over.

But she was already awake and it didn't end. It went on, curve by curve, a perfect thing as simple as keeping the bicycle upright through the ruts and steering between the stones, a perfect thing that asked nothing of her but the obvious and immediate, that she pedal hard on the gentle uphills and cruise the mild descents, that she keep Mike's lovely butt in sight, that she breathe the salt-freshened air.

Next was Sarah Vaughan singing "They Can't Take That Away from Me," which was simply a miracle. Jazz had been her father's only discernible passion. He could distinguish among the original takes of everything Charlie Parker had ever recorded, and he knew whether it was Zutty Singleton or Max Roach on the drums. Helen remembered sitting with her parents in the library on winter evenings, when darkness came early, while the LPs and 45s, ancient even then, spun with a trace of scratchiness in the sound. Her mother would be on the edge of the couch, ready to leap into service at the first sign of an excuse, but her father would loosen his tie, take his jacket off, and sink back in his deep cracked-leather chair with a vodka martini in his hand. Sometimes he would snap his fingers and nod his head as he listened, his glasses pushed back on top of his head, his steel blue eyes free for once of calculation. It had seemed possible for those moments that her father had a soul. There were family stories, amounting to myths, of Parker and Cora Rainey hitting the clubs in their youth, consorting with "Negroes" and drinking gin that still had the flavor of illegality and, unimaginably, dancing. It was hard to believe, but Helen even had a photograph of her parents in each other's arms in some smoky room, looking happy, free, and young. She had kept the black-and-white picture like a chunk of the One True Cross, a holy relic bearing witness to the incomprehensible truth: Her parents' marriage had once been supple, a living thing. There had been love at the root of all that dead ritual.

The trail bent away from the sea, into a deep fold of the hills. The cypresses began to yield to eucalyptus trees and Sarah Vaughan sang on.

"The way you wear your hat . . ."

A thrill ran up Helen's arms. It was almost too much.

"My parents used to dance to this!" she called. But Mike couldn't hear her through his helmet and the headphones, and he pedaled blithely on. It didn't matter. She felt giddy with amazement. The magic had happened. Mike had seen her whole somehow. Through luck, fate, or mystical intuition, he had plumbed some depth in her and found the music for it, knowing her in advance even of her knowledge of herself.

They made the sharp switchback in the crotch of the hill and started up the next rise, downshifting and pedaling hard as the Pacific opened up below them again. She was starting to get tired now, feeling the ache in her thighs, and mercifully, at the crest of the hill, Mike pulled off the trail. Helen braked beside him gratefully. She was glad to see that he was panting a little too. They took off their helmets, let the headphones fall around their necks, and smiled at each other. Mike's eyes were shielded by a pair of impenetrable cobalt sunglasses, two-hundred-dollar shades with titanium frames, prominently labeled "Gucci." Beyond them, a flat rock ledge jutted like a balcony over the sea. Helen could feel her heart in her chest, beating hard from the climb.

"Are you afraid of heights?" Mike asked, genuinely solicitous.

Helen laughed. "I'm afraid of everything. But I never let it stop me."

He took it as permission to get off his bike and move toward the precipice. Helen followed, feeling the space before them as a live, charged thing, a disconcertingly intimate presence. The cliff plunged straight down here; five hundred feet below, waves thrashed and churned amid a clutter of black rocks. The breeze was stronger at the edge, a palpable, probing caress, as if the gulf were reaching out. Helen felt naked to that touch, her breasts and thighs defined by the wind against the spandex, her nipples beading in the chill. She could hear the tape playing on through the headphones around her neck, a comforting murmur, tugging gently on her attention like a thread of memory. Beside her, Mike was silent, still enigmatic in the Gucci shades, his weight back on his heels, his face lifted slightly to the reddening light of the western sun.

Touch me, Helen thought. It was hard to get past her sense that he could read her mind, after the prolonged intimacy of the music. This was the moment, on this dangerous altar, poised above the sheer fall, warm from the ride and lifted in mutual offering. Her skin was starved for it, a longing sharpened to the verge of pain. Surely he could feel it, like heat.

But Mike was leaning landward, swaying in almost imperceptibly slow motion away from both her and the abyss. A retreat, a concession to the cliff. Helen realized that he was afraid, too. It was comforting, for once, to see a man's weakness. They would be afraid together.

She reached up and plucked his sunglasses off, startling him. Mike's eyes in the sunlight were sea-green, and Helen thought of Miss Pretty, her father's present on her seventh birthday, an old-fashioned rag doll with red yarn hair, a big stitched smile, and eyes of flawless jade. She remembered her astonishment that Parker Rainey had found her such a perfect gift. How loved it had made her feel. How seen.

Helen took Mike's hand and moved it to her heart. His palm was warm and she could feel her heartbeat made real against it, rapid but even, heightened by his touch.

"Umm." Mike smiled appreciatively, sliding his hand to cup her breast and feathering her stiffened nipple with his thumb. Helen sighed and arched toward him. His free hand moved to her waist, prudently easing her away from the edge, but she resisted, surprising him, and they almost staggered. He gave her a startled look.

"I like it here," Helen said. "With you."

Mike laughed uneasily. "A woman on the edge."

"It's all the edge, sweetheart."

Their eyes met. She could still feel the pressure of his hand on her waist, a steady gravity. She leaned against it, toward the cliff. They stood like that for a moment, locked in a small contest of wills, and then Mike relented, letting her go and taking a frank step toward safety.

"Do you want to get stoned?" he asked, like a parent trying to distract an antsy child.

It was so wrong that Helen just blinked and stared at him.

"I want to make love," she said. She sounded plaintive and she hated herself for that. It wasn't something she should have had to say.

Mike smiled and nodded affably, even indulgently, as if to say, Everything in due time. He crossed the ledge to his bicycle, pulled a little bag of works out of his day pack, and began to fix a pipe.

"I've got some killer stuff from Maui," he said.

The music through the headphones around her neck ceased just then, and Helen felt the click at her waist as the tape ran out. The sudden silence was unnerving; she realized how much comfort she had been taking in that steady background buzz, the ongoing evidence of Mike's soulfulness. She reached down and hit Eject, and the tape popped out of the cassette player. She went to flip it, glancing at the title strip as she did, then stopped. The label, in a hasty male handwriting, read "Melanie's Mix for Mikey, copy 2."

"Who's Melanie?" she asked, conscious of the effort it took to keep her voice casual.

"Just some girl," Mike said, his own nonchalance effortless. "She turned me on to those tunes. It's a nice mix, isn't it?" He had the pipe loaded and he cupped a hand around it against the breeze and let his lighter's flame play over the bowl as he took a hit. Helen watched him suck more air in on top of the smoke; he held his breath until he turned a little red, then let it out in a long hiss, like a punctured inner tube. He offered her the pipe, and she shook her head.

"She called you 'Mikey'?" she asked.

"Who?"

"Melanie."

"Oh. Yeah." He smiled, that bright white Keatsian toothpaste smile. "Everybody calls me 'Mikey,' eventually."

"I'll bet they do," Helen said.

Mike fired his lighter and took another hit off the pipe. His eyes had softened to a blurry aquamarine, rimmed with red, and Helen thought again of Miss Pretty. How she had torn that green-eyed doll to pieces when she'd learned it had been bought by her father's secretary. She'd shredded it down to the smallest bit of stuffing and scattered the shreds, until there was nothing left of that false gift but two perfect jade buttons.

Helen turned back to the cliff and flipped Melanie's cassette out into the wind. It spun away into the endless loneliness and Helen watched it until it disappeared. The breeze was stiffening. Her skin rose into goose bumps as the first fingers of fog began to drift past. Somewhere far off, she could hear the earnest whine of a motorcycle laboring through a switchback. Jimmy, no doubt, her absurd white knight, urging on his noisy steed. Chivalry was not dead; it was just stupid and brutal as a pit bull slamming against a chain-link fence. He'd be here soon enough, to save her from herself.

"Did you say something about making love?" asked Mike, with the magnificent equanimity of the freshly stoned, and Helen turned away from the cliff to face him. But she could still feel the vertigo, that old familiar emptiness, as if every direction now were just the same long fall.

"I think the moment's passed, Mikey," she said. "But I suppose we could have sex."

7

THE CRABS HAD FOUND the body and it wasn't pretty. The good news was that if you stood upwind you didn't have to smell it; the bad news was that there wasn't any wind. Rose kept moving, but the stench seemed to follow her. She had already thrown up twice, once immediately upon her arrival at the base of the cliff, figuring she might as well get it over with, and again when she got her first full breath of the putrefying corpse. Reduced to dry heaves, she kept her distance as much as she could. It would usually have earned her a lot of grief from the rest of the team, but this one was testing the toughest crime-scene macho. They were all wearing gauze masks, and even Chester had gagged. She'd never seen the AME gag before.

The body, a white male, had landed with perverse precision on the rocks near the edge of the debris line, far enough out into the water to be roughly handled by God knew how many high tides but not far enough to be carried away. It had been there a while, long enough to have bloated and split in several places. The guy had probably been attractive, Rose thought, even beautiful, a well-built twenty-something with an open, choirboy's face. But his head canted now at a savagely unnatural angle, and both dangling arms flopped with each wave's wash like broken wings. A fallen angel, his shiny pants crumpled pathetically around his knees, the silver of the spandex dulled to soggy gray.

The bicycle lay just beyond him, hung up on a black rock, with the front tire, half sunk in the shallows, spinning with the surge like an ineffectual waterwheel. It had survived the fall remarkably well and actually looked rideable.

"He didn't lock up the bike," Joshua noted, deadpan.

"Probably from out of town," Chester agreed.

"That would fit with him missing the turn up there. A local would have known to go right, not left."

"No helmet, either," Chester *tsk*ed.

Joshua nodded gravely. "You just can't emphasize it enough: Safe cycling begins with the proper equipment."

Rose let them talk. It was one of the unwritten laws of police work: The grosser the death scene, the worse the jokes. The photographer, not Perry this time, had finished taking his shots, but no one was in a hurry to approach the body. Chester had already pronounced the guy dead from fifty feet away and seemed to feel his work was done. The fog had settled, heavy and motionless, and the tiny beach seemed cut off from the rest of the world. You couldn't even see the top of the cliff. With the suffocating smell, the high tide, and everyone's sense that the death was probably accidental, it made for a kind of inertia. It was just too cold to step into the water for a closer look. Rose was shivering in her thin cloth coat. Joshua, wearing his jacket over a sweatshirt that said SFPD HOMICIDE: OUR DAY BEGINS WHEN YOUR DAY ENDS, seemed more comfortable, though that might just have been showing off. In any case, she was going to let him be the one to get his feet wet.

"I'm wondering about the pants," she said. "It's a little weird, isn't it? Around the knees like that?"

"Maybe he was taking a leak and got too close to the edge," Chester said.

"Pissing in the wind," Joshua seconded. "Never a good idea." The two of them giggled like third-graders.

"Would the wave action have done that?" Rose persisted.

"Or the fall. Snagged on a shrub on the way down or something." Chester shrugged. "Nature's got a sick sense of humor sometimes."

Rose passed up the obvious response and considered the body. The swarming crabs were the most horrible thing she had ever seen. Dozens of them, scuttling busily. She could feel the bile rising in her throat again. She and Joshua had already interviewed and released the hikers who had found the corpse, two college kids from Berlin who'd gotten more than they'd bargained for, looking for a novel view of the Golden Gate. The girl, whose English had been quite good otherwise, kept lapsing into German for her exclamations: *Scheußlich. Entsetzlich. Gräßlich.*

Rose was conscious of a stirring among the men behind her. The two guys with the gurney from the coroner's van were getting cold and restless, huddled against the rocks in full gas masks like stranded aliens. The EMT crew had turned around halfway down the trail and gone home at the first whiff of the body. The photographer had thrown up and fled, and the yellow-jacketed Crime Scene Unit, wearing floater masks, had already combed the rocks and sand twice, finding nothing. Everybody just wanted to bag the damn thing and get out of there.

"I guess we might as well get on with this," she said.

Joshua shifted. "I'm thinking only one of us really needs to go in."

"I couldn't agree more."

"Scissors, paper, rock?"

Rose laughed incredulously. "No way, partner. It's your turn."

"The hell it is. That car wash thing doesn't count. The guy hadn't even begun to stink."

"He'd crapped in his pants. It was like opening a toilet."

"I did the last floater," Joshua insisted.

Rose hesitated, then sighed. "Okay, so we choose for it." They held out their hands and swung them on the count. "One, two . . ." She shot out two fingers, scissors, because he usually went paper, but Joshua had made a fist. *"Damn."*

"Stone beats hardware, every time." He smiled.

"Bite me."

"I've got your back, Rose."

She bent resignedly to pull on a pair of the hip-length waders that the Crime Scene Unit had brought. Chester was watching her, amused and suspiciously motionless.

"Saddle up, big guy," Rose said.

"No way, sweetheart. My work here is done. I could have pronounced this guy from the top of the cliff."

"Don't you at least want to give us a preliminary take on the cause of death?"

"I'm betting the autopsy will show that it was a failure to keep breathing."

"You da man, Rosie," one of the CSU guys called cheerfully, from the relatively protected spot at the far back of the beach, where they were all sitting around with the collars of their yellow jackets up, smoking cigarettes to dilute the smell.

"Bite me, Billy," she called back, matching his bright tone, and they laughed.

Yeah, it was funny all right.

Rose turned to the water and started toward the body. Right away, the smell was much worse and she gagged again, trying not to show it, not wanting to give the guys that satisfaction. It wasn't fair. She'd been losing her breakfast every morning for a week now as her hormones started to kick in. Puking at life and puking at death. That pretty much seemed to cover the things you could throw up about.

"I'll tell you one thing, Rosie . . ." Chester called after her.

Rose paused, as a wave washed over her booted feet. "What's that?"

"It wasn't the fall that killed him."

"No?" she said, intrigued.

"No way. I'm thinking it was the sudden stop at the end."

Everyone laughed again. Rose rolled her eyes and continued toward the body, picking her way carefully along the rocky bottom and counting her steps from force of habit, for the crime-scene sketch. She had her notebook out, more for the comfort of holding on to something than from any sense that she'd be writing much down. The crabs held their ground until she was almost upon them, then scattered. The body seemed even sadder, somehow, without the grotesque distraction of their scurrying. More starkly what it was: the soggy, broken carcass of what had been a handsome young man, draped over a wet rock, staring at the sky from gutted sockets. Phlebas the Phoenician, a fortnight dead, Rose thought unwillingly; her undergraduate degree in English, normally useless, often came back to haunt her in situations like this. *Those are pearls that were his eyes.*

She forced herself to take a visual inventory. No helmet, as Joshua had noted. But everything else was expensive state-of-the-art. A silver cycling jersey, the zipper halfway down to reveal smooth pectorals, flaccid now but sculpted by obvious hours in a gym. Matching silver cycling tights, obscenely bunched around the poor guy's calves. Wool racer socks of royal gray, moisture-wicking acrylic booties, and cleated off-road biking shoes with a Pearl Izumi logo, Velcro straps, and nylon mesh uppers reinforced with suede and cordura nylon. No gloves, which seemed odd, given the obvious commitment to stylish cycling. But maybe the waves had stripped them off somehow.

Rose realized that she was getting used to the smell. She took off her mask, tentatively, and the guys on the beach hooted, thinking she was going to throw up again. But she could actually breathe without gagging. It was truly weird, what the human nose could get used to.

With the energy freed up by not suppressing nausea, she steeled herself to inspect the body. There was obvious trauma to the skull above the forehead, typical of an uncontrolled fall. The front of the corpse was purplish, the back side pale, which probably meant the kid had landed facedown and been flipped by the waves at some point after the lividity had fixed. The hands and wrists dangled eerily, and there were compound fractures on both forearms, apparently splintered in a futile attempt to break the fall. The wounds around the protruding shards of bone had been worked deeper by the crabs and gulls.

All the soft parts of the body—eyes, tongue, genitals—had been eaten away, and the ragged wounds gaped obscenely. Rose felt a wave of outrage at the indignity of it, along with a dizziness that she recognized as sympathy. And as sadness, as grief for the sheer human violation. It was the kind of emotion the pros always said would burn you out if you felt it, the kind everyone avoided like Mexican water. It was what made crime-scene humor so black and crime-scene banter so cold and hard. You couldn't feel it, the wisdom went. You had to keep it at a distance.

A single crab, already accustomed to her presence, made a tentative approach to the body again. Rose stepped closer to shoo it away. Beside the corpse now, close enough to touch it, she hesitated, then thought, What the hell, the photos in situ had already been taken; and she reached out and tugged the crumpled bike pants back up over the poor guy's hips.

This drew more catcalls from the men on the beach, but

Rose ignored them. They seemed very far away. She could feel a kind of hush settling over her, a dawning lucidity. It was one of the secrets of homicide work, the odd, impersonal quiet that lit everything around you at the most unlikely times. Somewhere beyond the revulsion and the defenses, beyond even the twisting knife of kamikaze compassion, things got clear and still. The carnage came into focus as a problem, as a puzzle. You stood there with death in that sudden clarity as if in the calm at the eye of a hurricane and you tried to figure out what the hell had actually happened. It wasn't something Rose talked about, this weird serenity that came upon her. It wasn't something every detective had. Jack had had it. Joshua showed signs of it. The best ones had it, and she was one of the best.

She could see the thin nylon belt around the body's waist now. A belly pack. A wave staggered her a little just then, the surge hitting her midthigh. The tide was still coming in. She regained her balance, set her feet, and heaved the corpse on its side, rotating the belt until the pocket appeared. There was a cassette player clipped beside it, much the worse for wear, the headphone wire stripped away. Through the fogged window she could read the label on the tape: "Melanie's Mix for Mikey." It hurt anew to think there was a girlfriend to contact.

Rose unzipped the belt's pouch and found a key ring, a slim, silver cell phone, and a wallet. The photo on the driver's license showed a handsome young man, rakish in a mustache phase. He'd had green eyes, Rose noted. Beautiful green eyes. His name was Mike Turner, and he'd been twenty-eight years old.

She bagged the wallet, phone, and keys; took the tape out of the cassette player on a whim and bagged that, too, then gave the body a last once-over. Turning it had exposed the right arm and Rose saw that there was something on the sleeve, a bit of unlikely blue-and-green color, a bug or something. A dragonfly, she thought. Weird. She shooed it and it didn't fly away and she realized that it was artificial. A fishing lure, a hand-tied fly, snagged on the spandex.

"You got something, Rosie?" Joshua called.

She waved him off impatiently. If he wanted a play-by-play, he could damn well get his feet wet, and she was trying to think it through. The obvious assumption was that the fly had hooked onto the sleeve while the body was in the water, but there was no fishing line attached.

Rose considered the thing for a moment more, wishing she had brought a camera. She didn't want to remove the fly without documenting its location on the sleeve, but she was afraid it would get lost in the shuffle of the body being taken to the morgue. At last she reached out and worked the hook free of the spandex.

She held the lure at arm's length to study it, thinking yet again that it was probably time to let vanity go and buy those reading glasses for close-up work. The fly was exquisitely crafted, but that wasn't the most interesting thing about it. It had been made into an earring and the white-gold ear wire, its loop half straightened as if it had been yanked off, had a smear of something dark on it that looked an awful lot like blood.

As she bagged the earring, Rose became conscious of an intermittent electronic beeping. One of those annoying, unplaceable postmodern sounds that nagged at the edge of one's consciousness, incongruous here. She checked her cell phone, and the victim's cell phone, and then her pager, but all the devices were silent. She cocked her head and listened. *Beep . . . beep . . .* It was coming from the bicycle, she realized.

She waded reluctantly toward the Peugeot, through deepening water that was coming closer to the tops of her boots now. The bike had some piece of electronic equipment on the handlebar—a Cyclocyber 500, she saw, as she drew closer. A bicycle computer, for Christ's sake.

"Rosie, what the hell are you doing?" Joshua hollered again.

"The bike's got a computer, and it's making some kind of weird noise!"

"What?"

"There's a goddamned computer on the goddamned bicycle!"

"WHAT?" Joshua yelled over the surf noise.

Rose ignored him and attended to the device. The tiny screen was flashing BATTERY LOW. She hit the most obvious button, and the screen switched and said, TRIP 1, CURRENT ALTITUDE: 1 METER. TOTAL ALTITUDE GAIN AND LOSS: 914 METERS. MAXIMUM ALTITUDE LOSS: 187.4 METERS. ELAPSED TRIP TIME: 157:31:24 . . . 25 . . . 26 . . ."

"I think we've got a way to figure the time of death!" she called excitedly, as the screen switched back to the low-battery warning. "Josh, do you know anything about bicycle computers?"

"What?"

"Shit," Rose said. She couldn't make any sense of the computer's minimalist buttons. She pondered the dilemma for a moment, then took out her cell phone and hit Seamus's work number on the speed dial. He answered on the first ring, as he always did. He was never anywhere but at his computer station it seemed.

"Hey," she said.

"Oh. Hey." He sounded distracted, but what else was new. Even with the lousy reception at the bottom of the cliff, she could hear his keyboard clicking.

"I've got a technical question."

"It's not really a good time, Rose."

A wave topped her boots, and cold water poured down her legs. There went those nice Eddie Bauer wool slacks that made her butt look so good, and the eighty-dollar loafers from Nordstrom's. Rose fought for patience. She and Seamus had finally had the fight about the chicken the week before. She'd left the chicken from their aborted special evening in the oven until it had withered and the whole house began to smell like a dead bird, but Seamus had never done the math. He thought a skunk had died under the kitchen floor or something and seemed prepared to live with that. Finally, on Friday night, Rose had taken the desiccated chicken out of the oven and arranged it with orange slices and parsley garnishes on the exquisite Celtic platter that Seamus's mother had given them for a wedding present. She'd thrown their Irish linen tablecloth over the dining-room table, laid out two place settings with their best silverware and china, then lit two tall white candles in silver sticks, plopped the chicken mummy between them, and settled in to wait for Seamus to come home from work. When he dragged in just after midnight he'd found her sitting there with the candles almost guttering and the air thick with decay like a neglected poultry crime scene. She'd been so mad by then that there was no chance of the conversation going well. Seamus had just thought she was nuts. And maybe she was. They'd been tense with each other ever since.

"I'm not asking you to be a decent human being, darling," she said. "I need your expertise. I'm standing here with a boot full of water, a guy who smells worse than that chicken, and a bicycle computer that's about to crap out on me."

"You're with a dead body?"

"And a dying computer. I need to save the data before the damn thing shuts down."

"Well, shit, I don't know. Hit Save."

"It's all icons."

Someone said something in the background at Seamus's end and he broke off to reply.

"Urgency, Seamus," Rose said. "Just tell me what the hell to do."

"Is there a Menu button?"

"It's all fucking pictures, goddammit!"

"There's no need to get testy, Rose. I'm just trying to help you out here."

The screen started flashing DATA LOSS IMMINENT. Rose held her tongue, knowing that Seamus would be Seamus. She wondered if the SFPD gave medals for marital heroism beyond the call of duty.

Seamus waited a moment more to make his point, then said in his best professionally patient tone, "Often the Menu icon is a little page with lines."

"Got it. Should I hit that?"

"Sure," Seamus said, which seemed unconsidered. But she punched the button and the screen switched to show a column of choices.

"More damn pictures," Rose said.

"One of them must be Save."

"Thanks, sweetie."

"That's just sarcasm," Seamus said. "Pure, unadulterated sarcasm."

The biggest wave yet washed through, wetting her to the hips and filling the second boot with water. Rose took a deep breath and said, "There's an icon of a little page with the corner cut off. There's a box. There's a doubled box. There's a little page with wings on it. There's an icon of a trash can."

"Try the doubled box."

"How do I scroll down? There's no mouse."

"Use the arrow buttons."

She hit the down arrow until the doubled box was highlighted. "Okay."

"Okay, what?"

"Okay, I scrolled down to the doubled box."

"Hit Enter."

"Icons, Seamus."

"Is this really that important?"

"You mean really truly completely important like whatever it is you do all day and night for strangers you don't like, or just minimally important like a marriage?"

"This is still about the chicken somehow, isn't it?"

Rose hit the right arrow button and the screen switched to show a split-screen display of data, TRIP AVERAGE data on the left, and CURRENT information on the right. She hit the left arrow to go back to the main menu and tried the icon of the page with wings. This time the right arrow led her to SAVE TRIP? She hit the right arrow again, and the screen prompted, SAVE CHANGES TO TRIP 1?

"Shit," Rose muttered, wondering if she had already altered the data. If so, she should probably not save the changes. But what if the complete trip data wasn't saved yet?

She went with what she knew and hit the right arrow again. The screen flickered busily, then went back to a display of the current altitude, temperature, trip totals, and elapsed time for a moment before going blank entirely.

"I think I got it," she said. "Whew."

"Is there anything else?" he asked, so patently not wanting there to be anything else that she almost blurted out, Yes, you prick, I want a divorce.

But Rose said, "Well, now that you mention it, there is. I'm pregnant."

There was a long silence. Even the clicking of the keyboard at his end had stopped. Rose took some pleasure in that. She wasn't sure she'd ever made him stop multitasking before.

"How pregnant?" Seamus asked at last.

"Completely. I am completely fucking pregnant."

"You know what I mean."

"When was the last time we made love, Seamus?"

More silence. A seagull landed on Michael Turner's chest and, as Rose stared at it in horror, stabbed at a ragged eye socket.

"Hey!" she hollered, and the gull took off. Another gull

swooped in to harry it, trying to get it to drop the piece of Michael Turner it had taken.

"What?" Seamus said.

"Nothing. Sorry. Weird scene here."

"Maybe we should talk about this tonight."

"Ya think?"

"I mean, as opposed to right now."

"I know what you meant. I'm sorry." His keyboard had started up again, she noted. Rose said, wearily, "Yeah, okay, of course. We'll talk tonight."

"Okay," he said, sounding way too relieved.

"Thanks for the help, Seamus."

"And thank *you*, for calling the PsiberSystems Inc. technical support hot line!"

In the past, it would have been funny. Rose said nothing. Seamus no doubt heard the flatness himself, because he quickly added, "Love you, Rosie."

"I love you, too," she said, wondering if either of them meant it anymore.

8

'M SORRY," Mike keeps saying, between coughs and sneezes. He feels terrible about her ear, and he doesn't seem to begrudge her the fact that she's sprayed him with Mace. "I'm sorry, I'm sorry, I didn't mean to hurt you."

His concern for her is weirdly endearing, even as he stands there with his pants around his ankles, his hard-on gone flaccid and his eyes red and streaming with tears. There is a deep, unlikely dignity to his solicitude and Helen feels a stab of confusion and remorse. It's like seeing something unexpectedly glinting in the trash. Maybe it is a diamond, maybe it is just cut glass. She would like to know. But of course Jimmy roars up on his bike just then and kicks the stand down and jumps off with his usual head of crazy steam.

Helen dabbed antiseptic on her torn ear lobe and winced. She still felt stupid about hooking the earring on

Mike's sleeve, but sometimes things just happened. She actually felt bad that she'd overreacted. It really hadn't been Mike's fault. He'd just been humping away, stoned and happy, and the barb had snagged on the synthetic net of his shirt, just as he'd been afraid it would, and she'd cried out and he'd yanked back and that was that. It had hurt so much she'd literally seen red, a bright crimson haze of pain and rage. It was different than the cold rage she felt about Melanie and the tape. That kind of rage freed her, made her calm inside. But the sharp hurt and the shock made her sloppy and stupid, and she'd hit him with the Mace. He'd still been staggering around the ledge apologizing when Jimmy rode up, the idiot cavalry on a Harley. Poor Mike, the look on his pretty face.

They hadn't even thought about the earring still being on his sleeve until it was too late to do anything about it. The tide was going out, but he'd landed on a rock and hung up. At least that's what Jimmy said; Helen hadn't been able to make herself look.

The whole thing had an element of terrible farce by then. They'd stood there by the cliff and debated whether to go put him in the water. Helen's urge was to hike down and clean up. She was her mother's daughter, after all, and never more so than when she'd made a mess. But Jimmy kept his head and said no, it's too risky, let the next high tide do the cleaning. And he was right, of course. He was a maniac sometimes, but he was a cool, practical man when the chips were down.

Her father had been the same way, at his best. Helen had cleaned the house for days after her mother had died, vacuuming and dusting and polishing like a madwoman. The Queen of Clean is dead, long live the Queen of Clean. But Parker Rainey had noted the frenzy and thwarted her compulsion by hiring a live-in housekeeper before his wife was in the ground, an obsessive-compulsive Swede with excellent references. That pretty much seemed to lay Cora to rest in Parker's mind. He'd taken Helen to Maui two days after the funeral.

The message was clear: Forget the damn vacuuming. Who went to Hawaii to grieve? Her father was treating her like a princess he'd just rescued from a dragon. It had been honeymoonlike. Ding-dong, the witch is dead.

They'd stayed at the Hyatt Regency in Kaanapali, in a fifth-floor suite with a doubled lanai and an ocean view, and the maids came in twice a day. Every morning they'd had coffee and five-dollar danishes in one of the place's many restaurants, then gone out to lounge on the beach in bright new bathing suits. Parker let Helen pick out her own suit at one of the hotel shops, with an air of letting her off a leash. She'd gone for an Ujena two-piece in Brazilian colors with minimal coverage that would have given Cora another stroke. Her first bikini. She was starting to get breasts and she felt naked on the beach, conscious for the first time of the eyes of men, of the assessing looks that they tried to hide. Helen could feel the attention like electricity, like something scathing and dangerous, and for a while she wore her matching sarong and one of her father's T-shirts until she was safely on her towel. But after a while she got used to it and she even began to savor the languid parade across the hot sand, with her sarong in her beach bag and Cora's silver crucifix bouncing in the beginnings of her cleavage and the sway of her slim hips exaggerated by the sand. She felt potent, at once exposed and inviolable, her eyes secret in the darkest shades, her skin already beginning to glisten and bake, while the male eyes swiveled to follow her.

They shopped and played tennis and every night they'd gone to the Pacific'O in Lahaina to listen to jazz. Parker bought her Shirley Temples, spiked them with vodka from his own drink, and taught her to tie the cherry stems into a knot with her tongue. In the dizzying rush of her first alcohol, Helen understood that her father knew his wife had probably not had to die that day. She'd never dialed 911, so she'd never know for sure herself. No one doubted Helen had been too distraught to act. But she felt in her bones that she'd killed her mother. She'd held Cora's hand and cradled her head as if she were holding her underwater, watching her mother's eyes go wild with desperation, and then calm with surrender, and then blank. She'd killed her. And somehow Parker knew.

They'd gone snorkeling one afternoon in Kapalua Bay. Helen had frolicked like a mermaid, reveling in the luminous water and the play of the colorful fish, in the languid, dreamlike elaborations of the coral. But every time she glanced toward her father, she found him watching her, his mouth frozen in an enigmatic O around the snorkel, his eyes magnified eerily through the mask. There was no judgment in his gaze; it was simply scrutiny, a consideration so steady and knowing that it amounted to acceptance and finally complicity. Like the looks of the men on the beach, it unnerved Helen at first, made her feel probed and even violated, a self-conscious stranger to herself; and then, as she grew accustomed to it, it made her feel invulnerable. Because the hunger in that gaze was his. Because it was she who led the eyes that followed.

And so she swam with a dawning sense of freedom, feeling the lazy power of the flippers driving her and the freshening caress of the water on her skin, and she dove deep when she pleased, and when she looked up she could see Parker Rainey suspended at the surface like a bug in silver jelly, floating helplessly in the light that was the sky beyond. Watching her, as if he were seeing her for the first time. She could forget about him entirely for long stretches, lost in the beauty all around her, but all she had to do was crook her finger and he would dive toward her like a fish coming to be fed.

Jimmy's favorite dinner was almost alarmingly simple: a thick steak seared black on the outside and dripping red within, a potato baked so dry it flaked, revived by a slab of butter, and canned lima beans. The lima beans had to be Del Monte; nothing else would do. Jimmy was a sort of idiot savant about lima beans and claimed to be able to distinguish between beans from a six-ounce can and the twelve-ounce cans he preferred. Helen had tested him on it, and it seemed he actually could tell the difference. So twelve-ounce cans it was. She hated lima beans. To her they looked like blood-fat ticks plucked from a dog, and they tasted like soggy cardboard. But Jimmy ate them with a serving spoon.

They didn't talk about Mike. They'd never talked about any of them. Jimmy didn't talk about something unless there were tactical considerations involved, practical details to be attended to, something to be done. But there was nothing to be done about Mike. There'd been nothing in the papers. The guy might never have existed. Except that he was still falling, in Helen's mind. She could see him flailing at the air as he went off the edge, as if there were something out there to grab. And she could see his eyes, the last startled glance at her. The bewilderment and the weird hurt.

They had apple pie for dessert, no ice cream. Jimmy didn't like foods that got messy and blended. He ate the way he lived, in short straight strokes that left clean edges. It gave him the slightly dizzying stability of a mosaic, a whole greater than the sum of its myriad chips of meaningless color. The occasional missing piece didn't affect the larger picture. Jimmy was the entire wall.

He talked about his job as he ate two pieces of pie. He was having problems with his foreman. What a surprise. Helen knew it was just a matter of time before Jimmy lost it and took a swing at the guy and got himself fired. But that was Jimmy. He'd find another job. He always did.

After dinner, Helen took Bubbles for a walk. Jimmy settled in with the TV; he never went out with Bubbles. In eastern North Carolina, no one walked their dogs. The dog let you know it wanted to go out and you opened the door for it and it went out and did what dogs did. And if it killed somebody's cat or tore up somebody's flowers or bit a neighbor's kid, well, you and the neighbor might holler at each other for a while and maybe it would come to fighting, but mostly not. Mostly the cats and kids were smarter in eastern North Carolina and people understood that dogs would be dogs. Jimmy really didn't see why the same system wouldn't work in San Francisco. Even now, the only reason he didn't let Bubbles roam free around the Richmond neighborhood was that he was afraid someone would kill the dog and eat it. Jimmy had strange ideas about the Chinese.

Still, he could not reconcile himself to the indignity of pooper scoopers and plastic bags, and so it fell to Helen to give the pit bull what exercise it got.

It had been fun when Bubbles was a puppy. They'd gotten the dog from one of Jimmy's cronies in Mendocino County, a transplanted redneck who grew dope on eighty acres above the Eel River and raised mixed-breed rottweilers, pits, and Presa Canarios for fighting. Bubbles had been the runt of his litter, a soggy little beanbag the color of bittersweet chocolate, with a splash of white on one side of his face and three white feet. His siblings bumped him aside in the scramble to feed and Jimmy's friend Don, who was a true psycho and mean as well, had already been talking about feeding him to the bigger dogs before he starved to death on his own. It was better for fighting dogs to kill their own food, Don said cheerfully.

Helen wished now that she'd just left Bubbles to his fate, but the puppy thing had happened. He'd looked up at her with his bleary black eyes and her heart had opened and she'd begged Jimmy to let her take him home. Jimmy just laughed, but he'd liked the idea. He said Bubbles would make a great watchdog and a lousy pet, and so it had turned out. Bubbles had been cute for about six weeks, and manageable for about six months, but now, at six years old, he was just a 110-pound shit-making machine who could kill a small child in a couple of minutes if you turned your back on him.

Helen headed south along Forty-seventh Avenue toward the park, hoping that Bubbles would hold off doing his business until they got off the pavement. The pit bull was easy on his leash, as nonchalant as a gunfighter with his slightly bowlegged trot, but Helen held the chain taut and kept her eye out for loose poodles, cats, and toddlers. Bubbles had once yanked a slack chain tight and torn a lazy Siamese to shreds before she could pull him back. She could feel his energy through the leash like the throaty mutter of an idling Harley.

She stopped at a corner store to buy the final edition of the *Examiner,* scanning the local section for signs that Mike had surfaced. But there was nothing. It was unsettling. Jimmy said no news was good news, but Helen couldn't see it that way.

"No, Jimmy, don't—" she yells as Jimmy storms up to Mike, but it sounds halfhearted even to her and Helen realizes it is the same thing she always says and that somehow over time the words have lost their meaning, have been ritualized into emptiness, into something more like "Amen."

And poor Mike never gets it. He just gapes at Jimmy, bleary-eyed and uncomprehending, still too decent to imagine what is happening, still saying, "I'm sorry, I didn't mean it," as if forgiveness could still matter. But Jimmy just shoves him toward the cliff. Mike staggers backward and Jimmy shoves him again, right up to the edge.

Bubbles gave a low growl, and Helen looked up. Another dog was approaching, a cocky little spaniel, straining at its leash. The owner was a young Chinese guy, clean-cut and thirtyish, still dressed in the slacks and button-down from his day job. Helen reined Bubbles in close and made room on the sidewalk, but the guy stopped near them and gave her a big smile. Dog owner rapport. If she'd been walking a beagle, she could have gotten laid before you could say American Kennel Club.

"Easy, Alfie," the guy told the spaniel, who was still snuffling and yipping, trying to get at Bubbles. Bubbles just watched the other dog with apparent indulgence, but Helen could see the alertness in his stupid, cunning eyes and she gave the leash another hitch.

"Don't mind Alfie," the guy said. "He doesn't mean anything by it. He's just too friendly for his own good." He gave her another smile. "Like his owner. Isn't that how it goes?"

"I guess it is. My dog's mean as a snake."

The guy laughed. "Pit bulls have gotten such lousy press. It's a shame, really. He looks like a sweetheart, with the white face and feet. Is he a purebred?"

"He's a mongrel, actually, and kind of volatile," Helen said. "Better keep your dog back."

"Oh, it's okay, they just need to sniff each other out."

Helen said hastily, "No, seriously, I—" but the guy had already given his dog more leash. Alfie surged forward exultantly and Bubbles, like a trap snapping shut, grabbed him by his floppy ear and began to shake him. The smaller dog gave a blood-chilling shriek.

"Call him off! Oh my God! Call your dog off!" the guy screamed and Helen wondered what planet he thought he was on. She kicked hard at Bubbles's mouth, which had no effect, then plunged into the fray and punched repeatedly at the hinge of the pit bull's jaw. Bubbles ignored the blows and kept swinging his big head savagely from side to side, his eyes calm and intent, and Alfie flopped in his grip, yelping pitiably.

The owner of the corner store ran out, screaming something in Chinese, and the dog's owner continued to wail and wring his hands. Blood was flying everywhere now. Helen punched again, just as Bubbles gave a particularly fierce shake, and the spaniel tore loose and flew into the gutter.

Alfie's owner immediately scooped him into his arms, heedless of the streaming blood. There was a ragged bit of flesh where the spaniel's ear had been. The poor dog kept squealing in pain and terror.

"I'm calling the cops!" the guy shouted. "I'm calling the cops! That dog is a menace! Oh my God, Alfie! Oh my God!"

"I'm so sorry," Helen said. "I'm so sorry." She had blood all over her hands and the front of her sweatshirt. Bubbles's expression of quiet focus had not changed from the beginning of the incident. His gory jaw worked a couple of times, apparently chewing on the ear, and then he swallowed and peered around amiably with his dull, calm eyes as if wondering what all the fuss was about. He looked a lot like Jimmy, Helen realized. Unperturbed by all the hand-wringing and emotional excess. Just doing what killers do.

"I'm calling Animal Control!" Alfie's owner screamed. "That dog should be put down!"

"I just can't say how sorry I am," Helen said and she set her feet to haul Bubbles away. He came along easily enough, trotting away with her as if he'd been born to the leash. She hated his bloody smugness as she hated her life now, with a helpless passion. But there was nothing to do but take the damned dog home.

"Oh Jesus," Mike says, in such a heartfelt way that Helen believes it is a real prayer. That seems worst of all: that ring of truth, the heartrending note of sincere appeal. Because that is what she's always wanted.

And then Jimmy shoves him again and Mike goes over and when she gets to the edge he is still falling and she turns away before he hits. And so in her mind's eye he is falling still.

9

A<small>S ROSE TURNED AWAY</small> from the bicycle and started back
toward the beach, a helicopter passed over the Golden
Gate and came in low over the water toward her. She
could see the distinctive blue-and-red logo of Channel 8
News on the chopper's side.

She hurried back toward the body, taking off her jacket
as she went. She didn't think the Crazy Eight crew were allowed to show a corpse on TV, but she didn't want to take
the chance. Someone out there cared about Michael Turner
and the last thing they needed was to learn of his death by
seeing his broken body on the late news. Both her boots
were full of water now and she felt like she was moving in
slow motion, like in a nightmare. The chopper had posi-
tioned itself for filming before she got to the body to cover
it and Rose tried to wave it off, a shooing motion as if the
helicopter were a big mosquito.

She could see the nose camera swiveling hungrily while she was still three steps from the body. STRAIGHT FROM EIGHT AT SIX AND TEN: WE GET THERE FIRST FOR YOU. No story too seamy, no image too inhuman. Before the camera could lock onto the scene, Rose raised her right middle finger as distinctly as possible, hoping to at least make whatever footage they got unairably obscene. She kept the finger in the air until she reached Michael Turner's body and laid her jacket over his face and chest. Then she turned her back on the chopper and slogged on toward the beach.

As she waded out of the water, soaked, exhausted, and furious, the men on the beach applauded. Rose hardly knew how to take that. It wasn't more teasing; the clapping was gentle and solid, like the applause for someone limping in at the end of a marathon, and she heard the note of genuine respect in it. It was actually moving. She'd never been applauded at a crime scene before.

"Good to go, Rosie?" one of the coroner's team asked with quiet deference.

"Bag him," she said. "Gently. And try not to give those guys in the chopper a shot of the face."

"Fucking vultures. I'd flip them off myself, if it wouldn't get my ass fired."

Rose hadn't actually thought of that herself, and she decided not to. "Somebody will need to bring the bike in. There's a computer on the handlebars, so be careful to keep it dry. We'll want that."

"You got it, Inspector Burke."

She turned away as the coroner's team and one of the Crime Scene Unit guys booted up. The chopper hovered annoyingly offshore, its bluster making conversation difficult. Amid the flurry of activity, Chester caught her eye and gave her a rueful nod.

"Nice work, Rosie," he said. "I hope you fucked up their footage."

Rose saw that she had shamed him, that he wished now he had gone out with her, if only to protect the scene. She shrugged. "You've seen one body splattered on a rock, amigo, you've seen 'em all. There was no need for more than one of us to be gagging out there."

"You're da man, girl," he insisted and turned away to call some unnecessary directions to the men retrieving the body.

Joshua was beside her, holding a blanket and looking concerned. Rose realized that she was on the verge of tears.

"I need a cigarette," she said, as he put the blanket around her shoulders. "Can you believe those ghouls in the helicopter?"

"The hell with them. You're shaking, kid. Let's get you out of the wind."

"These goddamn boots are full of water."

"Here, sit down, I'll help you out of them."

Rose allowed him to settle her on the sand. She could feel the cold grit right through her soaked pants. Seawater streamed out as Joshua tugged her right boot off, then her left. Her shoes came off with the boots and Joshua dug the loafers from the wet depths and made a small show of turning them upside down to dump the water.

"If this were a cartoon, a fish would fall out." He smiled.

"It's more like a Fellini movie with Smell-O-Vision." Rose slipped the ruined shoes onto her feet. Joshua gave her a hand and she stood up and drew the blanket tighter around herself as a shudder ran the length of her body. "Christ, did you see that seagull?"

Joshua nodded grimly. "Who in the world were you on the phone with?"

"Seamus."

He gave her a puzzled glance. "Odd time to chat."

"Just checking in. Good communication is the lifeblood of a relationship." Joshua continued to look blank, and Rose realized that her marital humor might be getting too black even for him. She said briskly, "The battery was dying on that bike computer, and I thought he'd know how to save the data."

She could see he wanted to talk more about the phone conversation, but he stuck to business. "You think there's something we can use?"

"There was an elapsed time for the trip and the clock was still running. We can probably get a good sense of the time of death, at least. And who knows what else."

"Smart," Joshua said.

"Yeah, I'm a fucking genius. You should have seen me out there, hitting buttons at random. Where's that cigarette?" And, as Joshua hesitated, "What? You gonna card me or something?"

Joshua wavered a moment more, then said, as if it hurt him, "Look, I know it's none of my business, but you really shouldn't be smoking in your condition."

"My 'condition'?" she laughed. "You mean cold, wet, and nauseated?"

"*Pregnant*, Rosie. It's bad for the kid."

She blinked, surprised and touched by his concern. But she said dryly, "Just one, partner. To get the smell out of my nose and the taste out of my mouth."

He shrugged and grudgingly produced the pack of Marlboros. Rose took one and they leaned together, cupping their hands around his lighter to keep the flame alive. The wind had finally picked up, but it was blowing the stench straight toward them. As the cigarette caught, Rose glanced up and found Joshua's eyes on her, unexpectedly close and still pained. She recognized the look. Jack had started to look like that after some guy had emptied an Uzi into the wall six inches over their heads when they kicked in the door to arrest him. He'd never let her go in first after that.

"Let's get you out of the wind," Joshua said again.

"Don't get all gooey and paternal on me, Josh," she said. "I'm a cop. And a grown-up."

"You're a goddamned human being with another life inside you, and you're shaking like a leaf."

She moved toward the sheltered lee of the cliff to keep him from taking her arm. They were both pissed off, suddenly. In the water, the coroner's team struggled unhappily with the body. Rose could hear them swearing and griping, even over the noise of the lingering news helicopter. What a fate, to be just another lousy part of some hourly wage worker's bad day. She took a drag on the cigarette and blew the smoke out through her nose, trying to burn the smell out of her nasal passages.

"So, what was so interesting out there?" Joshua asked, trying to normalize things.

She didn't trust herself to be nice again yet, but she took the plastic evidence bag out of her pocket and handed it to him. Joshua studied the artificial dragonfly for a moment.

"I don't get it," he said. "Where'd you find this?"

"It was snagged on his sleeve."

Her partner peered at the fly again. "Well, that's weird," he conceded. "I mean, just for starters, it's a freshwater lure, so what the hell is it doing—"

"It's an earring, Joshua."

He looked at the fly, opened his mouth once, and closed it. Rose continued, "It gets weirder. The guy had a ruby stud in his left ear and his right ear wasn't pierced. This isn't even his. And look, on the ear wire—"

"Blood," Joshua said.

"Sure looks like it to me."

They stood for a moment in silence. Rose took another hit off the cigarette. It tasted way too good, and she could feel the nicotine rush coming on. She felt dizzy and nauseated and slightly brilliant.

"So what are you thinking?" Joshua asked at last.

Rose shrugged. "I don't know. My old partner used to say, 'What's wrong with this picture?'"

"And?"

"What's wrong with this picture is the guy's got an earring stuck to his sleeve that isn't his."

Joshua mulled it over for a moment, then added, "And that he's at the bottom of the cliff rather than the top of it."

Their eyes met.

"Exactly," Rose said. It was nice to be in sync again.

She gave Chester a head's-up before he went up the trail with the body. The path was too rough for the wheeled gurney, and the coroner's team guys were griping about having to lug the stretcher. The AME seemed irritated by the suggestion that the death might require special attention, but he promised to get to the autopsy with all due speed, which meant in three days instead of four. He was obviously indulging her, still figuring the death was accidental. Rose resolved to be present for the autopsy, just to be sure Chester didn't mail it in.

Her shoes squished as she and Joshua started up the steep trail back to the top. Back at the beach, things were winding down. The Channel 8 chopper had finally run low on gas and buzzed away. The police divers had shown up and were sloshing around the rocks on the off chance that there might be anything else of significance in the shallows. It was probably futile, but it would be embarrassing if they'd missed another body or something. Most of the CSU team had gone on ahead to try to find the spot where Michael Turner had gone off the cliff.

A step behind Joshua, conscious of how dry he was, Rose drew the blanket around herself more tightly and shivered. She realized that she was still mulling over her conversation with Seamus. Obsessing, even. It was humiliating to be so preoccupied. She hated being a seething pot of female emotions. In all fairness, she couldn't have picked a worse time to break the news. But his reaction had been so maddeningly noncommittal. She'd been furious with her husband because she hadn't been able to tell him she was pregnant; and now she was mad at him because she had. Poor Seamus couldn't win.

At the trail's first sharp switchback, something down the slope caught her eye. Rose paused and saw that it was an audiocassette, with a jumbled spaghetti of tape trailing from it. The tape had tangled itself in a shrub at the edge of a sheer drop to the water below. She hesitated, thinking it was probably nothing, then stepped off the trail and started toward it.

"Jesus, Rosie, what the hell are you—?" Joshua began, just as she slipped and fell, skidding down the loose, rocky slope, tearing her wet pants and bloodying her knee. As she slid, Rose had time to wonder whether the fifty-foot fall would kill her or just maim her for life. The guys with the gurney were really going to be pissed off if they had to come all the way back down the trail to haul away her battered body; and if she didn't die, she would never live this down. But she came to a stop against the same last-ditch shrub the tape had hung up on.

"I meant to do that," she called up to Joshua, who had hurried to the edge of the trail and was peering over at her.

"Yeah," he said. "Very stylish. Are you okay?"

"I'll survive, but these pants are history."

"What have you got?"

"It's a tape."

"Yeah, that's worth dying for."

Rose reached into her pocket for some gloves, but she'd used her last pair in the water. She broke off the entire branch the tape was tangled in and held it up for a better look. She had no idea what she was looking for, but sometimes you just got lucky, even on a rotten day. The label read, "Melanie's Mix for Mikey, copy 2."

·   ·   ·

When Rose and Joshua finally reached the top of the cliff, the Crime Scene Unit had completed a perfunctory search of the area where Michael Turner had plunged off the edge and were posing for ironic photos next to a sign that said, PLEASE STAY ON THE TRAIL. Rose made them start all over again. It seemed obvious to her by now that Michael Turner had had a companion on his last bike ride. But the scene was clean.

She and Joshua waded through the knot of reporters that had gathered in the parking lot at Land's End, confirming only that they had found a body and that the death was under investigation. Back at the office, they gave Sandi Thanh the basics, and Rose got her knee patched up and changed out of her torn and soggy slacks into some borrowed sweatpants. It wasn't the most professional of looks, but it was better than leaving a wet stain every time she sat down. She and Joshua washed up as well as they could, but they both still reeked of the death scene and the rest of the detectives in the office gave them a wide berth.

They spent the rest of the afternoon trying to find someone who cared that Michael Turner was dead. But his personal data proved frustratingly elusive. The address on his driver's license was either outdated or false, and the billing address for his credit cards and cell phone was a P.O. box on Divisadero. The M. Turners in the phone book all appeared to still be alive. The redial button on Turner's cell phone reached a pay phone, also on Divisadero, and the only numbers programmed into the phone's speed dial were Chinese takeout joints and pizza places in the lower Haight. It was after seven P.M. before Rose and Joshua finally found a Pizza Hut that had Mike Turner's real address on file. Apparently the guy's most significant relationship in the world had been with the people who made his pepperoni-and-mushroom specials with a stuffed-cheese crust. He always ordered an extra-large. One of the delivery guys even re-membered that Turner was a good tipper, which seemed as close to a eulogy as the guy was going to get.

Reluctantly, Rose and Joshua left checking out Turner's apartment for the following morning. They'd been off the clock since five; Sandi Thanh had not seen fit to au-thorize any overtime for what still seemed like a biking ac-cident to almost everyone whose opinion mattered, and Joshua had a date he was already late for. He was sheepish about it, and Rose was surprised to feel a flash of grudging emotion that was way too close to jealousy. He picked up on it and got even more sheepish. It was awkward. They were both being ridiculous.

"Seriously, I could cancel," Joshua persisted. "It's just this setup by well-meaning friends anyway. She's an insur-ance adjustor. There may even be a conflict of interest in it. I mean, think about it—homicide, insurance . . . "

Rose laughed. "You're allowed to have a life, Joshua."

"I feel like I'm letting you down somehow."

"We're partners, for God's sake; we're not married. As long as you don't investigate any hideous deaths with this woman, I'm fine with you having other relationships."

"This trail is already cold. We shouldn't be wasting any more time."

"The trail's not going to get that much colder overnight. And the body's certainly not going to smell any worse. We'll pick it up tomorrow." She wondered why she was so reluctant to tell him, then decided it was more ridiculous-ness and said, "I should get home, too. I finally told Seamus today that I'm pregnant, and we have to have The Talk."

"You hadn't told him yet?" Joshua exclaimed. And then, even more incredulously, "Oh, shit, you told him on the phone while you were out in the water, didn't you?"

"What if I did?"

"Well—"

"I know, I know. But let's face it, it was too late to be going for style points. I'd already tried the candlelight dinner and the Significant Breakfast and let's-do-lunch and gotten nowhere. It's done, and that's what matters. At this point, I'm just happy to have told him before he noticed the bulge."

Joshua shook himself slightly, a suppressed shudder, like a wet dog trying to be polite. She could see that he was struggling to arrive at an appropriately supportive position and not finding much to work with. Finally he offered, "Well, I'll bet he was thrilled, huh? To hear he's going to be a father."

Rose felt a twisting stab of compassion. The poor guy was just trying to be decent and say the right things. It wasn't his fault that none of the right things applied.

She said simply, "It wasn't the best time to talk."

Joshua laughed gratefully, taking it for ironic understatement. "Well, it sounds to me like it's just as well we're not working any later tonight. You must in a hurry to get home, too."

"Yeah," Rose said, and wondered why she felt like crying.

She took longer than she really had to with the paperwork, staying at the office until after nine. But you could only avoid your life for so long, and Rose finally made herself get on the train. When she got home, there were five empty Heineken bottles on the kitchen counter, neatly replaced in the slots of their cardboard container. Apparently the six-pack had never made it to the fridge. Seamus was in the bedroom watching TV with no lights on, the last of the six-pack on the bedside table. In the flickering gray-blue light from the tube, she could see that he had his sullen look firmly in place. She was about three beers late, it seemed.

"Hi," Rose said, as he obviously wasn't going to say anything until she did.

"There's a message for you on the machine. Your partner."

He still hadn't looked at her. Rose said, as mildly as she could, "It can wait."

"That would be a change."

She blinked at the unfairness of that. Seamus answered his own messages slavishly at every hour and never turned off his beeper or his cell phone. You'd have thought he was an ICU doctor on call. But she decided to not rise to the bait.

"What are you watching?" she asked.

Seamus shrugged. "Nothing much. Just killing time 'til the news comes on."

He continued to attend to the screen, though. Rose came into the room and took her gun out of its holster. She ejected the magazine clip and checked the chamber and the safety. When she was sure the Smith & Wesson was clear, she laid it in the drawer of her bedside table, in its usual place under the needlepoint. This nightly ritual was usually good for a quip of some kind from Seamus, but her husband was still ignoring her. Rose closed the drawer and stood by her side of the bed through a couple of rounds of laugh-track hilarity, fingering her empty holster, then said pointedly, "How was your day?"

"Oh, it was wonderful," Seamus said, glaring at the sitcom. "It was fucking wonderful."

"Meaning, I take it, that it wasn't?"

He finally looked at her. "Meaning, I didn't get a goddamned thing done all afternoon, after that phone call. That was a helluva thing to do, Rose."

Rose felt a surge of relief that his anger was out in the open. Now they could just fight. She realized that she was ready for it, that she was even eager. "I'm sure PsiberSystems will survive you devoting a little of that expensive head space of yours to your actual life."

Seamus turned back to the TV. The sitcom had given

way to a car commercial, some high-decibel urgency over the latest APR. Rose said sharply, "Could you please turn that damned thing off?"

Seamus hit Mute, a frankly calibrated provocation, and continued to stare at the screen. Rose waited a moment, but he seemed determined, and she turned toward the closet and unstrapped her shoulder holster. She'd had it on for such a long time that it felt like her chest had a permanent dent. No wonder Amazons cut their breasts off.

Seamus sniffed uneasily, finally registering the stench from her hair and clothes. "Is that smell what I think it is?"

"You're not the only one who had a lousy day at work."

"Yeah, but dead people are *important,* right? It's only what *I* do for a living that's worthy of contempt."

Rose took a deep breath. "You know I respect what you do, Seamus. More than you do yourself, maybe."

"You don't respect it enough to not toss a bombshell like that in my face in the middle of a workday." She said nothing. "You couldn't tell me this morning?" Seamus persisted. "Or last night? How long have you known?"

"Since around the time we could still have eaten that chicken."

"*Jeezus,* Rosie!"

"Look, Seamus, what are we really fighting about here?" Rose asked, struggling for an even tone. "I mean, are you mad at the message, the messenger, or the mode of delivery?"

"Can you really sort it out that easily? *Shit,* Rose, you call me from a *crime scene* to tell me I'm going to be a goddamned *father*—"

"I never said you were going to be a father," Rose interrupted, wondering how they had gotten so off track, so quickly. But it wasn't quick at all, of course. They'd been off track for months. "We've still got to talk about that. I only said that I'm pregnant."

Seamus blinked, uncomprehending, and Rose reminded

herself that he was drunk. Her husband got surprisingly stupid when he was drunk, and lost his sense of humor completely. It was one more little irony simmering in the marital stew like a chunk of undercooked potato. She'd married him because he was so smart and so funny. But it didn't pay to dwell on that.

Seamus's wheels were still turning. Rose waited as patiently as she could. She wanted more than anything on earth to be in the shower, under water as scalding as her skin would bear. Her blouse still stank of the dead body on the rock, but she didn't want to take it off while they were mad at each other.

"Are you saying I'm not the father?" Seamus asked at last.

"Oh, for Christ's sake, Seamus," she snapped. "Of course you're the father. I'm saying I'm not sure I'm going to have it."

He blinked again, but his scowl lightened. With relief, Rose saw. With hopefulness, even. He hadn't wanted to be the one to bring it up, but he was glad she had. He wasn't really mad because of the timing at all; he was mad because he was afraid she wanted the baby.

The realization brought a surge of rage that almost staggered her. Quite simply, she wanted to kill him. And suddenly dozens of blood-smeared murder scenes made perfect sense: the bodies strewn across kitchen floors and flopped on beds and sprawled in broken heaps in bathrooms and garages, skulls crushed by baseball bats and hammers, bodies blasted until the gun was empty, or stabbed and slashed until someone's arms had given out: the passionate casualties of domestic wars. The messy blossoms of moments like this. It was absolutely humbling. She had a 9mm semiautomatic pistol in the drawer, under a needlepoint she hated from a mother-in-law whom she could barely stand, and she was perfectly capable at this instant of taking that gun out, slamming the magazine home with a practiced

ease, and emptying the clip into her husband. It was why
most homicides were so ridiculously easy to solve. Something snapped and someone died and half the time you
showed up at the scene and found the killer sitting amid the
carnage with the murder weapon on the floor, hanging his
or her head ruefully, stunned and numb and surrendered to
her or his fate, and even weirdly relieved that the worst had
finally happened, that it would all be so much simpler now.

Oddly enough, in the starkness of the moment, Rose
thought of Henry Pelletier, of the single neat wound that
had killed him, and of the fish knife in the dish drainer. It
just wasn't the way you killed someone who had pushed
you over the edge.

"Hey, look, you're on TV," Seamus exclaimed.

Rose looked at the screen. The late news had come on
and sure enough, there she was, up to her ass in the leaden
water off Land's End, wading clumsily toward Michael
Turner's limp body, her middle finger raised to the news helicopter's camera and her face a study in contempt. The
good news was that she'd accomplished what she'd wanted
to with the obscene gesture. The cameraman, apparently
delighted, had zoomed in on her and ignored the body during the moments when it might have been identifiable. The
bad news, unfortunately, was now obvious to the entire Bay
Area viewing audience. Rose wondered what channel Sandi
Thanh watched for the ten-o'clock news.

The filmed footage switched to a shot of the coroner's
team laboring up the trail with the bagged body on a
stretcher, and then to the Channel 8 reporter doing his
stand-up in front of the crime-scene tape in the Land's End
parking lot. Seamus released the Mute button and the reporter's voice kicked in. *". . . Police spokesmen declined to
comment on whether the death was an accident or the result of foul play, saying only that the incident is 'under investigation.' The identity of the victim is being withheld,*

pending notification of next of kin. This is Ian Furman for Channel Eight News . . . Jill, Ken, back to you."

The Late on Eight anchor team came back onto the screen, looking a little gleeful.

"Thanks for that report, Ian," the woman anchor said. "It looks like the investigation is in, uh, good hands."

The male anchor smirked appreciatively. As he began to read the lead into the next story, the phone rang.

"Don't pick up—" Rose said, as Seamus hit Mute and picked it up.

"Hello," he said. He listened for a moment, then covered the mouthpiece. "It's the *Chronicle.*"

"Shit. Tell them we already subscribe."

"No, no, it's a reporter."

"Of course it's a goddamned reporter, Seamus. Jesus. How the hell did they get our number?"

"Do you want me to ask him?"

Her husband seemed way too amused by it all. Rose said, "Tell him I can't comment on an ongoing investigation and refer him to the SFPD media spokesman."

"I'm sure he's more interested in why you flipped off Channel Eight."

"Seamus, for God's sake—"

As her husband turned his attention back to the phone, Rose's beeper sounded. She glanced at the caller ID, recognized the number for the metro crime desk at the *Examiner,* and turned the device off.

As soon as Seamus had hung up, the phone rang again. He reached for it, but before he could answer, Rose reached behind the bedside table and unplugged the line.

"Hey!" Seamus protested. "You're not the only one who gets calls on this line."

"Right. That's PsiberSystems with a computer emergency."

They could hear the phone still ringing in the kitchen,

until the answering machine picked up. It was another reporter.

"You're a star, Rosie." Seamus laughed. "This could make your career."

Rose just stared at him incredulously, wondering whether he really didn't get what this might do to her career. Or maybe it was the prospect of her career being wrecked that was making him so cheerful all of the sudden. But Seamus didn't register her look. He was already going around the dial, seeing if any of the other channels had picked up the footage.

"I'm going to take a shower," Rose said. Her husband nodded absently. She watched him for a moment as he worked the clicker like a kid with a video game, then she turned away and pulled her blouse over her head without undoing any of the buttons. She knew from hard experience that the smell would never come out entirely and she stuffed the blouse into a plastic dry-cleaning bag and dropped the bag into their bedroom's wicker trash basket.

She threw her bra into the basket, too, for good measure, conscious that her earlier sense of marital modesty had passed. She didn't give a damn, suddenly, whether Seamus saw her naked or not.

In the shower, Rose began to cry as soon as the door was closed. It took her by surprise; she had thought she was too angry and disgusted to cry, that she would be protected by her rage. But the tears came from somewhere deeper than the anger, welling slow and steady like the leakage from a faucet with a washer so worn you couldn't turn the handle hard enough anymore to shut it off.

Though she ran the water so hot it hurt, washed her hair three times, and scrubbed herself raw with a loofah sponge, she still felt vaguely dirty when she got out of the shower. But Rose realized that she felt clean inside. The tears had washed something away and she felt calm and sad and quietly lucid. She knew she probably should have been trying to figure out how to save her marriage, or at least her job, but she wasn't. She was thinking of Michael Turner's body on the rock, broken and abandoned, violated by the birds and the crabs and the elements, and of the almost unbearable pathos and indignity of the bike pants around the poor guy's knees. She was thinking that something like that didn't just happen. It was like the beer bottle six inches from the coaster on Henry Pelletier's coffee table, a cruelty too specific and calculated to be random. It was something someone had done. She wondered if Joshua was going to think she was nuts.

When Rose came back out into the bedroom, dressed for self-containment in a baggy T-shirt and sweatpants, Seamus had turned on the bedside lamp and was reading *InfoWorld*. He'd left the TV on ESPN at a low volume and was keeping one eye on the late baseball scores. It was all very business-as-usual. He actually gave Rose a smile as she approached the bed, and she realized that he thought they had already talked things through somehow. She wondered what he thought they had decided. But she didn't want to ask until she was sure she wouldn't kill him when he told her.

She opened the bedside drawer and took out the Irish Blessing needlepoint. Seamus sniffed, a little warily, and said, "I hate to say this, but I can still smell it."

"It doesn't matter. I was going to sleep on the couch anyway."

Her husband stiffened, clearly feeling that she was escalating things unreasonably, then he shrugged angrily and turned away. Rose closed the drawer on her gun and dropped the needlepoint in the trash on top of her ruined clothes. There didn't seem to be much point in saying "Good night."

The phone was ringing again in the kitchen. She stopped on her way to the living room to turn the ringer off. The message indicator was flashing "4," no doubt all from reporters. Rose moved to erase the messages without listening to them, then remembered that Seamus had said there was a call from Joshua.

She hit Play and listened to the first message. Joshua had called on his cell phone, apparently from a restaurant; Rose could hear plates and conversation in the background. It was like her partner to have continued to mull over the day's murder through all the exigencies of a blind date. She hoped Joshua had at least had the decency to wait until his companion had gone to the bathroom before he made the call.

"Just a weird thought, Rosie. I know it's totally off the wall. But I was just thinking—that earring, that fly-fishing thing? I was wondering if there's any way we could find out whether the fly came from the collection of lures in that guy's closet. You know, the one on Chestnut Street. That really clean scene, the fish knife thing. . . . I know, I know, you probably think I'm nuts."

10

H E WAS SITTING right across from her, on the other side of a giant fish tank. Helen had spotted him the minute she came in, and she knew that he had spotted her, but she purposely sat in what felt like the most inaccessible place, on the far side of the island bar, screened from him by the aquarium. She really shouldn't have been here at all, she knew, not for weeks, or even months. She was losing it; she was out of control. But here she was. The best she could do was to try to slow things down.

She could see him murkily through the tank, eclipsed by a lazily swimming angelfish, nursing a domestic beer and chatting up two women who looked like flight attendants on a girls' night out. He was about thirty—but weren't they all?—and attractive in a modest, nonobtrusive way, though he could have used a haircut. His clothes were stylish but not in-your-face fashionable, and he drank his beer out of the bottle. He seemed bright enough. In any case, he would do.

The Deep Six was a trendy place with an underwater feel. There were mermaids everywhere, on the walls and on the coasters and on the tiny T-shirts the waitresses wore. The lighting was low and the glass bar was lit from beneath with a wavering blue light, so your drink just seemed to float there on the unsteady surface. There were even mermaid-shaped ashtrays available on request, which seemed to suggest that the place had either decided to defy the no-smoking laws or paid somebody off. There was a sign near the cash register that said, NO LIFEGUARD ON DUTY. SWIM AT YOUR OWN RISK.

The crowd was young and well-to-do, and the specialty drinks expensive but immense, with cute names like "Davy Jones's Locker" and "Full Fathom Five." Helen was drinking something called "The Albatross" with a sense of private burlesque. Her father had called her his little albatross through most of her teenage years.

He'd come to her room for the first time the night they returned from Hawaii. Without ceremony, and self-conscious, like a defiant child with his first cigarette: just slipped in, in the darkness, and took her. Helen had realized she wasn't surprised. She had expected it. She even, strangely, welcomed it. It was the other shoe dropping, the payment for letting her mother die. It was a kind of penance, in its sick way. And it allowed her to hate him. Helen preferred that, on the whole. It was so much easier than hating herself.

After that, Parker came to her once a week at least, sometimes twice. They never spoke of it in the daylight, as they never spoke of Cora's death. Helen could handle that, as she could handle the smell of him, the weight of him, his oily, garlic-scented sweat, and the way his eyes would never meet her own, even in the dark. It fit her sense of their shared shame. But she hated it when he called her his albatross. That was like saying it was all her fault.

"Is this seat taken?"

Helen emerged from her reverie. The guy from the other side of the bar was standing beside her. He had pale blue eyes the color of new ice, her father's eyes. She could have killed him for that alone.

"Struck out with the stewardesses, did you?" she said.

"They're lawyers, actually."

"Both of them?"

"All three."

Helen glanced across the bar through the fish tank and, sure enough, the gaggle had grown. A trio, like the Fates in silk blouses.

"Way too complicated," the guy said. "I was never good at math." He sat down and looked at her nearly empty glass. "What are you drinking?"

"An Albatross."

"How is it?"

"A little dry," Helen said, which she thought would be too esoteric. But the guy laughed.

"Water, water everywhere, and not a drop to drink," he said.

Points for effort, she thought, deciding to ignore the misquotation. "'And every tongue, through utter drought, / Was withered at the root; / We could not speak, no more than if / We had been choked with soot.'"

"You win," the guy conceded cheerfully. He caught the bartender's eye and signaled for a round.

Helen watched him work, amused. "Did you buy drinks for the stewardesses too?"

"Lawyers."

"Whatever. You must be running quite a tab by now."

"I never touched my wallet." He leaned toward her, confiding. "The blonde bought one for *me*."

"You're kidding."

He shrugged modestly. "I suppose they thought I had promise."

"Until they got to know you, apparently."

"Ouch," he said. "Have mercy. I'm in a vulnerable place right now."

"You'd have to be an idiot to look for mercy in a bar," Helen said.

He laughed and raised his hands, palms up: guilty as charged. Their drinks arrived, another Albatross, and a Sam Adams for him. Helen sipped hers, letting the silence build. She was in no mood to help anyone out.

"So what's in an Albatross?" the guy asked.

"Irony, mostly."

"Jesus. I hope you're not planning on driving home."

She glanced at him, not quite willing to show amusement, then looked back at her drink. It was that, or the fish tank. There really weren't that many places to look in this bar, and she was beginning to feel a little claustrophobic.

He subsided, amiably enough. They sipped their drinks. The waitresses scurried to and fro in their tiny shirts with mermaids undulating across their breasts, sweating slightly as the place got busy. On the other side of the fish tank, a newly hopeful candidate had sidled up to the lawyers and was holding up three fingers to the bartender, who was ignoring him.

"There's an octopus in that aquarium," the guy offered. "Behind the coral. He was out a little earlier, floomphing around."

"'Floomphing.'"

"You know, how they move." He mimed an octopus in languid motion, using all his limbs. "They really do have eight arms. I counted. But I'm wondering what he eats."

"Is this the approach you used with the stewardesses?" Helen asked pointedly. "The octopus thing? Because I can tell you this right off, those girls are not here to discuss marine life."

"There was only one of them when I started. By the time the other two showed up and I realized it was a suicide mission, it was too late. And I happen to find octopuses fascinating. Octopi, rather."

"A 'suicide mission'?"

He shrugged. "Let's face it, nothing is going to work with three smart, pretty, fed-up women out on the town together and bent on making up for years of bad boyfriends by not giving a damn. I was a sacrificial lamb, atoning for the sins of my gender." He pointed through the fish tank. "You see that guy?"

"With the gold chain around his neck?"

"Dead meat. They'll string him up by that thing."

"It will serve him right," Helen said, conscious of a little shudder of memory, a frisson: the sickening tilt of Michael Turner's head as he lay on the rock at the base of the cliff. Dead meat.

"No argument, there," the guy said, apparently impervious.

They drank. At the end of the bar, a TV draped with fishing nets flickered with a muted sitcom. Without the laugh track, the show had the visual vigor of cardboard figures wilting in the rain. Helen turned back to the fish tank. She didn't see an octopus. It irritated her slightly, to catch herself looking for it.

"Mark," the guy offered after a moment. And, with a self-deprecatory smile as Helen looked uncomprehending, "My name. It's Mark."

"As in 'Twain'?"

"As in Matthew, Mark, Luke, and John, I'm afraid. My parents were New Testament maniacs and named all their kids after Evangelists."

"How clever."

"My sister Luke might disagree." He ignored her pointed failure to smile and forged on. "And you are—?"

"A fed-up woman bent on making up for years of bad boyfriends by not giving a damn."

He laughed. "And here I thought you weren't paying attention."

Helen shrugged. "I always pay attention. It's just so seldom worth it."

There wasn't much to work with there, and Mark acknowledged this by turning back to his beer. They'd both almost finished their drinks. Helen realized that she was a little drunk. Those Albatrosses snuck up on you. On the other side of the bar, the guy with the gold chain had ordered a dozen oysters on the half-shell and the lawyers were exchanging amused glances among themselves.

"Dead meat," Mark noted. "But who am I to talk?"

"My father used to call me his little albatross," Helen said, surprising herself.

He looked at her. "Really?"

"Really."

He considered this for a moment. Helen felt a small glow of satisfaction, to have finally pierced his glibness.

Finally he shook his head. "Maybe you should just have a gin-and-tonic on the next round."

"The Albatross comes with a cherry," Helen said. She plucked the cherry from her glass, popped it into her mouth, and tied the stem into a knot with her tongue. It took about ten seconds.

"Nice trick," Mark said, as she laid the neatly knotted stem on her napkin.

"Yeah, I'm a regular traveling circus."

The bartender, alerted by the cherry action, approached. "Another round?"

"Do you have anything without irony?" Mark asked him.

"Two more of the same," Helen said. "And give me an extra cherry."

"Whose tab?"

"Mine," Mark and Helen said simultaneously.

The bartender rolled his eyes.

"I believe the protocol is for the guy on the suicide mission to buy," Mark insisted.

Helen shrugged. "With stewardesses, maybe."

"Lawyers."

"Whatever. I prefer to feed the sacrificial lamb."

"I'm dead meat, any way you look at it," Mark told the bartender cheerfully.

"I'll bring the drinks," the guy said. "You folks work it out."

The octopus made an appearance not long after that, emerging from an empty conch shell to make a dash across the aquarium. It did floomph, Helen thought. She was surprised by how small the thing was, maybe two or three inches across. It was actually pretty cute. It was only out for a moment, and then it disappeared again into a hole in the tank's coral.

Mark seemed genuinely delighted by the sighting and started going on about what an achievement it was to keep up a large aquarium. He could name every species in the tank, from the Orange Spot Parrotfish to the Blue Caribbean Tang. Helen wondered what it was about her and men interested in fish.

"Did you know an octopus has three hearts?" he asked.

"No, I must say, I did not know that."

"Hardly anyone does. Plus, they have the most complex brain of all the invertebrates."

"Really?"

"Hearts and smarts."

"An ideal combination."

"Exactly. Very rare in nature."

"Even rarer in bars," Helen said dryly.

He laughed just the right amount, and she smiled back at him and signaled for another round of drinks. She was enjoying herself way too much. She hadn't been this drunk in years. She was ready to kill most men before the second beer.

"So what happened to your ear?" Mark asked, emboldened by her initiative.

Helen touched her torn lobe and shrugged. "Rough sex."

"Jesus. Who's your boyfriend, van Gogh?"

"It wasn't my boyfriend. It was—I don't know. A fling."

"Some fling."

"It was an accident, really. Not his fault."

"Still. I'd kick the guy's ass."

"My boyfriend threw him off a cliff."

Mark laughed. "Ah, well, there you go. So chivalry's not dead after all."

"You'd be surprised."

Their drinks arrived. Mark had switched to Albatrosses, and they were getting some mileage out of his failure to tie the cherry stems into knots. Helen was waiting for him to say something sexually suggestive about the nimbleness of her tongue, but he'd showed admirable restraint so far. She plucked the cherry out of her fresh drink and went to work. Mark was timing her by now, and when she took the knotted stem out of her mouth, he said, "Eight seconds. A new world record."

"I owe it to my father, really. He taught me everything a girl should never know."

"To your father, then," Mark said, holding up his glass.

She tapped it with her own. "'And I had done an hellish thing, / And it would work 'em woe: / For all averred I had killed the bird / That made the breeze to blow.'"

He gave her a sharp look. Helen went on, "'Ah wretch! said they, the bird to slay, / That made the breeze to blow.'"

"I thought you were the albatross," Mark said.

She shrugged. "I'm the whole damned poem."

"No, no," he insisted. "You can't have it both ways. Either you're the bird or you're the Ancient Mariner. If you're the bird, you're the symbol of life-giving something-or-other, which gets killed by human pride and stupidity, and if you're the sailor, you're the symbol of fucking up royally and the long journey to redemption."

Helen tried to sort that out and realized she was too drunk. It seemed to her that there was some actual insight in the observation. She'd assumed being the albatross was a bad thing for so long that it was going to take some time to consider an alternative view.

Mark persisted, "The albatross is a grace. If your father really thought of you as his albatross, he was probably recognizing that he'd screwed up somehow. That he'd been blessed with something as beautiful as you in his life and hadn't been able to live up to it."

Helen took a moment to make sure she wasn't going to cry, then marveled quietly, "I think that might be the nicest thing anyone's ever said to me."

"That's sad," Mark said.

On the TV screen in the corner, the ten-o'clock news had just come on. The nice black anchorman and the nice blond anchorwoman, with identical looks of grave solicitude. The lead story was headlined "Death at Land's End," and the stark background photo showed a broken bicycle on an offshore rock. They'd found Mike's body, Helen realized, with a weird little thrill.

The broadcast was muted and she considered hollering at the bartender to turn up the sound, then decided not to make a scene. The silent screen cut to some helicopter footage of Land's End, a sweeping context shot of sea and rocks, panning from the Golden Gate to a small beach crowded with police. A woman in hip boots and a surprisingly nice jacket was wading toward the rock where Michael

Turner lay like a sack of potatoes that had fallen off a truck. As the helicopter's camera zoomed in on her, she turned toward it and flipped the news crew off.

Helen studied her face. Even angry, the woman was pretty, and the look of sorrow and outrage on her face was exquisite. Helen felt a surprising sympathy for her. And a prick, like a needle's point, of shame. She really should have gone down the trail and cleaned up properly. Mike had been a self-absorbed asshole, but he'd deserved better than to be left to the gulls and the crabs. This woman, trying futilely to shoo the helicopter away, was doing something Helen should have done, giving Michael Turner a measure of dignity.

But it didn't pay to think about that. Shame and rage, grief and regret, it just didn't pay. There was no going too deep into any of that stuff without drowning. And that woman cop was going to drown, Helen thought. She felt too much. You couldn't care that much and survive.

A second shot showed the policewoman laying her jacket over the body's face and chest. Helen turned away from the screen.

"I've got to go," she said, gathering up her purse and jacket.

Mark looked dismayed. "So soon?"

"It's late."

"Can I give you a ride someplace, at least?"

"Sorry." She took her wallet out and tossed a twenty on the bar, considered it a moment, then dropped a ten on top of it.

"Was it something I said?" Mark persisted plaintively.

Helen said, "No, you were fine. You were great, actually. I'm going to think about what you said about the albatross."

"Well, you were great too. I had fun. And I'd love to see you again."

She hesitated, realizing she was tempted, then shook her head. "It's really best we don't."

"But—"

"No. Thank you. You're a sweet guy. Really, truly. A decent man. Too decent for the likes of me."

"A sweet, decent loser, you're saying," he said glumly. "Thanks for playing, better luck next time."

On the other side of the fish tank, the lawyers were building something silly out of the empty oyster shells, giggling among themselves. The guy with the gold chain looked on morosely. Dead meat, Helen thought. She should have gone for the guy herself. He would have been so satisfying to kill.

She turned back to Mark.

"Don't think of it as a game you lost," she told him. "Think of it as the night a miracle happened. Think of it as the night you found mercy in a bar."

She pulled her coat on before he could reply, turned briskly, and walked away, leaving him as you would leave a line snagged on a sunken limb. And in her heart she did something she had never done before: She cut him loose.

T HE HOMICIDE OFFICE on the fourth floor of the Hall of Justice was half full of inspectors at their desks by nine A.M., and they all stood up and cheered and clapped as Rose came in.

"Attagirl, Rosie!" "Way to go, Big Bird!" "Stick to your guns, girl!"

Uh-oh, she thought. Joshua was already hurrying toward her, with a *Chronicle* in his hand.

"This can't be good," Rose said.

"It's worse than that. You're page one, babe."

There she was, above the fold. The photo was grainy and had probably been pulled straight from the TV footage. SFPD Homicide Inspector Rose Burke Flips Off the World.

"Sandi Thanh wants to see you right away."

"I'll bet she does," Rose said, still studying the paper.

The caption below the photo read, "No comment!" which struck her as sort of clever, actually. She was definitely going to have to color her hair. You could see the gray from a fucking helicopter. Her raised hand exposed a patch of sweat at the armpit of her pale blouse and she looked like a hippo in those waders, despite the slimming slacks. If she'd known she was going to make the news, she'd have worn black.

"Can I have your desk, Rosie?" Dick Burke called.

"Go to hell, Dick," Joshua said, saving Rose the trouble. And then, quietly, to Rose, "I'll come with you. Sandi's really pissed."

"I got your message last night," she said. "I think you're right, about the Pelletier connection. I'd had a similar thought. We'll need to track down those tied flies from Henry Pelletier's closet and have forensics do a comparison of the—"

"We'll talk about it later, partner," Joshua said. "Let's make sure you've still got a job, first."

Lieutenant Thanh's office door was closed, which was unusual. Rose paused in front of it and took a deep breath.

"You'd better wait out here," she told Joshua.

"No way," he said. He had that ready-to-take-a-bullet-for-you look: my partner, right or wrong. The thing she'd had with Jack. Rose hadn't seen Joshua quite like this before, and the knee-jerk ferocity of his loyalty moved her. And scared her.

"Don't go off the deep end about this, Josh. I'm the one who fucked up."

"You didn't fuck up. And fuck anybody who—"

"Just don't make it worse," she said. "Okay? Let me take my medicine."

Joshua shrugged, still up on the balls of his feet, ready to fight. They were standing on either side of the door, in an inadvertent echo of the moment before a bust. As if in another moment they would draw their guns, do scissors-paper-stone for who went first, and kick the door in.

Rose stepped in front of the door, pointedly, to underline the fact that there would be no hail of gunfire from within, and knocked.

"Come," Sandi Thanh called brusquely, a sharp, irascible note. Rose and Joshua exchanged a last glance, and entered.

Their lieutenant was on the phone, her normally smooth brow scrunched in stoic concentration. She pointed to the spot in front of her desk and gave them a glare that said plainly, Just stand there. Someone was giving her an earful, and for several minutes all she said was, "Uh-huh . . . Yes, sir . . . Uh-huh." And then, apparently moving against the grain, "No . . . No, sir, I don't see it that way. . . . Not necessarily, no . . ."

Finally she said, "Well, that would be *my* call, wouldn't it?" And, with an edge, "Okay, fine . . . Fine, then. You do that. Sir."

She hung up sharply and took a breath, composing herself, then looked up at Rose and Joshua. "What the hell are you doing in here, Inspector Falkner?"

"I thought I'd save you some time, Lieutenant. 'Cause if you fire Rose, you're gonna have to fire me too. Might as well get it done in one fell swoop."

Thanh rubbed her eyes.

"Get out, Josh," she said wearily. "I understand where you're coming from, but—get out."

"The reason Rose is in that picture is that she was the only one with the balls to be in the water in the first place," Joshua insisted. He glanced at Rose. "Uh, no offense, Rosie."

"None taken."

Joshua turned back to Thanh. "And she was the only one with the balls to give those assholes in the chopper what they deserved. Rose just did what the rest of us should have been doing, she did the right thing, protecting the scene. And I'm not the only one who feels this way, I can tell you that. You may have to fire the whole fucking Crime Scene Unit. And the morgue crew, and the AME. I mean, we fucking *cheered* when she came back to the beach—"

"I'm not firing anyone at this point, Inspector," Thanh said. "Unless you're not out of this office in about three seconds. In which case, I'll be perfectly happy to oblige you."

Joshua opened his mouth to say something else, caught himself, and glanced at Rose. She cocked her head toward the door: *Go, for God's sake.* He hesitated a moment more, then shrugged and said, to Rose, "Holler if you need me."

It was another clear slam at the lieutenant, but Thanh let it go. Her face had settled back into its usual bulletproof serenity. She sat patiently as Joshua closed the door too hard on his way out.

"Sorry about that," Rose said, when the glass had stopped rattling. "He means well."

"I had the same partner for eight years when I was on the streets," Thanh said mildly. "I know how it goes. At least Josh kept his weapon holstered."

"Am I suspended?"

Thanh shrugged. "Not unless I am. But there are some seriously bunched knickers this morning at City Hall. So—we'll see."

Their eyes met. Thanh actually looked amused. Obviously she'd gone to bat for Rose and put her own butt on the line.

Rose drew a breath. "Thanks, Sandi."

"I don't think they've got the stomach to can the only two women in Homicide, frankly. But as I said, we'll see." Thanh smiled. "I wouldn't count on making sergeant anytime soon, though."

Rose felt a flicker of uneasiness. She realized that some

deep part of her had already started doing the salary math in the event of a divorce. But she shrugged and said, "That doesn't matter. I owe you, Sandi."

"They shouldn't have aired the footage," Thanh said. "The jerks. Everybody's panicked because they think it makes us look bad. But I've got some media contacts of my own. I know a guy at the *Chronicle* with an actual conscience, and he owes me a favor and a half. By the time he gets done spinning this, he'll have people thinking the middle finger in the air is the international symbol for 'Respect the dead.'"

Joshua was waiting for her three steps outside the lieutenant's office, still glaring at the world like a man ready to face Uzi fire.

"So—?" he demanded.

"So, calm down. Sandi's cool."

"How cool?"

"The coolest." Rose smiled. "She did suggest it might not have been the best career move."

He relaxed. "This is going to be a big disappointment to Burke and Fratello, you know. They're already dividing up your pencils and paper clips back in the squad room."

"Fuck 'em if they can't take a joke," Rose said. "Let's go work our case."

As they drove toward Michael Turner's apartment in the Haight, Rose called Jeff Tagliabue, the guy in the Computer Forensics Unit who had been working on the handlebar computer from Turner's bicycle.

"This is *really* a nifty gadget," Tagliabue told her enthusiastically. "State of the fucking art. I've been having a blast with it."

"Uh-huh," Rose said. She'd worked with Tagliabue before. He was a classic geek, a gangly redhead with ink-stained shirt pockets and one of the only beards in the SFPD. She'd learned that the best way to deal with him was to let him run on for a while.

"I mean, we're talking a watt function measuring energy expenditure, an altimeter, temperature gauge, actual speed, average speed, maximum speed, average maximum speed, all kinds of distance-to-speed functions. Water resistant, shockproof—"

"Perfect for riding off cliffs."

"Exactly! Takes a licking and comes up ticking!"

"Anything that might be of the slightest relevance to a homicide investigation?"

"Funny you should mention that," Tagliabue said, as if it had just occurred to him. "The time of death is a slam-dunk, of course. The bike hit the rocks at four twenty-seven P.M. last Tuesday, a little over an hour into the guy's ride."

"Okay. Great. Anything else?"

"Are you kidding?! This thing has a very sophisticated altitude-loss/gain-to-speed function. You can chart current speed against current altitude for every turn of the wheel, basically. It's fucking incredible."

"Mind-boggling," Rose agreed, rolling her eyes at Joshua, who'd been driving in silence, trying to make sense out of her half of the conversation. "What will they think of next?"

"I wouldn't mind seeing a relative acceleration function, myself—"

"Jeff, for Christ's sake, I'm fucking humoring you. What have you got?"

Tagliabue took a breath, momentarily subdued, but essentially undaunted, like a puppy on a leash. "Well, to make a long story short, when you chart your delta v against your altitude differential—"

"In English, amigo."

"—you can see immediately that the bike wasn't moving when the guy went off the cliff."

"What do you mean, it wasn't moving?"

"The velocity was zero. An hour and seven minutes into the ride, the guy pulls over for a rest or something. It's clear as a bell on the readout: speed zero, altitude change zero. Eighteen minutes later, the computer shows that the altitude changes by a hundred and fifty meters in about eight and a half seconds, but the speed is zero for the whole event. The wheels never turned."

"He went off the cliff from a standing start?"

"Essentially."

"Hard to picture someone doing that by accident, isn't it?"

"I'd say he was probably persuaded," Tagliabue said cheerfully. "But that's your job. Damn, this is a sweet little machine. I wonder where he got it."

The poignancy of a life interrupted never failed to hit Rose hard. When the landlord let her and Joshua into Michael Turner's second-floor apartment on Belvedere, two blocks from Haight Street, the place reeked of a neglected cat box and dead roses. An elegant young Siamese with soft blue eyes and a tail bent twice like a lightning bolt attached itself at once to their ankles, rubbing against their legs and purring furiously. Unless the place had slow mice, she hadn't eaten for over a week.

Rose squatted to rub the cat's ears as she looked around the apartment. It was a classic young bohemian's bachelor pad, with furnishings several notches down even from Henry Pelletier's incoherent bargain-days décor: a beached walrus of a couch, more or less green, a couple of unmatched lamps on the unmatched crates that served as end tables, and a beanbag chair, leaking beans. There were posters taped to the wall—Nirvana and Eric Clapton—and an expensive stereo system on a board-and-block setup in the corner, with dozens of CDs in uneven stacks on the floor nearby. The oblong garage-sale coffee table was strewn with magazines—*Biking World*, the most recent *Sports Il-*

lustrated swimsuit issue, well-thumbed, a token *Newsweek*, and some *Rolling Stone*s. Near the center of the table, a cheap vase held the empty stems of a dozen roses; the withered petals lay in heaps around the base.

Rose felt a stir of bloodhound energy at the sight of the expired flowers, the whiff of a trail. It seemed likely to her that whoever had given the roses to Michael Turner had also killed him. But there was no card.

"So who pays the rent if the guy is dead?" the landlord asked. He was a stubbly, squat, impatient man with a Bronx accent and a dirty white T-shirt, a transplanted cliché. "Is the city gonna pay the rent?"

Joshua shrugged. "I think you can take Mr. Turner's death as a de facto giving of notice."

"This place has a lease. He's six months into a two-year lease."

"That's fucking tragic," Joshua said, dangerously mild.

Rose moved on into the apartment, letting her partner deal with the aggrieved landlord. The cat stayed with her, weaving around her ankles, making it difficult to walk. The kitchen was off to the left, an elbow-shaped afterthought of a room with minimal counter space, an ancient, groaning refrigerator, and unwashed spaghetti dishes in the sink, licked more or less clean by the desperate cat. In the far corner, by the window, a Formica table sagged beneath an answering machine, a microwave oven, and a dying begonia in a pot.

The cat's feeding station was on the floor beneath the table, an array of empty bowls on a plastic "It's a Small World" Disneyland place mat. Rose pulled on a pair of rubber gloves and found a can of tuna-and-gravy cat food in the kitchen's only cupboard. The Siamese jumped onto the counter as she was opening the can, eager to assist in the process, and Rose almost shooed her off, then decided it couldn't matter all that much. The jingling name tag at the cat's throat read AGATHA.

Rose put the bowl of food down, along with some water, and took a moment to water the parched begonia too. It seemed futile, but so much of her life did right now.

The message light on the answering machine was flashing "9." As Agatha dug gratefully into the tuna, Rose sat down on the table's single chair, took out her notebook, and hit Play. There was a series of escalating messages from Turner's boss, culminating in him losing his job. Turner's mother had called, as had his sister, the calls apparently casual. Rose noted both numbers and saved the messages with a pang. She hated notifications; it was the worst part of the job, worse by far than facing the corpses themselves: to be the one who had to say, I'm very, very sorry, but the world is more terrible than you could ever have imagined.

The rest of the messages seemed routine, no smoking guns, no sultry calls from a femme fatale inviting Turner to get pushed off a cliff the previous Tuesday. A biking pal had called, proposing a ride in Marin, the mother had called again on Sunday, sounding a bit more urgent, and there were a couple of calls from someone named Bill, who had been in a band with Turner. He'd missed two rehearsals, but nobody was sweating it. Apparently they could do without out a saxophone player.

Joshua had gotten rid of the landlord and was in the apartment's single bedroom, sitting at the little computer desk by the window. He'd put on some rubber gloves and was trying to get into Michael Turner's e-mail.

"Shit," he muttered, as another guess at the password failed. "Shit . . . Shit . . ?"

It sounded like he had a rhythm going. Rose let him work and started in on the rest of the room. The queen-sized bed was unmade, and the sheet showed evidence of recent sexual activity. No platinum-blond hairs and no love notes in lipstick signed "Melanie." Rose left it for the CSU.

A pair of jeans and a T-shirt lay in a heap by the closet, probably from Turner's last change of clothes. The room's single bookshelf, a board on two cinder blocks, was dominated by books on mountain bikes and rock climbing, which had a tinge of irony in context. The closet itself was standard fare, light on formal wear, heavy on concert T-shirts, synthetic sports clothes, jeans, and corduroys. All men's clothing. And, poignantly, the saxophone.

The apartment's second phone sat on a rickety table beside the bed. The table's drawer held some condoms, a plastic bag of dope, consumer size, not wholesale, and a brown leather address book. Michael Turner was one of those people who ordered his contacts by the initial of the first name, which was a break. It made it easy to find Melanie Jurgensen.

"Shit . . . ," Joshua said. And, a moment later, "Shit!"

"Leave it for Jeff Tagliabue, partner," Rose said. "I want to go see a woman about a music tape."

Agatha slipped out the front door with them and refused to go back into the apartment. After wasting ten minutes trying to catch her, Rose and Joshua gave up and headed for their car. Agatha followed, just out of reach, but when Rose opened the passenger door, the cat slipped past her and settled happily on the backseat. Rose and Joshua stood on the sidewalk for a moment, pondering the dilemma.

"We could drop her at the SPCA," Joshua suggested.

"She's kind of cute."

"Don't even think about it, Rose. A victim's pet? That's probably breaking about forty regulations."

"It's not like she's evidence or something." He remained stubbornly silent. "What would you do? Grab her by the collar and stick her back in that apartment, so she can starve to death according to procedure?"

"We could call the next of kin and see if they'll take her."

"The next of kin are in Oregon."

"We could drop her at the SPCA," Joshua said again.

"Or just close our eyes and wish she'd go away?"

"You said it, I didn't. But frankly—sure."

"So you do that," Rose said.

He looked at her suspiciously. "What?"

"You close your eyes and wish she'd go away." She took the car keys out of his hand. "Meanwhile, I'll drive."

The address they had for Melanie Jurgensen was about a mile west of Turner's apartment, on a little side street off Parnassus, halfway up the hill toward the UCSF Medical Center. There wasn't a single free parking space in the entire neighborhood, and Rose finally parked by a fire hydrant and put the SFPD placard in the window. They left the cat curled up on the backseat and walked up to 1254, a squat white house built into the hillside. 1254-A, the apartment they wanted, turned out to be around the back. It was a garden in-law arrangement with a sliding glass door for an entryway. The backyard had a patch of well-tended grass the size of a beach blanket, and beds of bright orange poppies laced with wild irises. As Rose and Joshua approached, they could hear violin music from within the apartment. Something intricate and classical.

"Vivaldi," Joshua said. "Or is it Bach? Chester would know."

"This isn't it," Rose said, with sudden certainty.

He glanced at her. "It's the right address."

"No, I mean, Melanie. She's not the right one. She's not our gal."

"You figured that out on the walk from the car? Based on—what? Signals from Venus? Her touch with flowers?"

"I just know. Call it my gut."

"You have a very active gut," Joshua said. "You should probably take something for it." He stepped up to the sliding glass door, just enough off to the side to make it difficult to shoot him from inside, unsnapped the holster strap on the 9mm at his armpit, and knocked.

The violin music continued. Joshua knocked on the glass again, more firmly, and the music stopped. A moment later a young woman in well-worn jeans and a UCSF Med School sweatshirt approached the door and slid it open. She still had the violin in her hand and was holding it as if she might use it to defend herself, wary, and even a little edgy, at the appearance of a couple of coplike strangers. But not freaked, Rose noted. And not overly casual, in-your-face-nonchalant, as so many suspects were. A pretty girl, in her mid-twenties, with a freckled, slightly upturned nose that made her look younger, azure eyes, and coppery hair, cropped short and casual.

"Melanie Jurgensen?" Joshua asked.

"Yes."

He already had his badge out, presenting it with his left hand, keeping his right hand free. "I'm Inspector Joshua Falkner, with the San Francisco Police. And this is Inspector Burke."

She peered at the badge, then gave his gun hand a pointed glance. "Are you going to shoot me?"

"Only if you shoot me first," Joshua said, managing, with his drawl, to make it sound almost charming. But he didn't move his hand.

"We just want to ask you a few questions," Rose said.

"This is about Mike, isn't it?"

"Mike who?" Joshua said, going for spontaneous incrimination, but Rose said, "Yes."

Melanie gave a little tic of impatience and disgust, turned away from the door, and bent to pick something up. Both Joshua and Rose reached instinctively for their guns, but when Melanie stood up all she had in her hands was a paper grocery sack.

"You can tell that piece of shit that all he had to do was

ask for them," she said. "Jesus, fifteen minutes of law school and he thinks he's got the whole judicial system at his beck and call."

Rose leaned over and glanced into the doubled brown bag. It was filled with CDs and paperback books. Joan Osborne and John Grisham, the Rolling Stones and some white-boy rap.

"I don't know what he told you, but these have been sitting right there waiting for him for almost six months," Melanie said. "I've told him that half a dozen times, they're his for the taking. But I'm not a goddamned delivery service."

Joshua and Rose exchanged a glance.

"Uh, Ms. Jurgensen, just so we're on the same page—" Joshua said.

She glared at him over the top of the bag, still vexed. "Yeah?"

"I think you can probably keep the CDs."

She made them tea, which neither Rose nor Joshua particularly wanted. But they let Melanie Jurgensen putter, as she clearly needed to. While she banged around the kitchen, they waited on a low futon that probably opened up into a bed, a little self-conscious with their knees so close to their chests. There was a desk against the single room's far wall, stacked with medical texts and a computer, and a bicycle leaned against the other wall by the door.

By the time she brought in the matching cups and pot, in Japanese china on a black-and-red lacquered tray, Melanie had calmed down enough to give them a rueful smile.

"Milk or sugar?" she asked, as she set the tray down.

"I take it black, thanks," Joshua said, and added, with a Joe-Friday inflection, "I'm a cop, you know."

"This is green tea."

"Damn," he said, and Melanie laughed, almost unwillingly, like a child teased out of crying.

"Nothing for me, thanks," Rose said.

"I like a bit of honey," Melanie said. She crossed back to the in-law's tiny kitchen and took longer than seemed absolutely necessary to find the honey. Rose and Joshua exchanged a glance. If Melanie Jurgensen took a .38 out of the bread box and came back and shot them, or shot herself, it was going to be embarrassing trying to explain what they'd been doing having tea with a murder suspect. But they'd both pretty much decided she was clear.

When Melanie did return, carrying a plastic honey container shaped like a bear, her eyes were red around the rims. Joshua and Rose waited until she had poured them all cups from the common pot and taken a real swallow of her tea before politely sipping their own, as it would also have been contrary to procedure to get poisoned.

"So you think I killed him?" Melanie said, setting her cup down.

"Naw," Joshua said, as Rose said, "Did you?"

"I felt like it often enough," Melanie conceded. "Mike was that kind of guy. He'd drive you nuts. An ABNQ."

Joshua looked puzzled. "'ABNQ'?"

"Almost But Not Quite," Rose supplied. "Close, but no cigar, real relationship–wise."

"Exactly." Melanie looked at her tea. "He was so smart. And sweet, you know? He could be so damned sweet. Charming, funny. A good listener. Not like so many guys." She glanced at Joshua. "No offense."

"I think this tea may need honey after all," he said. "It's a bit strong."

Melanie studied him briefly, apparently intrigued.

"So you and Michael Turner dated?" Rose prompted her, giving Joshua a behave-yourself glance.

Melanie shrugged. "Nobody dates anymore. We hung out, we did things together. We were a thing."

"For how long?"

"Almost a year. He'd just dropped out of law school

when I met him. He was going to be an artist or something, but he didn't have any talent. He didn't even have a medium, really. He was just a nice, sensitive guy who smoked too much dope. Good in bed." She glanced at Joshua. "Again, no offense."

"I won't dignify that with a response," he said.

"When did you break up?" Rose asked.

"Last fall. He'd sworn to me he was going to get serious, go back to law school, start acting like a grown-up. Maybe even act like we had a future. And then . . ." She shrugged.

"He didn't," Rose supplied.

"Exactly. He was too damn happy being Peter Pan. So I got out."

"Was the parting of the ways, um—"

"Amicable?" Melanie gave a short laugh. "Did I threaten to kill him, you mean? Did I show up in restaurants and scream at him, did I stalk him, slash his tires, toilet-paper his house? Did I leave long harangues on his answering machine?"

"Something like that."

Melanie shrugged. "I was pissed off," she said. "I was bitter. I washed the sheets and threw out the matchbooks from our bars and put his fucking CDs in a bag. I drank a lot of margaritas and trashed him with my girlfriends. I made solemn vows to never love a charming fluff-ball of a man again."

"Did you ever send him flowers?"

Melanie looked shamefaced. "About six months ago," she conceded. "Right after we broke up. I was drunk. It was idiotic."

So much for the roses, Rose thought. She should have known. The vase had been dry as a bone.

She reached into her purse for the tape she'd found at the bottom of the cliff.

"Do you recognize this?" she asked.

Melanie glanced at the tape briefly, then did a double-take, and finally took it and studied the song list. "It's—yeah, it's a music mix I made for Mike. I mean, I didn't make this copy. I made the original tape."

"The master was in the portable tape player on his belt when he died."

"Jesus," Melanie murmured. And, after a moment, "And this—?"

"I found it on the slope near the same spot. I'm thinking maybe he had a date that day."

"That would be like Mike. Using my music mix to get laid. The least he could have done was change the damned label."

"Would you have any idea of who might have been on that bike ride with him?"

Melanie gave a short, hard laugh. "I didn't keep up. Some dimwit from the fruit section at the Marina Safeway, no doubt."

"The fruit section at the Marina Safeway?"

"That's how Mike met all his women," Melanie said. "Pick-up Central. He'd stand there by the cantaloupes and make double entendres." She shook her head at herself. "I should have known, really. I mean, what kind of relationship are you going to have with a guy who picks you up by the melons?"

"A serious man would stand near the broccoli," Joshua offered.

Melanie didn't even smile. "Exactly. Or in whole grains."

She picked up her teacup, found that it was empty, and set it down again. Rose gave Joshua a glance, and they stood up to go. Melanie kept staring into her teacup. She looked like she was going to cry again. Rose found herself wanting to say something comforting, but she couldn't formulate anything that seemed remotely appropriate.

She floundered for a moment, then finally blurted out, "Do you want his cat?"

Melanie glanced up at her. "What?"

"His cat. Agatha. She's sitting out in our car. I don't know what to do with her."

"I'm allergic to cats," Melanie said. "We always slept over here." She looked at the bag of CDs, which was still sitting by the door, and shook her head sadly.

"Maybe it's best he's dead, in a way," she said—tentatively, trying on the perspective. "That sweet, stupid guy. He was living off his charm the way you'd live off a credit card. There was going to be one hell of a reckoning at some point."

"It looks like there was," Rose said.

12

H ELEN FOUND HERSELF CLEANING. And cleaning, and cleaning, wielding the dust rag like a regimental banner in a suicide assault, gripping the handle of the vacuum cleaner as you would cling to the steering wheel of a car sliding on ice, conscious that she wasn't steering anymore, that the thing was out of control.

She lifted all the furniture and dusted every surface in every room. She bleached the bathroom grout and shined the outside windows through the burglar bars and polished the silverware, her maternal grandmother's silver, which she and Jimmy had never used. It was actually impossible to picture Jimmy holding one of her grandmother's Tiffany sterling salad forks, with the little inlaid bird singing amid delicate flowers on the handle. But Helen knew she wasn't polishing the damned silverware because the polishing mattered. She was cleaning as her mother had cleaned, because she was slightly mad, and to stop would be to feel the weight of that.

The thing was, her life wasn't working anymore. Had it ever? Helen wondered. It had; she was sure it had. Her knight had come, once upon a time. He'd slain the dragon, according to the script, and they'd lived happily ever after for a year and a half. But it turned out there was another dragon. There was always another dragon. The fairy tales didn't mention that.

And so he killed the next one for you, and the next, and the blood soaked into the ground more slowly every time and the dragons reappeared more quickly and happily ever after lasted eight months, four months, a week and a half. Until suddenly one day you woke up and happily ever after was a faded dream and you realized you were living with the dragon. That maybe you had been all along. That it was the knights who'd been dying. That you'd been trapped in this magic cottage for a thousand years, scrubbing blood with blood, trying to get it clean enough to lift the spell.

In the bedroom, Helen shined Jimmy's bowling trophies for the second time in three days, and dusted the lightbulbs in the lamps. The rest of the surfaces were spotless. Even in the grip of madness, she was running out of things to clean.

"It's got to stop, Jimmy," she'd said.

She stood for a long moment in the center of the room, looking at herself in the immaculate mirror. Her skin was pink from scrubbing, and her face was free of makeup. Even her hair would bear no more washing; every trace of artificial color was gone and the short, sassy cut that had seemed so crisp in Malaysian Cherry was merely ragged in her natural dun. She looked like a novice nun just out of the shower, simple, drab, and draped in innocence. She looked like someone's fortunate daughter, immune to evil by a miracle of birth.

"It's got to stop."

Helen stooped and pulled the chest from beneath the

bed. Jimmy said it was stupid to keep it there, and of course it was. Maybe it really was that simple for him: stupid or smart, caught or not caught. Maybe, for Jimmy, the ghosts didn't need a home. Maybe he could live with the way they'd filled the air before she'd started keeping the chest locked away, the way they might sneak in with the next song on the radio or in the light through clouds just after rain. At least with the chest she could close the lid for a while. She could pick her moments to fight, or to grieve, to loathe herself, or to regret—whatever she did when she had to face the ghosts. Because Helen knew by now that sometimes there was nothing to do but face them.

"How?" he'd said.

The chest was cedar in a rosewood finish, with an engraved brass latch, an incongruous double-armored stainless-steel combination lock with hardened shackles and hand-carved Oriental dragons on all four sides and the top. A "hope chest," Cora had called it when she gave it to her daughter for Helen's eleventh birthday, though it was too small to accumulate much of real usefulness and, even at eleven, Helen had wondered what a hope chest was doing with dragons on it. She'd come to think of it more as a private Pandora's box. The first thing she'd ever stored in it was the diamond ring she'd slipped from her mother's finger the day Cora had died.

The MasterLock's combination was keyed to her parents' wedding anniversary. The lid's hinge gave a distinctive creak when Helen opened it, a ghost's plaint in a minor key. A soft cedar aroma wafted from within, tinged with copper from the traces of blood. The chest held fewer than a dozen items, most of them mundane, and none anywhere near as valuable as her mother's engagement ring. Michael Turner's titanium-framed Gucci sunglasses lay beside the remaining earring of the set made from Henry Pelletier's hand-tied dragonflies. There was her father's copy of *The Family Album of Favorite Poems,* the pages grayed near the center where "The Rime of the Ancient Mariner" lay, and toward the end, along the edges of "Gunga Din" and "The Raven." Her father's taste in poetry had been limited to the darkly epic, relentless, and rhythmic.

"How you gonna stop it, Helen?"

There was a Timex watch that had been Wesley Freundling's, the crystal smashed and the hands frozen at nine twenty-seven on a forgotten date. A sweat-stained CAT hat that had belonged to Billy Church. A gardenia corsage, carefully pressed, given to her by Joel Severence on the night he died. A key to the apartment of Robert "Don't Call Me Bob" Maugham, who had never given his key to anyone before. Chet Buford's bear claw still dangled from the necklace chain that had been strong enough to choke him; Ken Joseph's Phi Beta Kappa key, which he'd worn everywhere, nestled beside the eight ball that had broken Dennis Mackay's skull. And there was a tiny purple teddy bear, won for her at the San Mateo County Fair by a guy whose name Helen could not recall, though she could still see his face in death, the shocked, slightly reproachful look that lingered there, muted like a footprint in the sand, touched once by a receding tide and left.

She spread the items on the bed, balancing one against another, still trying to remember that poor boy's name. She was ashamed of herself, to have forgotten. The fog had come in, and the spring afternoon was as bleak and gray as a New England November. And the horror was with her, the quiet, helpless horror, and the knowledge that she was lost.

The last thing in the box was a framed photograph of herself as a child. Helen held it up in the chilly light, trying to remember what the picture looked like. But the image was obscured, as it had been for years, beneath a cracked glass splattered with dried blood, because her father had been holding the photograph when Jimmy shot him from behind, like a coward, like a monster, like her long-awaited knight.

"I don't think you can stop it anymore," he'd said.

13

W ELL, THAT WAS AN interesting little relationship semi-
nar, wasn't it?" Joshua said as they walked back to the
car from Melanie Jurgensen's apartment.

"You've got to stop hitting on murder suspects, Josh,"
Rose told him.

He shrugged. "That wasn't a hit. A tap, at most. Besides,
you said she wasn't the one."

"You're trusting my intuition suddenly?"

"Only with women who play the violin."

They reached the car. The cat had curled up in a splash
of sunshine on the backseat and was dozing contentedly.
Joshua went to the driver's side, subtly reasserting himself,
and Rose tossed him the keys. Agatha looked up lazily as
they got into the car, then lay back again and closed her
eyes.

"That cat is way too fucking comfortable in here," Joshua

said. He put the keys in the ignition and looked at Rose. "So, where to?"

"Do you think it's possible that Turner and our gal actually hooked up in the produce section of the Marina Safeway?"

He looked dubious, but he started the car. "It seems like a long shot. But I suppose it's the best long shot we've got."

"I wonder if they've got surveillance cameras," Rose said. "I wonder if they tape."

They could see the cameras as soon as they walked into the store, but the manager was reluctant to discuss them, ostensibly on constitutional grounds. A pear-shaped man stuffed somewhat sweatily into a white shirt, balding in unrelated patches on the top and back of his head, with a hint of Elvis in his sideburns, he wanted paperwork. His name tag read C. THURMAN, STORE MANAGER, SERVING YOU SINCE 1987, and he had clearly risen to his level of incompetence.

They stood in his cluttered, glass-walled office, arguing the Bill of Rights. Thurman felt that both the First and the Fourth Amendments applied, as well as the Safeway Informational Request Form. Rose couldn't tell whether he was protecting the civil liberties of his customers, as he claimed, if he was unwilling to expose the extent of the store's security system to public awareness, or whether he was just exercising his small bureaucratic right to obstruct. She had wanted to kill him pretty much from the moment they walked into his office, so she let Joshua handle the negotiations with his usual soft southern style. Her partner's patience amazed her sometimes.

"I'm certainly willing to refer this to our regional office," Thurman said, for the third or fourth time. "They'll probably have our legal team research it for us, and—"

"Or we could get a warrant," Joshua said pleasantly.

"You could certainly do that," Thurman conceded, echoing his tone.

They stared at each other for a moment. Joshua didn't want to get a warrant, Rose knew; it would take the rest of the afternoon even if they could find a judge to sign off, and the grounds were pretty flimsy. But she didn't think Thurman wanted to call his regional manager either.

She said, into the silence of the impasse, "Mr. Thurman, do you think your average Safeway customer is prepared to appreciate the delicate constitutional issues here, if it became widely known that a serial killer has been stalking victims in your produce section?"

Thurman glanced at her. "What do you mean?"

"Well, I mean, hypothetically. Like, if an article were to appear in the newspaper to that effect, or on the evening news: 'A Murderer Among the Melons! Safeway Stonewalls Police Efforts to Catch a Killer,' something like that."

"Well, first of all, there's no real evidence that anything of the sort has—"

"Yeah, but you know how the media can be." Thurman stared at her unhappily; Rose persisted, "Do you think it would help your sales figures or hurt them?"

"Well, obviously, it wouldn't, um—"

"Maybe you could ask your regional manager, when you call him."

"Her," Thurman said. "But I don't really see any need for that, or for bringing the press into it. This is obviously a situation where we want to work as closely as possible with the authorities, with the utmost discretion."

The store's video security center was a paranoid's delight, a cramped womb ten degrees warmer than the store outside the door, stuffed with gadgetry and reeking acidly of old coffee and male body odor. The only light was the flickering gray of eight black-and-white monitors, four each on either side of the narrow aisle, their images shifting every ten seconds from one section of the store to another. The room was manned by a Mutt-and-Jeff pair of cheerful maniacs in drab olive uniforms, a big guy named Stan and a stooped little guy named Terry. A peculiar subculture was immediately evident; both men had the air of submariners who had not surfaced in quite some time.

Thurman hurriedly introduced the guards to the police officers, made a show of telling them to give Rose and Joshua anything they needed, and fled, no doubt to create a credible paper trail. Rose noted that his scruples over the Bill of Rights seemed to have evaporated. She had the sense Thurman needed to do something simple and soothing right away, like receive a consignment of canned goods.

Against expectation, Stan seemed like the brains of the pair, though the impressive effect of his equipment-laden cop belt was somewhat diminished by an empty holster. A crew-cut slab of a man with a face made rugged by old acne scars, he guided them through the security overview with obvious pride and no small amount of glee. The eight monitors revolved through views from twenty-four separate cameras, he informed them, covering every square inch of the store.

"Including the produce section?" Rose asked.

"Every square inch," Stan repeated solemnly, as if she'd questioned scripture. He was, Rose realized, the primary source of the room's appalling stench. She leaned back as far as politeness allowed.

"Do you recognize this man?" Joshua asked, producing the blow-up of Michael Turner's driver's license photo. Stan and Terry glanced at it and both nodded at once.

"Fridays," Terry said. "Late afternoon. Almost every week."

"And the occasional weekday," Stan added. "You get to know the faces pretty quickly, especially with the, uh—"

"Browsers," Terry supplied, and the two of them giggled.

"Browsers?" Joshua said.

Stan shrugged. "Not everybody comes here to buy food, if you know what I mean. It's quite a scene out there sometimes."

"We could make a fortune renting rooms by the hour," Terry offered cheerfully.

"Do you videotape?" Rose asked.

Stan exchanged a conspiratorial glance with Terry, then gave Rose a wink.

"Well . . ." he drawled. "I could tell you that—" He leaned toward her, narrowing the gap between them again, and lowered his voice to add, "but then I'd have to kill you."

Terry snickered appreciatively.

"Not without a gun in your fucking holster," Joshua noted quietly.

Terry's snicker stopped short. Stan gave Joshua a long, uneasy look, trying to figure out whether to tangle with him or make a joke of it, before he said, with a trace of petulance, "I'm licensed to carry. But the store doesn't want us armed."

"Of course," Joshua said.

Stan didn't seem to know where to go from there. Rose, trying to breathe shallowly and fast losing patience herself, prompted, "So you *do* tape?"

"Well, shit, of course we tape," Stan said sullenly. Apparently he had decided to lower the standards for disclosure.

"What's the point of spotting shoplifters if you can't back it up with hard evidence?" Terry demanded. "We tape everything. We tape the fucking *bathrooms*."

"Shut up, Terry," Stan said.

"Right," Terry said, genially enough, as if he'd been reminded to take his medication.

"Do you keep your back tapes?" Rose asked, riding through the byplay.

Stan hesitated, then shrugged. "For a while."

"'A while'?"

"A while." Rose held his gaze stubbornly, and he conceded, "A couple weeks."

"You mean, like, fourteen days?"

"Whatever." She looked at him and Stan said, with some defensive heat, "We're not the FBI archives, for Crissake. We've only got so many videotapes. We keep the damned things a couple of weeks, more or less. Then we start taping over them again."

Rose and Joshua exchanged a hopeful glance. Two weeks might be enough.

"Got a live one," Terry exclaimed from his station at the monitors. "Camera three."

Stan swung around instantly. "Hold view."

Terry hit a button and the shifting monitors paused on a young white man in a 49ers jacket lingering in front of a refrigerated case, hands in his pockets, glancing left and right, and left again.

"Dairy aisle," Terry noted importantly.

"Cheez Whiz, Cheez Whiz," Stan agreed, and the two of them giggled. Apparently it was an in-joke of some kind. They watched intently as the kid on the screen hesitated a moment more, then made his move and stuffed several slabs of packaged cheese into the jacket's capacious pockets.

"Gotcha, baby," Stan said. He took a handheld radio from his belt and fingered the transmit button. "Jonesy, we got a spill on aisle two. Male, red jacket."

The radio crackled instantly in reply. "Roger that. Aisle two."

The kid on the monitor was already easing away from the dairy cooler. They watched as he spotted the store guard coming toward him and hurriedly reversed his direction. Terry hit another button, and the monitor switched to a different camera view for the guard catching up with him. The kid started shaking his head immediately and launched into what was apparently an animated explanation of the un-usual circumstances.

"You have the right to remain silent." Terry smiled.

"If you give up the right to remain silent, anything you say can and will be taken as bullshit," Stan added, and they giggled again.

"Where do you keep your back tapes?" Rose asked.

"Huh?" Stan said.

"Your surveillance tapes from previous days. Where do you store them?"

Stan looked uneasy. "I don't know if Mr. Thurman—"

"Mr. Thurman has already discussed this with us and of-fered the store's full cooperation. As he told you."

Stan hesitated a moment more, then shrugged and led them grudgingly to a closet in the room's dimmest corner. He opened the door and yanked the string on the naked ceiling bulb. The harsh light revealed a tiny unshelved space, the floor strewn with videotape cassettes, many of them heaped rather than stacked, in no apparent order. It looked like a beach on the first low tide after a shipwreck.

"Yikes," Rose said.

"We've been meaning to get around to organizing things a little better."

Joshua plucked a cassette from the nearest pile of flot-sam and squinted at the label.

"This is dated three years ago," he said.

"It's hard to keep up with the labeling sometimes," Stan conceded.

After a brief survey of the chaotic cache of videotapes, Rose and Joshua decided to divide their efforts, with one of them going back to the office to follow up there. They did scissors-paper-stone for who would stay and sort through the tapes, and Joshua lost.

"God help me," he said. "Just me, and Starsky and Hutch

here, and ten thousand mislabeled videos of people steal-
ing cheese."

"Keep your cell phone on, so I can reach you. And call
me if you find anything."

"This is a circle of hell, Rosie. It could take weeks just
to find out it's a dead end."

"I'll get back as soon as I can to help out. And I'll ask
Sandi for overtime. Unless you've got another date?" Joshua
made a vulgar sound indicating that this was unlikely. Rose
laughed and said, "How was it with the insurance gal last
night, by the way?"

"Oh, it was wonderful," Joshua said gloomily. "Absolutely
fucking wonderful. Everything you could hope for from a
blind date with a CPA."

Rose stopped at a pet store on the way back to Bryant
Street and bought a plastic cat pan, some kitty litter and
a pooper scooper, canned and dry food, and plastic bowls.
Agatha nosed around the acquisitions for a while, scratched
at the bag of dry food, and resettled herself hopefully beside it on the passenger seat. At the Hall of Justice, Rose
put her in the plastic kitty litter pan and carried her inside.
She badged the guard at the metal detector, who hesitated
before opening the gate for her.

"I'm not sure you can bring that cat in here, Inspector."

"She's a material witness in a homicide investigation."

"And I'm the fucking Tooth Fairy," he said politely. He
wavered a moment more, then let the gate swing open. "If
anybody asks, you came in the back door."

"If anybody asks, we're probably both screwed," Rose
told him.

She set Agatha up in the coffee room on the fourth floor,
closed the door to keep the cat in, and went to her desk.

The Homicide squad room was nearly empty, which meant that any number of San Francisco residents were dead. The only other person in the room was Dick Burke, the world's most obnoxious man, and Rose readied herself for more comments on her recent celebrity. But Burke just said, "Hey, Rosie, didja hear about the rape/murder downtown?"

"No. We've been chasing down leads in the Marina."

"Sad, sad scene. They found the victim at the corner of Bangor and Leaver."

Rose sighed.

"Get it?" Burke persisted. "Bang 'er and leave 'er?"

"I get it, Dick. You're an asshole."

"Yet strangely attractive, right?"

"I'm sure your wife wakes up every morning thanking God."

"You don't know the half of it," Burke said smugly, and mercifully got back to work. Rose sat down at her desk and checked her in-box and messages. The Crime Scene Unit report was in on Michael Turner's apartment—a hodgepodge of fingerprints, but nothing immediately helpful. Rose hadn't counted on much there anyway; whoever they were after, it was someone savvy enough about evidence to avoid leaving casual prints. She forwarded the set of elimination prints she and Joshua had taken from Melanie Jurgensen and moved on to the rest of her messages.

Chester Sparks had scheduled Michael Turner's autopsy for the following morning. Jeff Tagliabue had written up his analysis of the bicycle computer data. The Forensics Lab had replied to her request for a blood typing and DNA analysis of the traces of blood on the earring they'd found on Turner's body: the blood type was O-negative, the most common, and it would be six weeks, at best, before a DNA analysis could be made, pending approval from the chief of the Homicide Section. There was a supplementary report from Forensics to the effect that the string used to tie the artificial fly found on Turner's body was "consistent" with the string used in the flies in Henry Pelletier's tackle box, and that there were strong "stylistic similarities" between the two samples. Which was worth zero in court, Rose knew. Someone downstairs had mailed it in.

She e-mailed Sandi Thanh, requesting the go-ahead for the expensive DNA test, then started writing up her notes from the interview with Melanie Jurgensen.

"So where's your partner, Rosie?" Dick Burke asked from across the room.

"Working our case," Rose said pointedly, not looking up.

"Ah. Well, that's a relief."

Rose gave him a grudging glance. "What's that supposed to mean?"

Burke shrugged. "Oh, you know."

"No, Dick, I don't know."

"Well, it's just . . . I mean, with the high casualty rate among your partners and all. I was just afraid the poor guy might have eaten his gun or something."

Rose stared at him for a moment, then stood up. She unbuckled her shoulder holster, set her gun on her desk, and started walking toward him.

"What?" Burke grinned, rising from his own chair and spreading his hands invitingly. "You gonna beat me up, Rosie? You gonna punch me out?"

Burke was a big man and Rose went up on her tiptoes to hit him, leading with a straight right jab to his prominent nose, hitting him hard and fast, figuring she was only going to get one punch in and wanting to make it count. She could feel the cartilage give beneath her fist. Burke yowled and staggered, both hands coming up to cup his face, and she followed with a short left to his solar plexus. Burke doubled over and Rose hit him again, a right hook to the exposed side of his head. As he crumpled to the floor, Sandi Thanh hollered from the doorway.

"Hey! Knock it off, you two!"

Rose stepped back, panting a little. On the floor, Burke groaned and struggled to his knees, his hands still cupped over his face, blood seeping out now between the fingers.

"Ah, Jesus, Jesus, Jesus," he moaned. "Jesus, Rosie. You broke my fucking nose."

"Oops," Rose said. Her knuckle was killing her; she'd hurt her hand on that last punch. Burke had a very hard head. But she wasn't going to let it show.

"What the hell is going on here?" Thanh demanded.

Rose shrugged and looked pointedly at Burke, who took a moment to find his feet again, still cupping his nose. He met her gaze briefly, his eyes bleary with involuntary tears, his face smeared with blood. Then he turned to Thanh.

"Nothing," he said.

"Nothing, my ass!"

"Just one of those things, Lieutenant. I must have . . . slipped."

"You slipped all right, you prick," Rose said.

"Shut up, Rose," Thanh said. She looked at Burke and said, as if intrigued by the idea, "Slipped, you say?"

He shrugged. "Accidents happen."

"I've noticed that the floor gets slick in here sometimes," Thanh said tentatively.

"Must have been a wet spot," Burke said.

"Must have been," Thanh agreed. She hesitated a moment, then ventured, "I certainly can't see any point in generating a bunch of paperwork about it."

"I can't see any point in making a big deal about it at all," Burke said. He found a handkerchief in his pocket and started sopping ineffectually at his face.

"Well, then," Thanh said briskly. "Looks like we've all got to be more careful. Dick, why don't you take the rest of the afternoon off, stay on the clock, of course, and get that nose taken care of. Run the paperwork by me, we'll figure out a way to get it covered as job related . . . And Rosie—in my office. Now."

"Lieutenant—"

"Now," Thanh said.

In her office, Lieutenant Thanh went to a minifridge in the corner and pulled out two bottles of Evian water. She gave one to Rose and sat down on the edge of her desk, gesturing for Rose to take a seat. Rose hesitated, then sat down reluctantly. She'd left her holster on her desk and felt naked without it.

Thanh opened her water, took a long swig, and crossed her slim brown legs.

"You seem a little volatile lately, Rosie," she said.

"He made a crack about Jack."

"You can't hit everybody who makes a crack about Jack."

Rose gave her a stubborn shrug: Maybe she could. Thanh waited, then sighed and shook her head. They sat for a moment in silence. Rose went to open her water bottle and found that she couldn't. Her right hand had already swollen around the knuckles. It looked like a bad potato. She put the water bottle between her knees and opened it left-handed.

"Is everything all right at home?" Thanh asked.

"Not really," Rose said, struck, as she often was, by the piercing quality of the lieutenant's intuition. She felt a brief surge of dizziness, just thinking about where to start, then shook her head and left it at that.

Thanh gave her a long moment to say something else, then sighed again and hopped off the desk. She went around behind it and sat down, back in business posture, as if to say, Okay, have it your way.

"So this cliff-diver thing, Bicycle Boy—" she said. "You're really thinking it's a homicide?"

"He went off the cliff from a standing start. We've got several indications that someone else was with him. A woman." Rose hesitated, then said, "Joshua and I both think it might be the same one who killed Henry Pelletier."

"A female multiple?" Thanh said. "Doesn't seem likely. It's probably just an epidemic of pissed-off women." She raised one thin, exquisitely plucked eyebrow at Rose and smiled. "Maybe there's something in the air."

Rose conceded the point with a sheepish grin, but insisted, "My gut says there's a connection."

"Your gut told you to break Dick Burke's nose. You might want to get a second opinion once in a while." Thanh hesitated, then said, "Well, run with it. Take a look at some of our unsolved back cases. Check VICAP. But low-key, okay? Try not to get the FBI too interested yet. And for God's sake don't say anything to the press. That's all we need, a bunch of headlines screaming about a female serial killer on the loose, to go with your little we're-number-one episode."

"Okay, boss," Rose said. She stood up to go.

"And Rosie—" Sandi Thanh said.

She paused. "Yeah?"

"I don't think Dick Burke is going to be in a big hurry to talk about that little slip of his. I don't think you should be either."

Rose stood for a moment studying the bottle of water in her left hand, then confessed, reluctantly, "I think I might have broken my hand."

Her lieutenant laughed.

"Duh," she said. "The guy's got a head like a fucking rock."

*B*ack at her desk in the Homicide squad room, Rose found the jacket she had used to cover Michael Turner's face, freshly dry-cleaned, in a clear plastic bag draped over her chair, along with a single long-stemmed red rose. A note attached to the dry-cleaning ticket read, *"From the guys in* *the morgue, to the fastest finger in the West—we love you, Rosie."*

She tore open the plastic and sniffed at the jacket. It still stank of death, which reminded her, perversely, that she had to call Michael Turner's mother. But first, she found a slim vase for the rose, filled it with water, and set it on her desk. And then, just for a minute or two, while the office was still empty, she put her face in her hands and cried.

14

THE MOMENT HELEN WALKED into the Deep Six, she knew Mark wasn't there. The empty jolt of disappointment told her that she had been nursing the hope that he would be, despite what she'd been saying to herself for days while she fought the urge to return. But she realized that she was glad, too, genuinely glad that Mark wasn't at the bar. That surprised her. It was a strange, bleak gladness that made her feel lonelier than she had ever felt before. She thought it was probably the most wholesome emotion she'd felt in decades.

She'd timed her arrival well. Happy hour was winding down and the casual after-work drinkers, the hasty conquests, and the early-round losers were clearing out, while the serious later crowd had yet to begin arriving. Helen sat down in the same spot she had sat in before, with a view of the aquarium and the TV. The bartender recognized her instantly, which was something she usually tried to avoid. She knew she should leave, as she had known she shouldn't come. But she kept her seat and even gave him a smile when he brought her an Albatross unbidden.

"Sad and beautiful tonight," he noted, as he walked up. Not a come-on, simple bartender rapport, a perceptive cut above the usual.

"Just sad," Helen demurred.

He shook his head, disagreeing, set her drink on a napkin, and moved away, politely leaving her to herself. Helen sipped the Albatross and considered the aquarium. The octopus was nowhere to be seen, but the rest of the colorful population circled languidly. A beautiful blue fish, with a yellow tail tipped in black, lay unmoving on the sand at the bottom of the tank. Helen thought it might be dead, which for some reason made her want to cry. She was definitely losing it.

"'Alas! thought I, and my heart beat loud, / How fast she nears and nears—'"

Helen glanced to her right and found Mark beside her. He gave her a wink and continued, reciting grandly and a little self-consciously, "'Are those her sails that glance in the Sun, / Like restless gossameres?'"

"You've been doing some homework," Helen said.

"I had to do something after you stole my heart and disappeared."

She groaned. "Oh, God, *please*. Don't be an ass."

"Don't be a big fat meanie," he said. "Admit it, you've been sitting here hoping I'd show up."

She'd killed men for less presumption, of course. But Helen had to concede the guy had a certain erratic charm. She hadn't been called a big fat meanie since the second grade.

They fell to talking at once, easily, almost giddily, like old friends, reviewing their already rich store of in-jokes and amusing each other with obscure lines from "The Rime of the Ancient Mariner," which Mark really had mastered with comical thoroughness.

"You changed your hair," he noted, not long after they had settled in.

"No," Helen said. "I stopped changing it."

"Ah. Well, it looks great."

"It looks like shit," Helen said. "It looks like last year's straw hat."

"I love the way you take a compliment," Mark said.

The bartender seemed genuinely pleased to see them re-united and comped their second round of drinks, throwing in a dozen gratuitous oysters. Mark grinned with surprised delight as the man set the plate down, and thanked him extravagantly. But as the bartender walked away, pleased with his good deed, Mark, still smiling, muttered out of the side of his mouth to Helen, "I actually can't stand oysters."

She laughed. "You're kidding."

"Nope. Too much like slugs."

Helen tugged an oyster loose from its shell with her fingers, slopped it through the cocktail sauce, and popped it into her mouth. She gave him a sly smile with her mouth full, and swallowed voluptuously.

"Don't toy with me," Mark said.

"You *look* like an oyster eater." Helen reached for another oyster and gave him a mischievous glance. "Like that guy in the gold chain last time."

Mark picked up the small fork and clumsily worked an oyster free, ran it tentatively through the cocktail sauce, and looked at the concoction for a long moment. Then he set it down.

"You laugh," he said, a little morosely. "But that guy went home with someone that night."

"No! With one of the stewardesses?!"

"Lawyers. No, it was the redhead down the bar from him." She furrowed her brow, trying to recall. "White knit blouse, sort of clingy?" Mark prompted. "Dangling turquoise earrings, shaped like teardrops. Freckles to die for."

"Her? No way. She was way too together for a guy like that."

"It was getting late. He bought her a martini on last call and apparently it looked better to her than going home and feeding the cat." Mark shrugged. "Never underestimate the power of human loneliness: 'Alone, alone, all, all alone, / Alone on a wide, wide sea! / And never a soul took pity on / my soul in agony.'"

Helen considered that for a moment, then said, "What in the world were *you* still doing here at last call?"

He laughed. "What the hell do you think I was doing? Jesus, woman. I was waiting for *you.*"

Helen met his eyes and realized she believed him. That was unsettling, and she didn't know what to do with it. She turned away, to the aquarium.

"I think that fish is dead," she said sadly, after a long moment.

Mark made a little sound of impatience, apparently at the distraction.

"No, seriously," Helen insisted. "It pains me."

He glanced grudgingly at the tank. "The damselfish?"

"Is that what it is?"

"She's not dead. Her gills are moving. She's probably playing possum."

"Fish play possum?"

"You see that other, similar-looking fish? The bigger blue one? That's an Indonesian Blue Devil. He's got her cowed."

"Really?"

As if on cue, the blue-and-yellow fish on the sand stirred and eased upward slightly. The bigger fish instantly charged it; there was a brief flurry, a blurring of sand, and the smaller fish ducked back down to the bottom and was still again.

"That tank's too small for the two of them," Mark said. "Damselfish are very territorial."

"That's terrible."

"It's nature."

"That doesn't make it less terrible. That poor beautiful thing—"

"A damsel-in-distress fish." Mark smiled. "What they really need to do is put a knight-in-shining-armor fish in there."

"I don't think it's funny at all," Helen said. She was near tears and Mark saw it and subsided. They fell silent, a little painfully. The bartender cruised by, noted their untouched drinks-in-progress and the tension, and discreetly moved away.

"You are a very complicated woman," Mark offered at last.

She glanced at him. "What do you mean?"

"You don't give a damn about anything in the world, as far as I can tell, but you're ready to cry over a lousy fish in somebody else's aquarium."

"I'm not that complicated," Helen said. "I give a damn about just about everything. I'm just fucked up." And, to her horror, she did begin to cry then, the tears welling quietly but steadily. She tried to stop it and realized she couldn't and an electric jolt of fear ran through her, because the tears seemed to say too much and it was all right there like streams of text, running down her cheeks for all the world to see.

The many men, so beautiful!
And they all dead did lie;
And a thousand thousand slimy things
Liv'd on; and so did I.

Mark cocked an eye at the bartender, who turned away and studiously busied himself wiping the counter at the far end of the bar. Two guys a few seats down toward the TV had picked up on the scene and were peering at them with open curiosity. Mark glared at them until they turned away.

"Christ, I'm pathetic," Helen muttered, groping for a napkin and dabbing ineffectually at her eyes. "God help me. I'm a fucking joke."

She reached for her purse, intending to bolt, but Mark intercepted her hand and used her momentum to guide her off the stool toward the center of the floor. Before Helen quite knew what was happening, his arms were around her and they were moving gently. Swaying—dancing, she realized. She couldn't even hear any music at first and then she registered something jagged and industrial over the bar's tinny sound system, a sort of blare with a beat, which Mark was ignoring entirely.

He was a perfect eight inches taller than she was, and she buried her face against his collarbone, her nose near the pocket of his cotton shirt. He smelled of cigarettes, and something soothing. Vanilla, maybe. Helen wondered how he could smell like vanilla.

"What are we dancing to?" she asked after a moment.

He smiled. "A different drummer."

"Seriously."

"I'm thinking . . . Ella Fitzgerald. 'They Can't Take That Away from Me,' maybe."

She laid her cheek on his breast again and felt his chest expand as he breathed in the smell of her hair. She felt calm now, quiet inside, and dangerously content. The tears had lifted one of her contact lenses loose and she blinked to settle it and felt it come out. She let it go. She couldn't even remember what color her eyes were supposed to be today, and suddenly she just couldn't make herself care.

"Are you okay?" Mark asked after a while, solicitously.

"Yes. Yes, I am. Thank you."

"Do you want to get out of here?"

"No," Helen said. "Let's just keep dancing."

15

Rose found some ice for her throbbing hand and took two extra-strength Advil, then strapped her gun back on and settled in at her desk. There were several surprisingly conciliatory messages from Seamus in her voice-mail box, deftly nuanced pleas for marital attention, but she knew that if she called her husband back right now, she'd have to tell him she'd just punched Dick Burke and that she'd been thinking all day about divorce, and Rose decided to put the call off.

Instead she spent an hour and a half poring over unsolved murders in the SFPD Homicide files. The backlog was daunting at first, but she quickly narrowed it down, looking only at young, single, white, male victims, and eliminating obvious drug killings and robberies. There were surprisingly few candidates once she'd applied those criteria. She found only one case of possible relevance, from the previous July. Ken Joseph, thirty-two, an architect, Stanford class of '91, had been stabbed to death in his North Beach apartment after what looked like a date gone very wrong.

A single, clean wound, Rose noted with a chill, skimming through the autopsy report. Either anomalously deft or very lucky: one to the heart, an upward thrust under the breastbone with a weapon of opportunity, an eight-inch Henckels chef's knife of German stainless steel, pulled right from the wooden block of the matched set in the victim's kitchen. Joseph had been between marriages and dating widely and somewhat exuberantly, by all reports, but the ex-wife and all the recent girlfriends who had been identified had come up clean. There was a report from a single witness of a glimpse of Joseph with the woman he had picked up at a Lombard Street bar on the last night of his life. A bottled redhead, maybe, very attractive in a maddeningly vague way.

The only thing missing from Joseph's apartment had been his Phi Beta Kappa key, though that had not been noticed until his mother tried to find it for the funeral. The place had been wiped down so well that the investigating team had seriously checked out the cleaning woman. The killing had been considered a transient girlfriend's crime of passion, and the investigation eventually ran into the sand for lack of evidence.

Rose copied the crucial pages of the file and spent the rest of the afternoon and into the evening wrestling with the massive VICAP Crime Analysis Report Form. The FBI's Violent Criminal Apprehension Program in Quantico, Virginia, kept a nationwide database of unsolved murders and other violent crimes, collecting, collating, and analyzing the scattered data in a clearinghouse way that allowed the detection of serial violence patterns invisible from the local level. Filling in the blanks on the questionnaire, Rose felt increasingly foolish at how thin her theory of a multiple murderess really was in light of the hard evidence she could present. She had remarkably little real information. There was no similarity in method, time parameters, geographical location, weapon, or cause of death. The links among the cases amounted to an unusual earring in the wrong place, a suspiciously thorough absence of clues in ostensible crimes of passion, and a gut sense, completely incalculable, that the beer bottle ring on Henry Pelletier's coffee table correlated somehow with the mean indignity of the bicycle pants around Michael Turner's knees. It seemed pretty flimsy in black and white.

She was trying to edit the apologetic note out of her "Narrative Summary" when her phone rang. She picked up, wincing as she used her right hand, which had already turned a lurid sanguineous purple around the swollen knuckles.

"Rosie?"

"Josh?" She could barely hear him over the raised voices, rowdy and cheerfully profane, of Stan and Terry in the background of the Safeway's security room. It sounded like he was calling from a sports bar, midgame. "What's up?"

"Cancel that dinner date, baby." Joshua seemed exuberant, and possibly intoxicated. Maybe he *was* at a sports bar, Rose thought, amused. Maybe Barry Bonds had just hit one into McCovey Cove.

She said, "I've got no dinner date, partner. Seamus isn't even speaking to me at the moment."

"I'm sorry to hear that," Joshua said. "But maybe it's just as well. I think we've got her."

The security center smelled worse than ever with an overlay of beer. The boys had in fact broken out some Budweiser and half a dozen long-neck empties cluttered the room's minimal flat surfaces. C. Thurman had gone home, and the night manager, a kid who didn't seem old enough to drive, obviously ran a looser ship. He was sitting in one of the room's chairs with a look of beatifically indulgent authority on his young face, three tiny pewter skulls running up the curve of his ear, and the vivid edge of a black-and-red tattoo peeking out from beneath his crisp white shirtsleeve. Stan, Terry, and Joshua lounged more sloppily on the consoles with fresh bottles in their hands, loud and easy with each other. Above them, the monitors flickered unattended. It would have been a great time to steal some cheese.

"Jesus, Joshua," Rose exclaimed. "Are you out of your fucking mind?"

"When in Rome." He shrugged. "Besides, I'm off the clock. This bit of selfless service is my gift to the city and county of San Francisco."

"A case got damaged in transit," Stan told her. "We couldn't let it go to waste. It's practically, uh—"

"Janitorial," Joshua supplied.

"Exactly," Stan said, pleased. "Janitorial."

"It's a public service," Terry chimed in. "We're facilitating interagency cooperation."

They'd apparently all worked through the urge to shoot each other. Rose, yielding to the fait accompli, said, "I just hope they don't tape the security room."

"We *are* 'they,'" Stan informed her cheerfully, which struck Rose as true, surprisingly profound, and scary.

"Is that beer cold?" she asked. Joshua gave her a quick, chastising look, *What about the baby?* She shrugged back at him, *Who are you to talk?* and opened a Budweiser.

The video was flamboyantly mislabeled in bold black ink, "Aisle 7, 3:47 P.M.–9:47 P.M. 8/26/97," but the footage was of fruits and vegetables nine days before, and it was almost certainly their gal. She was dressed down in jeans and a baggy flannel shirt, like a movie star trying to slip past the paparazzi, and her hair was cropped short, an indeterminable brunettish shade in the grainy black-and-white, but definitely not platinum blond. It was her carriage that made Rose immediately sure it was the same woman whose back and breasts had so fascinated Alfred Powell. She held herself like a dangerous person, a hot knife in a world of butter.

And she was camera-shy. She stood chatting with Michael Turner in front of the melons, her back to the surveillance with frustrating consistency.

"She's got the video spotted," Rose fretted.

"Doesn't matter," Joshua said smugly. "She turns right at the end. We got her face."

They watched Turner and the woman banter for another minute and a half, while the superimposed clock ticked in the corner of the film. It was fascinating and eerie in context, a dime-a-dozen pick-up dance that they knew would end with the dancer dead. Michael Turner played it out charmingly enough, straining cheerfully for effect, while the woman seemed cool and only intermittently amused. The negotiations ended on an uncertain note, and she moved away without ever exposing herself to the camera. But at the last possible moment, Turner took a parting shot, apparently effective, and she turned with a grudging smile to reply.

"Freeze it there," Joshua said, and Terry obligingly hit Pause.

"Gotcha, baby," Stan breathed. "Come to Papa."

Rose stared at the face on the screen. The woman was older than she'd expected—not a lethal twenty-five-year-old at all, but something closer to Rose's own mid-thirties, despite the Winona Ryder pixie cut. The quality of the video image was frustrating, but the woman's beauty shone through the grainy black-and-white. She had a surprisingly tender mouth beneath the clear lip gloss, and an even more surprising vulnerability in her gaze. Her iciness, it seemed, took some work: the makeup, though subtle, all labored toward a hardening effect, the eyes etched in black and chilled with some silvery shadow, the exquisite cheekbones shaded into hauteur, and the brows plucked to a fine cold line like a crack in ice.

"Awesome tits," Terry noted.

"Shut up, Terry," Stan told him.

"Okay," Terry said.

"Is this all you've got?" Rose asked Joshua.

He looked hurt. "Jesus, Rosie, I spent six hours in video hell getting that. It's a fucking passport photo."

"You know it's her, I know it's her. To a jury, she's just another pretty face making conversation in a supermarket. Where's the link? Where's the smoking gun?"

"Check out her jewelry," Joshua said. "Terry, magnification two."

Terry worked his magic, and the monitor image jumped to a closer focus. The resolution was terrible, but it was good enough, and Rose's arms tightened into gooseflesh. It wouldn't hold up in court any better than anything else they had at this point, but the dangling dragonfly earrings were unmistakable.

They plunged back into the morass of videotapes, looking for footage of their suspect at the cash register, hoping she'd used a credit card. Rose quickly understood Joshua's unhappiness at returning to the archival closet; sorting through the tapes was tedious, eye-wearying work, complicated by the now beery efforts of Stan and Terry to help. The elimination process went more quickly with a solid date and time frame, but there was still a daunting amount of mechanical labor involved. They worked for an hour and a half, setting aside video after video without result, before they hit their limit and decided to take a break and grab some dinner.

Ignoring Stan and Terry's broad hints about joining them, Rose and Joshua slipped out of the store and walked toward Fort Mason. Night had settled on the city, cool and clear, and the marina was bustling. They found a bar with a view of the bay and settled at a table by the window.

"I feel like I've spent eight hours in a porno store, putting quarters in a peep machine," Joshua said. "Jesus, the stuff that goes on in the aisles of a supermarket . . . I mean, who *knew*?"

"I've got this urge to pocket a package of hot dogs and some feta cheese," Rose said.

Joshua shook his head mournfully. "No wonder Stan and Terry are such wackos, watching that shit go down, day after day."

"If you look too long into the abyss, the abyss looks into you."

"Exactly," Joshua said. "Jeezus. Give me a good clean homicide anytime."

The waitress arrived and Joshua ordered a cheeseburger. Rose settled for a salad. They explored various rationalizations for having another beer.

"It's Juneteenth," Joshua declared at last. "The SFPD supports the richness of our multicultural something-or-other."

"Juneteenth is next week," Rose noted, but it seemed close enough, and she added, to the waitress, "Rolling Rock."

"Make it two," Joshua said. "In celebration of our African-American heritage." As the woman walked away, he said to Rose, "I'd have pegged you for imported."

"That's Seamus. I'm a domestic gal all the way."

"What was Henry Pelletier's refrigerator full of? Heffelpuken? Deutschpissch?"

Rose shrugged, aware of a sudden dip in her mood. The mention of Seamus had killed her appetite for banter. She knew that she should call and at least tell him she was working late, if not have an actual conversation and try to repair some of the damage, but she just didn't want to. That couldn't possibly be good, that she didn't want to talk to her husband.

Joshua picked up on the change in the weather instantly and fell silent. Just offshore, a ferry chugged past Alcatraz, lit like a party barge; across the black water of the bay, the waterside towns of Marin sparkled, patches of diamonds snug in the darkness of the coastal hills. They could see the square brick of lights that was San Quentin, near the end of the Richmond Bridge.

"I think I might have found some more of our gal's work in the back cases," Rose said at last.

"Really?" Joshua asked, intrigued, but begrudging her avoidance of discussing the mood shift. Her partner was the only man she knew who would rather talk about relationships than serial murder.

"A date-killing last summer. Single white male enjoying the fruits of divorce until somebody stuck him with a chef's knife. One stab, clean kill. Immaculate apartment."

"If it really is our gal . . ." Joshua voice trailed off. He mulled it over, then shook his head. "I mean, one killing, you can overlook it, right? Everybody has a bad day once in a while. Two killings, well, what the hell, it's the nineties. But *three* dead guys . . . I think at some point you've just got to say, This girl's got a problem."

Their beers arrived. They both nudged the frosty mugs aside and drank from the bottle. When the waitress had passed back out of hearing, Rose said, "Sandi doesn't buy the serial angle, but she said to run with it—"

Her partner rolled his eyes. "Great. Meaning, we can put in a ton of extra hours with no overtime pay, and if we're right, she'll be a fucking genius."

"—and I sent off a VICAP form. Twenty-four pages of embarrassing gaps and details we don't have. It felt like one of those half-done crossword puzzles you find in the old flight magazine on an airplane, where somebody's only filled in the easy clues."

"So in six weeks, or six months, the FBI can either tell us they don't know shit either, or come steal our case." Joshua shook his head. "Jeez, Rosie. I should have gone back to the office myself and let you do the mud wrestling with Stan and Terry. I'd have gotten us overtime, at least, and kept the fucking Feds out of it."

Rose laughed and took another hit off the beer. She was feeling cheerful again, unexpectedly. It felt great to be in work mode with Joshua, mulling the angles. The pall of the morbid security room was fading, like a bad dream; the Rolling Rock tasted good, cold and crisp. And Seamus could take a flying fuck at a rolling doughnut.

"What the hell did you do to your hand?" Joshua asked, as she set the bottle down.

Rose hesitated, then said, "I punched Dick Burke."

Joshua laughed appreciatively. "No, seriously."

"Seriously."

"Jesus . . . *Really?* What does *he* look like?"

"His nose looks like my hand, only flatter."

"This happened in the office? Was anybody else there?"

"Sandi walked in right about the time he hit the floor. We all discussed it and decided he had slipped."

Joshua was silent for a moment, then ventured, tentatively, "Not that you need a particular reason for slugging that asshole, as far as I'm concerned, but just out of curiosity—?"

"He—" Rose's throat caught, to her dismay, a little choked sob. She cleared it briskly and took a breath. "He said something about the casualty rate among my partners."

"Meaning Jack?"

"Meaning Jack. And . . . you."

Joshua opened his mouth to respond, then ducked his head and fell silent. Rose didn't prompt him. She was unnervingly close to crying; she felt as if someone had opened her chest and her heart was exposed, beating red and vulnerable for all the world to see.

Joshua was leaning back in his chair, exercising a patient, unobtrusive delicacy, giving her space. Rose took a breath and let it out. "Look, Joshua, I don't know what you've heard about me and Jack Brady—"

Her partner shrugged, pointedly noncommittal. "I don't give a fuck about squad-room gossip. I never knew the man. I know there was some kind of stink about an unrighteous shoot, right before he died—"

"Right before he killed himself," Rose said quietly.

Joshua met her eyes, a pained, steady, acknowledging look. She was conscious of the soft pure blue of his eyes. Carolina blue, like a sky at midday. "It's not like we don't all look into that hole once in a while," he said. "I heard Jack Brady was a good cop. And I know he was your partner. That's good enough for me."

"I know there's a lot of talk," Rose said. It was strange, trying to talk about Jack with Joshua, like tearing open wounds from a previous marriage. She hesitated, then said, "The shooting *was* unrighteous. And it was my fault."

"Bullshit," Joshua said instantly.

"No. It's true. We went into a suspect's house, me first. I hollered, 'Police!' and the guy reached for what we thought might be a gun and Jack shot him. Bam-bam-bam, three to the chest. Just blew him away. But it wasn't a gun. It was a cell phone."

"It happens," Joshua said. "And if it hadn't been Jack who shot him, it would have been you."

"No. That's the point. I could see it was a cell phone as soon as he went for it. Jack fired too soon."

"That's not what you told the review board, is it?"

"Fuck the review board. I'm telling you the truth."

Joshua was silent. He held her eyes for a long moment, then looked away.

"So he was one beat too quick on the trigger," he said at last. "I say again, it happens. Nobody wants to know about it, but if you've ever been in that spot, you know how it can go down. You wait to see if it's a cell phone or an Uzi and maybe you're dead, and your partner too. It *happens*."

"He shot that guy because he was afraid I was too slow," Rose said. "Because he was protecting me. Because he'd lost perspective. And he shot himself because he couldn't live with that."

"He loved you," Joshua said quietly, with such naked conviction that it shocked them both.

"Yeah," Rose said. "And I'm not sure I can live with *that*."

They held each other's gazes for an instant, then looked away, past their reflections in the window glass, at the lights beyond, and the watery darkness.

Their dinners arrived. The waitress set the plates down, took in their preoccupation at a glance, and scurried away without a word. Neither Rose nor Joshua even glanced at the food.

"I wonder if you can smoke on that deck out there," Rose said at last.

Joshua looked pained. "Come on, Rosie. Really. The baby—"

"You're not my fucking gynecologist, Joshua."

He shut up, looking like she'd slapped him. Rose stood and plucked the Marlboros out of his breast pocket. She pulled one cigarette free, tossed the pack on the table, and headed for the back door. She was already out on the deck when she realized that she hadn't taken his lighter and that she had no matches. She went to the wooden railing and stood there looking down at the foamy water sucking and receding around the pilings, holding the unlit cigarette, breathing fast and shallow, trying not to cry.

Behind her, a rectangle of light showed briefly on the boards as the back door opened and closed. Joshua came up beside her, his lighter out, his hand cupped, and Rose stabbed the cigarette between her lips and bent to accept the flame. She straightened as it caught, took a deep, deep drag, and blew the long stream of smoke out over the water, toward the black hills of Marin.

"Seamus doesn't want the damned kid anyway," she said, and then she did begin to cry. The cigarette fell out of her hand and Joshua kicked it off the deck into the water and took her in his arms.

16

HELEN AND MARK danced until last call, speaking little, savoring the precious hush that had settled upon them, moving together in a way that somehow was not like moving at all, but like a kind of stillness that just grew vaster as they sank more deeply into it. The last song before the sound system shut down was some Hawaiian guy doing an incongruously wistful cover of "Somewhere Over the Rainbow," complete with a ukelele, and as they swayed to the aching sweetness of it, Helen could feel Mark's heart against her face, a steady, heightened pulse, like a homing beacon. She didn't want the dance to end and it was ending and she began to be afraid.

The bartender just waved his hand when they came back to their seats, indicating that the final round was on him. He set the Albatrosses down and moved away, beginning to break down the spill trays and stow the bins of cherries and sliced limes in the refrigerator beneath the bar. There was no one left in the Deep Six except a few other late-starting couples, the cocktail waitresses cashing out, and three sailors running on rum, Red Bull, and wishful thinking. As the heavy front door swung outward for a lone departing drinker who'd finally decided to cut his losses, Helen caught a glimpse of Jimmy's truck, idling in a tow-away zone on the other side of Van Ness, the headlights black, the tinted windshield opaque, glinting coldly with reflected streetlights. Just before the door closed, a red spark winked in the black rectangle of the truck's side window, like a de-mon's eye; and then the door thumped shut, and Helen shuddered, still feeling the sting of that watchful ember, as if it had touched her own skin and left a blister.

Mark, touchingly oblivious, raised his glass. "To the ac-tual color of your real eyes."

Helen blinked, disconcerted. She'd been wearing only one colored contact lens since losing the other when they'd started dancing and several times Mark had tilted his head at her goofily, with one eye closed, pretending to be dizzied by the disparity.

Now she took the remaining brown lens out. They looked at it for a moment, cupped upside down on her fingertip like a little piece of clear mud, and then Helen flicked it away. It felt like the last, flamboyant piece of a striptease. For the first time in fifteen years, she was out in public without someone else's hair and eyes, naked in her natural coloring.

"That was impetuous," Mark said.

She shrugged. "I'm an impetuous gal."

"The hell you are. You're wound tighter than a Superball."

Helen met his gaze, conscious of her unprotected eyes. "I'm an impetuous gal wound tighter than a Superball."

He laughed. "Just don't bounce away again, okay?"

"I won't," Helen assured him, surprising herself. It sounded like a marriage vow.

Mark caught the note of solemnity and sobered instantly. They turned to their drinks, humbled into a sudden, mutual silence.

Across the room, someone began shutting down the lights, and the restaurant sank into a blue-lit darkness. The other customers were drifting toward the exit. In the aquarium, still brightly lit by a spotlight over the bar, the damselfish stirred again from her spot on the bottom, and the Blue Devil promptly charged and cowed her back into place. Watching, Helen felt a surge of sympathetic despair, of helplessness. There was nowhere to go.

The bartender cruised by, glancing pointedly at their still-full glasses as he pulled the bus pan from beneath the bar.

"Closing it down, folks," he said.

"We're finishing up," Mark told him and the guy nodded and moved away with the full pan, back into the kitchen. Mark took out his wallet and laid two twenties on the bar, hesitated, then added a third.

"I felt like he was very supportive of our relationship," he said.

"What's going to happen to that poor fish?" Helen asked.

Mark glanced at the aquarium and shrugged. "It's not as brutal as it looks. He doesn't want to kill her, he's just protecting his turf. In the wild, it would be simple. She'd swim away and find a patch of reef of her own. She'd mate up with a damselfish Prince Charming and lay half a million eggs every few months and live happily ever after."

"But in the aquarium?"

Mark hesitated, then conceded, "She'll probably starve to death. If she doesn't get torn to pieces first."

"I can't *stand* that."

Mark considered that for a moment, as if weighing it out, then glanced toward the kitchen. The bartender was still out of sight. He stood up, moved to the waitress station at the bar, and ducked under the counter.

"What are you doing?"

"Shhh." Mark grabbed a glass and filled it with water, then went to the aquarium. There was a small, handled net on top of the tank. He picked it up, stood on his tiptoes to raise the lid, and neatly snagged the Blue Devil in the net. Another glance at the kitchen; still no sign of the bartender; and Mark dumped the wriggling Blue Devil into the glass of water and ducked back under the bar with the glass in his hand.

"We're out of here," he said with a wink, heading for the door.

Helen followed hurriedly, marveling at the adrenaline zinging through her system. She was terrified that they'd get caught, which struck her as absurd. She'd stood by unmoved, her pulse rate steady while her boyfriend killed people in cold blood, and here she was freaking out as the accomplice to the kidnapping of a fish.

"Good night, folks," the bartender called, as they reached the door. "Thanks."

Mark waved cheerfully with his free hand. In the aquarium, the damselfish stirred and flapped its fins, tentatively, rising from the bottom, feeling out the sudden free space.

Mark and Helen pushed out the door onto the sidewalk. As they stood there, getting oriented in the cool night air, they heard the bolt on the bar door's lock click shut.

"No retreat," Mark smiled. "The bridge is burned behind us."

"You're a maniac," Helen said.

"A woman like you needs a maniac, I think."

"What in the world are you going to do with that fish?"

"Damned if I know," Mark said. "I really hadn't thought this through. It's not like there are rehab programs for Blue Devils with a history of domestic violence." He considered for a moment, then handed her the glass with a flourish. "Milady, his fate is in your hands."

Helen stared down at the Blue Devil circling in the water like a moth caught in a lamp. The fish looked tiny and touchingly vulnerable now that it wasn't dominating an even smaller fish. She felt an unexpected surge of compassion. She wondered if it would be able to live in a goldfish bowl. She wondered what it ate.

Across the street, Jimmy's truck roared into life, then settled into the distinctive throaty mutter of its idling. Jimmy had left the lights off, as he always did. They'd done this many times; they had it down to a sort of science. Usually by this time Helen knew at least three reasons why she didn't mind a bit that the man she was with was going to die.

Beside her, Mark waited, quietly expectant. Her move.

"I can't go home with you," Helen said. "You can't come home with me. It's been lovely. Like a dream. But it has to end right here."

"Are you talking to me, or the fish?" Mark asked.

She met his eyes. "I'm serious."

"I know you are. You're too damn serious."

"No," Helen said. "I'm not serious enough."

They stood for a long moment without speaking. A police car cruised by, slowing to look at them, then driving on. Helen had a weird urge to flag it down. To just tell the truth and take what came. To be done.

"Let it go," Mark said, quietly fervent. "Whatever it is, whoever it is that's hurt you in the past. Let it go, for once in your life."

She felt the tears sting her eyes, and blinked them back. "You don't understand. It won't let *me* go."

"No. It's your decision. It's always your decision."

"No," she said. "Not tonight. Tonight it's out of my hands. You're just going to have to trust me."

Mark opened his mouth to reply, then closed it and nodded, as if it hurt him.

"Okay," he said. "I'll trust you."

"I'll call you," she said. "Soon. Tomorrow. What are you doing tomorrow?"

Mark smiled ruefully. "Skipping work and waiting for you to call, apparently."

"I don't even know what you do."

"It doesn't matter what I do," Mark said. "I love you. That's what I do, from here on in."

Across the street, Jimmy revved the engine once, impatiently. The fish swam around and around in the glass in her hand, colorless in the bad light, a living shadow in fruitless dead-end motion.

Helen asked, "Would you kill for love?"

Mark blinked, then laughed and shook his head indulgently, as if she were a child. "Nobody kills for love," he said. "What would be the point? But I'd die for love."

"Would you?"

He smiled. "In a second."

Helen took a breath.

"Go home," she said. "Walk that way and turn at the corner. Don't look back. I'll call you."

"I can't just leave you—"

"Trust me," she said. "Just go."

Mark hesitated, then shook his head, turned, and walked in the direction she had indicated. Helen stood on the sidewalk with the fish circling in the glass of water in her hand, watching until he was out of sight. He turned and looked back twice, as she had known he would, and it wasn't until he was well around the corner and she was sure he was gone that she crossed the street to Jimmy's truck.

"What the hell was that all about?" Jimmy demanded, when she got in. "Jesus. I was starting to think you expected me to come over there and take the guy out right there on the street."

"It was nothing," Helen said. "A tease. I think he might be gay."

He sat for a moment in silence, gripping the wheel with both strong hands. In the streetlight, Helen could see the scar across the knuckles of his left hand, from the time the knife had slipped. She sat quietly, surrendered to what would come. If he was going to hit her, he would do it now.

The windows of the truck cab were steamed up, dense with the humidity of his rage, except for the little circle he had rubbed clear to be able to see across the street.

At last, Jimmy let out his breath in a long slow sigh, rolled down the window, and lit a cigarette.

"What's that in the glass?" he asked, in a more conversational tone.

"A fish," Helen said. She leaned her head back against the seat and closed her eyes. Jimmy waited, but she left it at that, and after a moment he shook his head, amused, as he so often was, at her inexplicable ways.

17

TIME HAD GOTTEN a little strange. It seemed to have eased
to a quiet stop, like the moonlight on the water of the
bay, a bright stillness ruffled by passing moments, but
essentially unmoving. Rose had no idea how long she'd
sobbed in Joshua's arms, or how long she'd been standing
on the deck with her face against his chest, even after she'd
stopped crying. Way too long, she knew. Long enough to
begin to smell him, to breathe in the comfort of the soft
skin at the base of his throat. Long enough to feel both of
them relaxing into the embrace, to feel the subtle mutual
tuning of their bodies begin. Long enough to feel that unnerving stir within herself, the flicker of a visceral response.

But she couldn't make herself move away, and Joshua
showed no sign of wanting her to. The sense of relief was
deep. It felt like defeat, to have yielded to her confusion and
grief, but an unforeseeably sweet defeat, a surrender that

somehow healed. Rose felt loved, seen, and held. It really was that simple, and it was entirely sufficient. She didn't want anything else. She just wanted the moment to go on forever.

And so it made perfect sense to her when her cell phone trilled. Because that was reality. Because this moment was stolen, not paid for. Because the bills always came due.

She leaned back and met Joshua's eyes. His rueful, tender look said it all. She pulled the phone off her belt on the third ring and punched it on. "Burke."

"I'd like to report a missing person," Seamus said. "My wife seems to have disappeared."

Rose liked the way Joshua let her go—not with a guilty start, like someone caught in a dirty secret, but gently, unhurriedly, releasing her to talk without denying the immensity of what had just happened. Leaving the warmth still alive between them. As if there were room for how complicated everything had just gotten, and time for living with that.

"Could you describe the person in question, sir?" she said to Seamus.

"Five-foot-four, hundred twenty-five, young beyond her years. Face like an angel, great body, good with a gun. Beautiful black hair. A few strands of gray, highly overrated. Eyes like fresh coffee. A patient, kind, and loving woman, pushed beyond all human limits by her asshole husband."

"We get a lot of those, actually."

"None like my Rosie," Seamus said. "She's a Taurus, if that helps."

Joshua lit a cigarette and leaned on the rail. Calm, looking at the moonlight on the water.

"Well, I'm certainly sympathetic to your situation, sir," Rose said into the phone. "But I'm afraid you've reached Homicide, not Missing Persons. There's really nothing I can do until this woman kills someone."

"That's just a matter of time, if her husband doesn't shape up."

Rose laughed. "That's my line, sweetheart."

"I love you, Rosie," Seamus said, suddenly earnest. "Jesus. I'm so fucking sorry. I've had my head so far up my ass lately it was starting to look like my colon would have to be wired for e-mail."

At the rail, Joshua blew a smoke ring into the moonlight, watched it wobble and unravel, then dropped the butt on the deck and ground it out. He gave Rose a supportive wink and tapped his chest and nodded toward the restaurant to indicate that he was going inside and she should take her time. She nodded back uneasily, wishing she had something to say to him that wouldn't sound completely idiotic. But he was already moving away.

As the door closed behind Joshua, Rose said to Seamus, "How many beers have you had? And, more important, what kind of beer? And where can we order more?"

"I'm sober as a suffragette," Seamus said cheerfully. "Does a man have to be drunk to love his wife?"

"Well—"

"I've just been thinking. Unprecedented, I know. I've been contemplating my life. Our life. And I want you to know, it's your decision. I'm with you, I'll back you all the way, one hundred percent, no matter what you choose to do."

"Really?"

"Absolutely," Seamus said. "I think you should color your hair any damn color you want to."

Rose laughed. This was a Seamus she recognized, the Seamus she had loved. She wondered what the hell had happened.

"Well, I love you, too, darling," she said. "But you should know, I haven't ruled out magenta."

"So where the hell *are* you?"

"The Marina. We may have caught a break on this cliff-diver case, but it's buried in several tons of mislabeled Safeway surveillance tapes."

"Any idea what time you're going to be home?"

"I don't know," Rose said, and apologetically, "The case is sort of . . . burgeoning."

Seamus laughed. "'Burgeoning'! Isn't that some kind of wine?"

"It looks like we may have a multiple killer on the loose."

"If it's not one thing, it's another, I guess," Seamus said.

"This appears to be several."

"Well, you do what you have to, obviously. I'll keep the home fires burning."

"How was *your* day?" Rose asked, conscious of the effort it took even to remind herself he'd *had* a day.

"Well, certainly nothing as exciting as a pile of dead bodies. Just a maiming or two, really. The network was down for an hour and a half, blah, blah, blah. Thompson's all over me about an upgrade that would take months even if there wasn't anything else going on. I told him I've got all the extra work I can handle." Seamus hesitated. "Actually, I'm thinking of quitting."

Rose laughed. "Yeah, me too."

"No, seriously," Seamus said. "I hate this fucking job. It's been nine-tenths of the problem with us, I swear. It's fucking killing me."

"*Quitting?* As in, no longer working there?"

"As in, ceasing to be in their employ. As in, having a damned life again."

He was serious, Rose marveled. She was silent for a long moment, trying to figure out why the prospect of Seamus quitting the job she had wanted him to quit, for over a year now, made her so uneasy.

"I thought you'd be thrilled," Seamus said.

"I am. Thrilled."

"Yeah, I can tell."

"No, I am. It's just—I don't know. . . ." Through the window, she could see the waitress putting their food into styrofoam boxes. Apparently Joshua had decided to cut their losses on dinner.

She said, "I'm just distracted, sweetheart. It's been, well, you know—"

"One of those days."

"Exactly."

"I think that's *my* line," Seamus said, though the joviality was starting to sound a little forced. Rose hesitated, frustrated at being unable to muster the proper emotion. It was the baby, she knew. She'd already done the math at some deep level and had been counting on Seamus's nice regular corporate paycheck through the maternity leave. But she was afraid to say that. They still hadn't talked about it, and she didn't want to squander the sudden wave of goodwill.

Inside the restaurant, Joshua picked a French fry out of the to-go box, waiting patiently. Rose realized that what she really wanted was to talk to him, to go in there and have another beer and try to sort things out in her head. But she knew that was exactly the wrong thing to do, that it would be saying the marriage was over.

She took a breath and said, "Seamus, we've got to talk about the baby."

"Earth to Rose: *Duh.* I've been sitting here since six o'clock, waiting to talk about the damned baby."

"Yeah, but—" The electronic call-waiting bleat sounded in Rose's ear. She glanced into the restaurant to see if it was Joshua, but her partner was still sitting at the table quietly. He had finished his beer and started on Rose's now.

"Shit, I've got another call," she said to Seamus.

"I'm sure it can wait, for once."

"I'm in the middle of a serial murder investigation, Seamus. I should at least see who it is."

"So, see," he conceded wearily. Rose felt a surge of irritation. He took one evening off, out of the last year, to get home before her, and suddenly he was the World's Most Long-Suffering Job Widow. She punched the button to switch lines and said, "Burke."

"Detective Rose Burke?"

"This is Inspector Burke, yes. Who's calling?"

"I'm Special Agent Marvin Swain, with, umm, the National Center for the Analysis of, uh, Violent Crime. Well, VICAP, specifically. The, uh, FBI?"

"I've heard of it," Rose said dryly. The poor guy sounded flustered; she had an urge to help him along. "What can I do for you, Agent Swain?"

"Uh, Marvin, please."

"Marvin," Rose repeated a trifle impatiently. "What can I do for you, Marvin?"

"Well, umm . . . Earlier today, you submitted a VICAP Crime Analysis Report on a, uh—umm—"

"Murder?"

"Homicide, yes," he said, pleased. "A couple of homicides, actually."

"Yes?"

She heard papers shuffling. Rose glanced at her watch; it was almost ten o'clock. If Swain was on the East Coast, he was working very late. She had an urge to click back to her other line, to see if Seamus had hung up on her. What she really wanted to do was just go home, not stand here wasting time with some Quantico wonk.

"You didn't specifically request a, uh, Criminal Personality Profile evaluation—" Swain noted at last, tentatively. It had the flavor of bureaucratic nit-picking. "But, uh—"

"They told me I had to go through the local field office. I was going to work up a package tomorrow. Though to tell you the truth, it sounded like an awful lot of work to throw a bunch of paper into a hole."

In the restaurant, Joshua's cell phone apparently rang, because he took it off his belt and punched it on. Swain, still muddling, said, "Yes, well, see, I'm in sort of a funny position here. I'm not really supposed to be initiating this kind of criminal investigative assistance without a more specific, umm—"

The call-waiting beep sounded in Rose's ear. Seamus, she thought; he'd probably hung up and called back. She resisted the urge to click over and said, "Agent Swain, my marriage is falling apart on the other line. Is there something important you actually had to say to me tonight?"

"Well, see, the thing is, I think we've got a few other cases that might be the same guy."

"I'm pretty sure our guy's a gal," Rose said. "I made that clear in my report."

"No, no, I—umm—"

Joshua came out the back door just then, looking exultant. "Stan's got her."

"What?" Rose exclaimed, as Agent Swain echoed in her ear, "What?"

"He's got her," Joshua said. "He found the fucking tape, our gal at the cash register, in glorious black and white. We've got her, Rosie."

"I've got to go," Rose told Swain.

"Can I at least fax you, umm—"

"Yeah, yeah, fax away," Rose said. "SFPD Homicide, attention me. I've really got to run, Marvin."

"Okay, then, I'll, uh—"

Rose clicked over to the other line, but Seamus was gone. He hated being put on hold. She would like to have called him back, but Joshua was already moving back through the restaurant, snatching up the to-go bag as he went. Light-footed, practically skipping; he looked like Gene Kelly in love. Rose stuck her phone in her pocket and followed. She couldn't help feeling it, too, a sudden lightness in her own step, the sheer exhilarating rush of closing in: They had her. They fucking had her. There would be time for Seamus soon enough.

18

JIMMY CIRCLED THE BLOCK TWICE, looking for a parking space along the crowded Richmond district curbs, cursing the street-cleaning schedule as if everything were normal, as if they were coming home late from a movie or something, as if he had not just spent hours sitting in a chilly truck cab waiting to kill the man she came out of the bar with.

Jimmy finally found a spot and jammed the truck into it, banging the bumpers a bit more than necessary. They walked to the house in silence, with Helen still holding the ridiculous Blue Devil in the glass. Inside, she set the glass on the counter, well back from the edge, so that it wouldn't get spilled if Jimmy hit her. But Jimmy seemed determined to be decent, to act as if nothing had happened.

They undressed for the night, brushing their teeth, even

flossing. As they settled in the bed, Jimmy said, "I could get you an aquarium for that fish."

Helen was silent. She was actually moved. The resiliency of Jimmy's simple world, his capacity for the insistence on a normality that amounted to forgiveness, always amazed her.

"It's a whim," she said. "It's just a whim. We don't need to make a whole big deal out of it."

"I wonder what the hell a little fish like that eats," he said.

Later, he reached for her tentatively; when she responded, he took her into his arms and made love to her, emphatically enough, reasserting his turf, but with a note of hurt and baffled tenderness as well.

Helen felt the tears start, as he moved in her. Because it was over, it was dead now, and Jimmy didn't know it. She thought of her mother lying in her arms on the living room floor, how Cora's breathing had grown gentler and slower, and how she had glowed when it finally ceased. It had been so beautiful, it had taken Helen a moment to realize that quiet radiance was death. This lovemaking was like that, a lovely thing aglow with departing life.

Back in the Safeway's security center, Stan had the video cued. He was so proud and excited, like a big happy kid who had found a particularly cool turtle or something, that Rose found herself liking him briefly. Terry had gone home, but the young night manager was there, and two more guys in uniforms, the graveyard security crew. They all huddled around the monitor as Stan ran the tape for Rose and Joshua.

"That's our gal, all right," Rose marveled. The tape showed the woman at the cash register, buying a six-pack of Rolling Rock and, incongruously, a cantaloupe. Rose leaned closer to the monitor as their suspect paid for the items.

"Shit, she paid in cash," she said.

"She gave him a card," Joshua said.

"No, she gave him a twenty—look, there's the change, bills and coins."

"She gave him *something*."

"A coupon?"

"Run it again, Stan," Joshua said, and Stan rewound the tape. They watched the transaction backwards, in fast motion, then the tape rolled forward again.

"Stop it there," Rose said, and Stan hit Pause. The image on the screen blurred slightly as the tape froze, but clearly the woman was handing the cashier something. "Right there, what is that?"

"It ain't no coupon," Stan said. "It's a plastic card."

"It's a Safeway Club Card," the night manager said authoritatively. "You can see the logo."

"What the hell is a Safeway Club Card?" Joshua asked.

"Oh, it's our special shoppers' club," the guy said, slipping easily into the corporate pitch. "On top of Safeway's already low prices, members get special discounts on thousands of items every week. You just present your Club Card at checkout and the savings are automatically deducted from the total. Plus, if you spend more than two hundred fifty dollars, you get a hundred twenty-five bonus miles on the United Mileage Plus—"

"We're not looking to buy the damn thing," Rose said. "We just—"

"Oh, it's free of charge! All you have to do is complete the membership form and—"

"For Christ's sake, man," Joshua said. "Would you have this woman's membership form? Could we find out who the hell she is?"

The night manager looked uneasy. "Well . . . Mr. Thurman would be pissed."

"Fuck Mr. Thurman," Joshua said.

It took another hour and a half to track down the register

tapes and isolate the transaction, then backtrack to the club membership number, but in the end it came up clear and simple. Safeway Club Card #3181957 was registered to a Helen Rainey, of Forty-seventh Avenue in San Francisco. It even had her phone number.

"Shall we give her a call?" Joshua said.

Rose met his exuberant look and smiled. "I'd hate to disturb her beauty rest. I'm thinking we just drop by."

Jimmy thrashed through the short night, woke before first light, and banged around the kitchen for a while, then came back to the bedroom and told Helen he was going to work early. She knew what that meant: He would stop at the 7-Eleven and buy a couple of quart bottles of Budweiser, park the truck by Ocean Beach, and drink and brood and watch the pelicans until the beer ran out. Then he would go in to work and find an excuse to punch someone. Probably his foreman. It was simple frustration, Helen understood, the maddening sense of an undropped shoe. If he had killed Mark, Jimmy would have slept late, awakened tender and cheerful, and made them both a good North Carolina breakfast of greasy things and grits; he would have gone to work and been a model carpenter and come home with an armful of bright cheap flowers from the roadside stand on Nineteenth Avenue. As it was, Jimmy would lose his job today, because no one had died last night.

Helen tried to go back to sleep after he left, but it was useless. She finally slipped out of the bed just after first light, wrapped Jimmy's shabby bathrobe around herself, and padded barefoot out to the kitchen, where the Blue Devil still circled in its glass. She considered it for a moment, then went to the living room, took the fishbowl full of matchbooks from the coffee table, and brought it back into the kitchen. It wasn't an aquarium, but it was better than that glass.

She dumped the matchbooks out onto the counter. There were dozens of them, from dozens of bars: a little history of looking for love in all the wrong places, the footprints of her madness. She rinsed out the fishbowl and filled it with water, then dropped the Blue Devil in. It seemed happier with more space. She found some cornflakes and crumbled them up into the water, and the fish nibbled at them contentedly.

The pile of matchbooks still lay on the counter, and Helen looked at it. She was tempted to just strike a match and toss it on the pile: to pack a few things and take her fish and leave the place to burn. To let Jimmy come home to the ashes. But that was a fantasy. Nothing was that simple.

Bubbles started barking frantically in the backyard and slamming against the chain-link fence. A moment later, the doorbell rang. Helen glanced at the kitchen clock: six twenty-three. It was Mark, she thought, with a little surge of joy. There was no one else in her life who would show up at this hour. There was no one else in her life at all.

She hurried to the door and opened it. A man and a woman stood on the porch, decently dressed but distinctly rumpled.

"Helen Rainey?" the man said.

"Yes?"

"I'm Inspector Falkner and this is Inspector Burke. We're with the San Francisco Police."

She recognized the woman now. It was the one who had been on TV, the one in the water with Michael Turner's body. So this was it, Helen thought. She actually felt relieved.

"Is there some kind of problem?" she asked.

$\int$ HE WAS CERTAINLY A cool customer, Rose thought with
grudging fascination, watching Helen Rainey through
the one-way window that peered into Interrogation Room
3. Their suspect sat alone at the scarred wooden table, her
legs crisply crossed, tending to her nails with an emery
board as casually as if she were in the waiting room at a
dentist's office. She hadn't even called a lawyer. She'd taken
the time to dress well before they came downtown and
looked defiantly stylish in a pleated black blouse, tinted red
and yellow on the front and sprinkled with tiny mirrors,
black gabardine pants with no pockets, and black suede ankle boots with silver half-moon ornaments, sharp toes, and
two-and-a-half-inch heels. Her black handbag had leather
fringe hanging from a black leather lotus flower. Hippie
chic. The purse had probably cost four hundred dollars, and

all Rainey seemed to have in it was makeup, cigarettes, and Kleenex.

"I don't think she's going to self-destruct," Joshua noted laconically from the chair against the wall, where he'd been nursing a series of cups of coffee for the last hour and a half.

Rose felt the implied critique; it had been her idea to let Rainey sweat for a while. She said defensively, "She's so nonchalant, it's practically a confession."

"I don't think a jury will buy it. Doing your nails is covered by the Fifth Amendment."

Rainey finished with the emery board and started touching up her peach-colored fingernail polish. Rose shifted fretfully, conscious of her own frayed edges. She knew her eyes were veined with red; her hair felt like straw, and she was still wearing the unflattering olive-dun pantsuit she had put on at six A.M. the day before. It seemed incredibly petty, but she hated to go into the interrogation room at such a fashion disadvantage.

"Five more minutes," she said.

Joshua hesitated, then shrugged and let the chair rock back on two legs until it hit the wall behind him with a thump. Stoic, indulging her. They were both tired, on the verge of irascibility; looking at Joshua now, barely containing her own frustration, Rose tried to picture herself crying in his arms the night before, and couldn't. It saddened her that she'd lost that image, that the sweet, deep moment had been swept away in the rush of events. She hadn't even thanked him for catching her fall, and now it seemed too late.

They'd gotten Mel Simmons, the deputy city attorney, out of bed at dawn and made a case for arresting Rainey outright, but even the flimsy evidence they had was all circumstantial and he'd advised them to hold off. It would be weeks, possibly months, before the DNA results came back for the blood on the earring they'd found on Michael Turner's body. Alfred Powell's photographs were inconclusive. The videotape from the Safeway proved only that Rainey flirted briefly with Michael Turner. They had nothing, essentially. They hadn't even been able to get a warrant to search Rainey's apartment. They'd brought her in hoping that she would panic, but it didn't look like she was going to.

The scrape of a chair in the interrogation room, amplified over the intercom, made both of them turn back to the window. Helen Rainey had risen to her feet and was approaching the mirror. She walked right up to the glass, directly in front of Rose, and stared into it, apparently checking out her makeup job. It was all Rose could do not to flinch; she had to remind herself that their suspect was only looking at her own reflection. But Rainey's assessing look seemed to penetrate the one-way glass. The two of them were exactly the same height and their faces, no more than a foot and a half apart, were eerily eye to eye. Rose found herself meeting the other woman's gaze as if she were being seen.

"Start the music, Josh," she said quietly, without looking away.

"I thought you said—"

"Forget that. Just start it."

Joshua let the chair's front legs fall back to the floor with a clunk. Rainey heard it, Rose noted: The other woman's surprisingly mild gray eyes widened ever so slightly in startled reaction. But she quickly brought her face under control. And smiled, straight into the mirror.

Joshua crossed to the sound system's panel and hit Play. The master copy of the tape Melanie Jurgensen had made for Michael Turner kicked in, and the first cathedral notes of Madonna's "Like a Prayer" sifted through the interrogation room's scratchy speakers. Rainey glanced back at the source of the sound in the high corner behind her, then turned again to the mirror, still smiling. Coldly, knowingly, amused: conceding that the music was a clever ploy.

"Life is a mystery, everyone must stand alone . . ."

Rainey held Rose's gaze, blindly, through the mirror for another long moment, then turned away and walked back to the table. She sat down and crossed her legs, opened her purse, and took out a pack of cigarettes.

Rose glanced at Joshua, as Rainey lit up. He gave her a wry smile.

"We can bust her for smoking, at least," he said. "I suppose it's better than nothing."

"She'll crack," Rose said. "Let's get to it."

She'd never felt so calm. Helen marveled at the feeling. She had always thought that when the time finally came, it would be chaotic, a tumbling ride through river rapids, cold and harsh and loud. Colliding with rocks, swallowing water, disoriented and battered. But this was simple and even gentle, an effortless floating on a smooth, sunlit stream. She'd planned for this day, dreaded this day, weirdly, perversely longed for this day, and now it was here and it was nothing, nothing at all. It was like a drug without a buzz; it was like a new kind of weather, a suffusing atmosphere, luminous and mild, lit strangely from within. Everything was clear and quiet and obvious.

When the two cops came into the room, Helen could see instantly that the guy was in love with the woman. It was something in the way he moved around her, as if she were made of precious glass. He reminded Helen of Jimmy on a good day: an attentive puppy, eyes wide and devoted, trying to guess the ways to please and failing, but failing endearingly. The woman wore a wedding ring and looked fatigued and drawn.

"Sorry to have kept you waiting so long, Ms. Rainey," she said.

"I assumed that was your intention." Helen took a drag off her cigarette and blew a long tendril of smoke toward the harsh fluorescent ceiling light. "I don't suppose I could have an ashtray?"

The guy suppressed a smile at the impertinence: a weakness, there; he was way too sympathetic. The woman met her eyes coolly. Helen waited for her to tell her to put the cigarette out, but after a moment the detective just shook her head, a little wearily, refusing not the ashtray but the game itself. She took a seat across the table, getting down to business. The guy cop settled amiably against the wall, standing with his hands in his pockets, letting his partner lead. Helen shrugged and flicked her ash onto the floor.

"I suppose that at some point you will tell me what this is all about," she said.

"You know what this is about," the woman said. Quietly, not insisting, not accusing, just stating it. It had almost the tone of an exchange between friends, of girl talk: *Let's cut the bullshit, shall we?* She leaned back in her chair and waited. Helen did the same, pointedly mirroring, but glad for the propping of the cigarette, for something to keep her hands busy. Carole King came on the music system, "Where You Lead, I Will Follow," and Helen had a sudden, vivid image of Mike's beautiful butt, the gluteal muscles working beneath the taut fabric of his bicycle pants as he pedaled up the hill above Seal Rock.

"What was your name again?" she asked the detective.

"Burke. Inspector Rose Burke."

Helen smiled. "An Irish rose."

"A rose of Sharon, actually. My maiden name was Goldstein."

"Ah."

They fell silent again. The cigarette was down to the filter, and Helen hesitated, then stubbed it out on the table's surface, leaving a black scorched spot. Her mother would have spun in her grave. Neither of the cops said a word. She dropped the butt on the floor and reached for her purse to get another cigarette, but Burke dispassionately beat her to the bag and slid it across the table out of reach. Helen conceded the point by settling back in her chair.

"So—" she said. "Am I under arrest?"

"No," Burke said.

"I can go, then?"

"Yes."

Helen blinked in surprise, then snapped, "I wish you'd told me that an hour and a half ago."

"Oops," Burke said laconically.

Helen stood up. Neither of the cops moved, and she hesitated, feeling a perverse surge of outrage.

"You don't have a thing, do you?" she said. "You don't have a fucking clue."

Burke finally stirred. "Oh, we've got a clue," she said. She reached for the manila folder she had brought into the interrogation room, slipped a stack of several glossy photographs from it, and spread them on the table in front of Helen. "Do you recognize any of these men?"

Helen looked down at the array. Henry Pelletier's driver's license photo, blown up blurrily to eight-and-a-half by eleven. Michael Turner's expired student ID picture, ditto. And, unexpectedly, a snapshot of that preppie guy, the architect in North Beach. What was his name? Something Joseph. Kevin? No, Ken, that was it, like Barbie's partner. Ken Joseph. How the hell had they tracked *that* down? Someone had done his homework.

She said, "Nothing really rings a bell."

"Maybe these will jog your memory," Burke said, placing a second set of three photos before her, matching them neatly with the first set: before and after shots. Henry Pelletier, pathetic in his gory bed; Mike on the rock like a broken bird, Icarus with his bike pants around his knees; and Ken Joseph on his living room floor, the look of bewildered reproach he'd died with fixed upon his features. She could still remember the way the blade went in, the black snake tattoo on Jimmy's forearm flexing around the muscles as he gripped the knife, and Joseph's little *oof* as he doubled over. He'd sunk to his knees with his hands folded across his heart like an altar boy, his lips moving in speechless prayer, his eyes fixed on Helen's while the light emptied out of them. It seemed like it had taken him forever to die.

Helen looked up and met Burke's fierce, steady gaze. The detective had coffee-brown eyes, almost black. Sad eyes, Helen thought, dark with some kind of grief, fathomless as a lake at night. In another life, they could have been sisters.

"Nope," she said. "Sorry."

"You fucking monster," Burke said.

"Easy, Rosie," the other detective said gently from his spot against the wall.

"You don't know me," Helen said. "You don't know anything about me."

"I know what happened to your ear."

"What?"

"Your ear," Burke said. "That's a nasty wound you've got there. Like an earring got torn right out of it or something."

Helen touched her healing lobe involuntarily.

"We've got your blood," Burke said. "We've got your DNA. We've got pictures of you in Henry Pelletier's apartment on the night he was killed, courtesy of his sicko neighbor across the street. We've got surveillance tapes of you picking up Michael Turner in the Safeway."

"Sounds like you should probably arrest me," Helen said. "I wonder why you haven't?"

"We've got a witness," Burke continued. She glanced at her partner. "Joshua, would you mind bringing her in?"

"My pleasure," the guy said, and left the room.

The two women, left alone, were silent.

"A witness," Helen said at last.

"Yup."

"This should be interesting." Burke said nothing. After a moment, Helen offered, "I saw you on TV."

The detective stirred. "Cleaning up your mess, you mean? Poor Michael Turner. Did you really have to yank his pants down before you pushed him off that cliff? Are you really that hateful?"

"You must have ruined that pantsuit," Helen said. "You should have let your partner go out there. He seems so . . . amenable. So eager to please."

Burke looked at her incredulously, then said, "Joshua is a truly decent man. He can't imagine how evil you really are. He's got that southern woman-on-a-pedestal thing, see. But I can imagine it. I know myself. So I know you."

"Then you know how useless it was, dragging me in here, expecting me to panic."

"Oh, I don't know," Burke said. "Pressure is a funny thing. It builds, you see. It just builds, and builds, and builds. It makes people do funny things."

They were silent again.

"Is this conversation being recorded?" Helen asked.

"What do you think?"

"There's something I want to tell you. Off the record."

Burke smiled, amused. "I can assure you that anything you say to me in this room is just between you and me and the prosecuting attorney of the city of San Francisco."

Helen was struck by the easy blackness of her humor and thought again how nice it would have been to be friends with this woman. But it was way too late for that. "What if I told you that it's my insanely jealous boyfriend who's been killing these poor guys? And that I've been too terrified to turn him in?"

"I'd say, Nice try. I'd say, You seem a little too composed and well dressed to me, for a sexual hostage in fear for her life."

"Maybe victims come in more shapes and sizes than you're prepared to understand."

Burke leaned forward, suddenly fierce. "Listen—" she snapped. "I don't give a fuck about your unhappy childhood. I don't give a fuck about your issues with men. I don't give a fuck about your psychology at all, frankly, except in whatever way it helps me get you off the streets. And I'm perfectly prepared to understand who the victims are in this case. I'm the one who had to deal with their bodies, remember?"

Helen hesitated, then said, "Have you ever been in love?"

Burke blinked, taken aback, then shrugged and settled back in her chair. "I'm married."

"That's not what I asked."

The detective smiled faintly. "Touché. Of course I've been in love."

"I never had been. Until the other day. It changes everything."

Burke shook her head. "Love's just love, dearie. It's not magic. Nothing changes the way things really are. And nothing changes what you've done."

"Everything," Helen insisted. "It changes everything."

Burke was silent for a long moment. Then she said, "Maybe it does. But probably not the way you wish it would."

"Who knows? They say it's never too late for a happy childhood."

"It's too late for Henry Pelletier and Michael Turner," Burke said. "It's too late for Ken Joseph."

The door opened just then, and the other detective came back in. Helen looked for the witness, a little uneasy in spite of herself, but she saw no one. It took her a moment to realize that the guy was carrying a cat, and another moment to recognize Michael Turner's beautiful Siamese.

Helen kept her face impassive, feeling absurdly exposed. Falkner set the cat down on the floor and she walked straight to Helen and rubbed against her leg. Helen looked at Burke, and found her smiling, that same black humor, that weird camaraderie.

"You remember Agatha, don't you?" the detective asked. "You made an orphan of her."

"*This* is your witness?"

Burke shrugged. "I'm hoping we get a sympathetic judge."

Helen laughed and shook her head. "You really don't have shit for evidence, do you?"

"No," Burke said. "You've been ever so clever and neat. But we will. It's just a matter of time, now."

"I'm free to go, then?"

"I can't stop you." The detective held her eyes. "Yet."

"You should try a little henna in your hair," Helen said. "That gray's no big deal, really. The henna would jazz it right up."

Burke looked startled, briefly, and even a little hurt, and Helen felt sorry for her for a moment. But the detective recovered and even managed a smile. Conceding the point. "Actually, my husband likes the gray."

"Of course he does," Helen said. She reached for her purse and turned toward the door. Burke's partner stepped quietly aside, clearing her way, and Helen gave him a smile. "Nice meeting you, Detective."

"Somehow I find that hard to believe, ma'am," he said mildly. He had a lovely southern accent, like Jimmy's North Carolina drawl, only softer. "But it's certainly been interesting."

Helen gave him another smile and moved to the door. Burke waited until she'd touched the knob, then asked quietly, "Are you going to run?"

She paused, considering it, then said frankly, "I've got nowhere left to go."

Burke stooped and gathered Agatha into her arms. The cat lifted her face and the detective bent to rub her nose against the cat's nose, then raised her head again to meet Helen's eyes.

"Then I'll see you soon, I guess," she said.

"Think about that henna," Helen said. "There's really no need to let yourself go." And she went out.

20

WELL, *THAT* WENT WELL," Joshua said, when the door had closed behind their suspect.

Rose flopped down in the chair that Rainey had sat in, still holding the cat, and said nothing. She felt sick to her stomach. Maybe it was morning sickness, maybe it was revulsion. Or maybe it was just the knowledge of how badly she had blown it.

"We should have waited," she said at last. "We should have waited until we had something solid. We jumped the gun."

Joshua sat down across from her, wearily. "It was worth a shot. Who knew the woman was made of ice and stone? I never saw anyone that cool in my life. She never even blinked."

"We shouldn't have let her go."

"We didn't have anything to hold her on."

"We should have made something up."

"We should have waited," Joshua said, with sane finality.

It was the truth. They had moved too soon and tipped their hand, and accomplished nothing except to let Rainey know they were on to her. They sat in silence, contemplating that. The air in the interrogation room still smelled of cigarette smoke and, faintly, of jasmine and gardenias, of Helen Rainey's complex soft perfume.

Rose stirred at last.

"I guess I'll go tell Sandi where we're at," she said. "Much as I dread it."

"Why don't you go home and get some sleep?" Joshua said. "I'll handle Sandi. It's my turn, anyway. You did the last round, and you didn't even get us overtime."

Rose looked at him. "You need sleep as much as I do."

"I've got some kind of second wind, for some reason. I think it's the coffee. I might as well run with it. I'll give Sandi the edited version of the fiasco, get some paperwork done, and go home and crash myself, when the caffeine gives out."

"We really should keep pushing."

"We pushed too damn much today already, I'm afraid." And, as Rose wavered, "Look, Rosie, she's not going to kill anybody else in the next few hours. We'll get her. But not if you're crapped out. Go get some sleep."

Still Rose hesitated. But Joshua was right. They'd pushed things to the limit and beyond, for the moment. They were exhausted and Rainey was rested and crisp and smelled of L'Air du Temps. They'd done everything they could. It was their suspect's move now.

"She looked fresh as a fucking daisy, didn't she?" she said. "I hate that."

"I don't know why all the criminals seem to keep saner hours than we do," her partner agreed. "I think they eat better, too."

"That goddamned blouse with its pretty little mirrors. That goddamned phony hippie purse."

"We should have made her come down here in her sweatpants."

"I should have told her how cheap she looked as a platinum blonde. Jesus, what *was* all that shit about my hair?"

"Fuck her," Joshua said stoutly. "And the fuckin' horse she rode in on."

Rose stood up, with Agatha still in her arms. The cat, half asleep, stirred briefly and settled again. Rose moved toward the door, where she paused, wanting, again, to thank Joshua for being there for her the night before, for the healing moment in his arms. But to do that, she felt, would make that moment over. It would move it into the category of *de nada,* of partners having each other's backs, all in the line of duty. It would make it history, and business, and friendship. And she wasn't sure she wanted it to slip away into that.

Joshua was looking at her, a quiet look that made her realize he was thinking of it too.

"Just for the record—" he said. "I happen to love your hair just the way it is."

Rose felt the sting of tears rising and turned to the door. She definitely needed to get some sleep.

"I'll leave my cell phone on," she said.

She took the train home with Agatha in her arms. The N-Judah streetcar driver gave the cat a long look, then shrugged and let her board. When Rose got home, she set the cat down and went straight to the bathroom, where she clung to the toilet rim and puked up what was left of the salad and beer from the night before.

Holy shit, she thought. *I'm really pregnant.*

When she looked up, Seamus was standing in the bathroom doorway.

"You're not at work," she said stupidly.

"No." He smiled. He crossed the floor, knelt beside her on the tile, and touched her cheek. "Welcome home, sweetheart."

Rose would like to have responded in kind, but just then she threw up again, moving into dry heaves. Seamus held her hair back for her, tenderly, like a good date at a frat party.

"I can see why you're so ambivalent about getting into this," Rose said, when the spasms had passed.

"What's a little nausea, in the long run of a marriage?" Seamus shrugged. "Puke away, my love. Let the hormones rage. It's going to be a beautiful kid." She looked at him, startled, and even incredulous, and he smiled. "Is that so unthinkable? She'll have your looks and brains, and my, uh—"

Their eyes met in amusement as he groped for a word. "Deep, unrelenting emotional cluelessness?" Rose prompted.

Seamus laughed. "I was going to say humility, actually." He stood up and flushed the toilet; as the mess whirled away, he held out his hand. "Come on, sweetie, let's get you cleaned up and into bed."

Rose took his hand, feeling her exhaustion, her tongue running over her teeth against the sour taste. As he pulled her up, she said, "I let a serial murderer walk back out onto the street this morning, Seamus."

He put his arms around her. "We all have bad days."

"And bad weeks," she said, more pointedly than she had intended.

He met her gaze without rancor. "And bad months," he conceded. "We've just got to muddle on."

Rose put her face into the curve of his shoulder, breathing in his familiar scent with a sense of complete incongruity. It had all just gotten too complex for her, she realized. She had no idea what was going on anymore. Anywhere.

"I'm a fucking mess," she warned, into his shirt.

"Tell me something I don't know."

"I'll probably cry."

"I'll probably cry too," her husband said.

Mark answered halfway through the first ring, as if he had been sitting beside the phone, waiting to snatch it up "Hello?"

"It's me," Helen said.

She heard the silence on the other end, and then his long sigh.

"Jesus," he breathed. "Jesusjesusjesus. Thank God. I was going to die. I was literally going to fucking die, if you didn't call."

"You may die yet," she said.

They lay quietly together in the unfamiliar daylight. It was delicious and strange to be in bed on a weekday morning—like a snow day or something, Rose thought, a gratuitous release from routine that felt vaguely illegal. Seamus had turned off the ringers of all the phones as if it were a religious ritual and led her to the bedroom by the hand. They had been shy with each other, a sweet shyness that made everything fresh, taking off their clothing one piece at a time, rediscovering each other's bodies tentatively, tenderly.

Seamus's hand moved on her skin, still damp with their mingled sweat, languidly fondling her shoulder, tracing her collarbone and easing down her sternum. His thumb caught the fullness of her breast and he lingered there, then moved down her belly, pausing again, the flat of his hand warm over her womb; his fingers sifted through her pubic hair and he slid one finger along the wetness between her legs.

As Rose shuddered in pleasure, Seamus smiled into her hair, and his hand moved on, easing across her thigh and up and over the curve of her hip, a long tender caress running back up to her shoulder that left a trail of goose bumps along her arm.

Rose sighed.

"I could get used to this," she murmured.

Seamus chuckled. "I wonder how long our unemployment checks would hold out."

"Maybe we could get into computer fraud or something, so we could work at home. I know a couple of the guys in the tech division; they might let us slide for a while."

"Sounds like a plan."

She leaned back enough to see his full face. Seamus's blue Irish eyes met hers, and she could see the light in them, the light she had thought was gone.

"I love you," she marveled.

He laughed. "You make that sound like such a huge surprise."

Rose hesitated. But the desire to not mess the lovely moment up was not as deep as the desire to make it realer, deeper, truer. They'd lived too long with settling for pleasantness, keeping the fleeting decent moments like spunglass ornaments on the rickety shelves of all the things they weren't saying, until they were afraid to say a true word for fear of shattering everything. "I've never doubted that I loved you, Seamus. But I've doubted that love was enough. I've wondered if love was worth it. I've wondered if I was good enough at it, and if you were, wondered whether we were both just too immature and fucked up and selfish to make a marriage work. I've doubted we were capable of being grown-ups. And—" She stopped and shook her head. It seemed like too much to say, even throwing caution to the wind.

"You've doubted that I loved *you*," Seamus supplied.

"I've . . . wondered."

He was silent for a moment, and his eyes flickered, looking past her now, somewhere inward. Rose thought she had probably gone too far. But there came a moment when too far was the only place worth going anymore. So she waited, telling herself to breathe, and finally her husband's eyes came back to hers.

"It's funny," he said. "Not ha-ha funny, just . . . funny. The things that are so obvious to me. The things that aren't clear to you. That you could wonder, that you could doubt for a moment that I love you—"

"The last couple of years have been no picnic, Seamus. Didn't *you* wonder?"

"I wondered every fucking day. But not about whether I loved *you*." Seamus hesitated; Rose saw him weighing it out, considering the risk, and making the same decision she had. He took a breath and said, "The thing is, Rosie, for the longest time now, every time I've tried to get closer to you, it seems like there's a dead body in the way."

My God, Rose thought. But he was right, of course. They were there, in her mind's eye, always: sprawled grotesquely, splayed, slumped, and shattered, the corpses that were her daily work, the unanswered questions lying in pools of blood, the mysteries in the exit wounds and the blatancy in the ruptured flesh of ended lives. She brought her work home, inevitably; it poisoned her dreams and sat at the dinner table grinning like a skull. She lived with it, she took it to heart and suffered it, way more than she should have. She'd faulted Seamus for his own careerism; but at least her husband's preoccupations didn't stink of death.

She began, stammeringly, "God, Seamus, I'm so sorry. I know the job has been—"

"I'm not talking about the job," he said. "I'm talking about Jack."

Rose blinked, stunned and then appalled, inclined to resist, but overwhelmed by a sudden wave of fear, a terror that it was true. That it was fatal and that there was no way out.

"You think I'm so dense," Seamus went on. Not accusing; gently matter-of-fact, and even with a sort of camaraderie. "That I'm . . . How did you put it? Clueless, emotionally. That I'm just this chain-working techno-dolt. I don't know when or why that started, how we slid into that. But once we were in it, it seemed like there was no way out. You'd just decided, you'd locked in this view of me, this—I don't know, this *contempt*—"

"It was never contempt, Seamus," she said hurriedly, stung. "Frustration, maybe. Hurt, despair, resentment—"

"Call it what you will. You'd put me in this box in your mind and I knew it, and it made it harder and harder for me to say anything at all, because I'd feel myself bumping up against that box's little sides, every time I tried to talk. And after awhile, I was just too angry to even start, too angry to even try. I—" His voice caught; Seamus took a breath and was silent a moment. Then he shook his head and said simply, "There was nowhere to start."

"I'm so—God, Seamus, I'm sorry, I'm just so *sorry*. I had no idea. I never meant to shut you out, never. I just thought we had lost it. I mean, I thought it was *your* damn job. I thought you didn't care anymore."

"How could I not care that you were sleeping with your partner?"

"What?!"

He met her eyes. "You heard me. Did you think I was an idiot?"

Rose gaped at him. "You—you think I slept with *Joshua*?"

Seamus, remarkably, smiled, a genuine smile of amusement, laced with sadness. "No, Rosie. For what it's worth, I think you're *going to* sleep with Joshua. I think you *slept* with Jack."

She recognized that smile, Rose realized: she'd been noticing that mild, resigned, slightly weary smile for a long time. Had wondered where it came from, and what the hell it meant. "No—*no*—my *God,* no—Seamus, Jesus, I—I don't even know what to say. I—"

"It's all right, Rose," he said.

"All *right?!*"

He smiled again. "Well, it took me a while to come to terms with it, I admit. I thought about killing him for the longest time. That would have been ironic, I guess: a real open-and-shut case for you, that one."

"Jesus, Seamus—"

"You'd come home and it was always, Jack said this, Jack said that, Jack is so fucking funny, Jack is so fucking thoughtful. 'Oh, I just had a couple of beers with Jack. Oh, no need to cook, Jack and I already grabbed a sandwich.' It used to drive me nuts. I'd think, Well, shit, I can't compete with a man who can be funny and sensitive about dead bodies. I can't compete with having beers together after wading through the gore. I'm just a fucking computer geek. Just a dull old husband. All I can be funny and sensitive about is fixing the toilet."

"Jesus, Seamus, I'm a Homicide cop. And so was Jack. There's a camaraderie there, sure, but—"

"He shot that guy for you. Your white knight. And you lied for him at the hearing. You put your whole career on the line for the guy."

Rose opened her mouth, then closed it.

"You'd come home with your wedding ring off," Seamus said. "You still do, half the time. You'd come home with your hair wet from a shower, smelling like Irish Spring soap. You'd go to work in stockings and come home with bare legs, go to work in low heels and come home in sneakers."

"I take my ring off when I pull on the rubber gloves at a crime scene because I'm afraid it will tear the glove. I take showers at work a lot of the time because I don't want to come home smelling like road kill, and I never even paid any

attention to what kind of soap I use. I take off my stockings—
shit, I don't even *remember* ever taking off my goddamned
stockings. I probably knelt down in some poor splatter case's
blood that day, I don't know." Rose heard herself, stopped,
and took a deep breath. "Seamus, this is crazy."

"Is it?" he said. "There's a time for the truth, Rose. It actually feels good, believe it or not. Makes you miserable,
then sets you free. So you tell me, truly: Am I really crazy?
You were in love with Jack. It almost killed you when
he died, it fucked you up for years. Hell, it's *still* fucking
you up."

"No."

"And now you're in love with Joshua," Seamus said.
"Maybe there's just something about looking at death together every day that makes that kind of bond. Maybe it's
getting shot at together. I don't know. But I know it's there."
He faced her, his gaze open, quiet and focused. "Look at
me right now, Rosie—look me in the eye and tell me that
I'm crazy. Tell me I'm making this shit up."

Rose met his eyes, feeling a kind of helplessness, a despair. It seemed to her that there was just enough truth in
what Seamus was saying to ruin their marriage, but not
enough to heal them. But what was the alternative? They'd already lived with it swept under the rug, warping every step
they took for years. The truth was going to have to be enough.

She said quietly, matching his tone at last, "I never slept
with Jack, Seamus. I never even came close, I swear to God,
I was never even seriously tempted. It just wasn't that kind
of thing. But you're not crazy. I—did love him. I just didn't
know it, I couldn't admit it even to myself, until—"

Her cell phone trilled just then, from her purse, on the
table beside the bed. They looked at each other incredulously, and then Seamus smiled, that same unnervingly resigned smile, a humor black with defeat. "You'd better get
that, right?"

"Fuck it," Rose said. "It can wait, whatever it is."

· The phone rang five more times, a seeming eternity. Rose vowed to reset her voice-mail pickup to fewer rings at the first opportunity.

When the ringing finally stopped, she said, "It wasn't until he killed himself that I really—"

The phone began to ring again.

"*Shit!*" Rose leaned over, took the phone out of her purse, and punched it off. But as she leaned over to put the phone back into the purse, her pager beeped.

"Sounds like something's really up," Seamus said.

"I'm a Homicide cop, for Christ's sake. How urgent could it be? The people we deal with are already dead." But she took the pager out and looked at it. 9-1-1-1-1-1, Joshua's coded version of a Pearl Harbor headline, a five-star red alert on breaking news.

"Shit," she said again. "I'd better call."

"Of course."

"I'll make it quick. And then—we'll keep talking, right?"

"Of course," Seamus said, not sounding entirely convinced. He rolled away and slipped out of the bed.

Rose watched uneasily as he rummaged around for some boxers and a T-shirt. "Seamus?"

He pulled his boxers on. "Yeah?"

"I love you."

Her husband looked at the PsiberSystems T-shirt in his hand—psianide blue, he always called it—and sighed.

"I love you, too," he said. "Now call your fucking partner. You're a Homicide cop, for Christ's sake. I'm going to go fix us some lunch."

Joshua answered instantly. "Rosie?"

"What's up?"

"It's fucking unbelievable. You know that FBI wonk you sent the package to the other day, the dweeb at VICAP?"

"Mr. Personality? Swan, Swain, something like that?"

" 'Call me Marvin.' "

"That's the dweeb all right."

"He faxed you some stuff."

Rose felt a surge of impatience. She could hear Seamus banging around in the kitchen, and all she wanted to do was get out there before he really worked himself into a state. "He thinks our gal's a guy, Josh. He's got his head up his Quantico ass."

"He's got ten, count 'em, ten cases that fit our profile exactly. I mean, it's fucking airtight. He's got blood from the killer, DNA, almost certainly a white male, on one of the early killings. Apparently it took our boy a while to learn how to handle a knife. He's got a pickup truck with North Carolina plates, seen near several of the California scenes. He's got two clean sets of *fingerprints,* even. It's the same guy, Rosie. There's no doubt about it."

"Well, good for Marvin. I still don't see what any of this has to do with Helen Rainey killing Pelletier, Turner, and Joseph."

"Funny you should ask," Joshua said. "The prints they've got come up in the database for one James Rehoboam Pesh, the prime suspect in the nineteen ninety-one murder of Parker Rainey in Raleigh, North Carolina."

Rose was silent for a moment, conscious suddenly of her heart thudding in her chest. "Holy *shit,*" she breathed at last.

"Exactly."

"Her—father? Husband? Brother?"

"Father. Pesh was her boyfriend. Blew Daddy away and disappeared. They held Helen for a while as an accessory, but couldn't make it stick. She ended up with a shitload of cash from the inheritance and played the grieving daughter for about a year and a half. Then they both dropped off the fucking map. Until a few years later, when an awful lot of bachelors on the make started dying in immaculate apartments in northern California."

Rose realized she was on her feet. She couldn't even remember getting out of the bed. "My God, Josh, we let her walk!"

"Not far," he said grimly. "I talked to Sandi and Simmons. We've got warrants for both of them."

"I'll be right down."

"No, meet us in the Richmond, the boys are already putting on the armor here and we're heading for Rainey's place any minute. We're gonna set up on the corner of Forty-seventh and Balboa and go in from there."

"I'll be there before you are, then. Bring a vest for me, will you?"

"The flowers motif or that nice little number in red?"

"Surprise me," Rose said.

Helen finished her final cleaning and put the chemicals away beneath the sink. The gun was where it always was, right behind the bottle of Murphy's Oil Soap. There'd never been any chance of Jimmy finding it there.

She took the 9mm out, cocked it, and checked the action, then inserted the ammunition clip. The magazine held eight bullets, though she'd never been able to imagine using more than one or two.

Bubbles charged in through the back door as soon as she opened it. It was early for a walk, but the dog was nothing if not stupid. Helen let him career past, then followed, through the kitchen and into the front hallway, where the leash hung from its hook. Bubbles was waiting impatiently when she got there, his big pink tongue lolling.

"Not today, sport," Helen said, and raised the gun. Bubbles peered at the unfamiliar object, his dull black killer's eyes flat and blank. It was surprisingly easy to pull the trigger. The noise was tremendous in the confined space. Bubbles's body dropped right where it was, twitched briefly, and then was still.

Helen looked at the dead dog for a long moment, her ears ringing. The wall behind the dog was a bloody mess; she hadn't thought of that, but no doubt there were a lot of things she hadn't quite thought through. Like whether any of her neighbors were at home, and if anyone could have heard the shot. But it was too late for fine points now.

She stepped past the pit bull's corpse into the living room, where she settled on the couch with a view of the front door. Laying the gun carefully on the cushion beside her, she took *The Family Album of Favorite Poems* from the coffee table where she'd placed it earlier. The book fell open to "The Rime of the Ancient Mariner," as it always did.

> *I woke, and we were sailing on*
> *As in a gentle weather:*
> *'Twas night, calm night, the Moon was high;*
> *The dead men stood together.*
>
> *All stood together on the deck,*
> *For a charnel-dungeon fitter:*
> *All fix'd on me their stony eyes,*
> *That in the Moon did glitter.*

It seemed to Helen that it was a toss-up who would show up first, the ghosts, or Jimmy; Mark, or the police. She was rooting for Mark, of course. But somehow it didn't seem to matter that much anymore. She only knew the unlocked door would open at some point, on a fate she felt had been settled long ago. And at least she would never have to listen to that damn dog's barking again, or hear him fling himself against the chain-link fence.

The pang, the curse, with which they died,
Had never passed away:
I could not draw my eyes from theirs,
Nor turn them up to pray.

And now this spell was snapt: once more
I viewed the ocean green,
And look'd far north, yet little saw
Of what had else been seen—

Like one that on a lonesome road
Doth walk in fear and dread,
And having once turn'd round, walks on,
And no more turns his head;
Because he knows a frightful fiend
Doth close behind him tread.

In the kitchen, Seamus had set down a bowl of tuna fish and some water for the cat and was sitting on the floor beside her as she ate. There were sandwich fixings spread out on the counter, a loving, extravagant array, which caused Rose a pang. Her husband looked up as she came in, already dressed, buckling on her shoulder holster.

"You might have mentioned that we had a guest," he said.

"My bad. Seamus, meet Agatha. Agatha, Seamus."

"The pleasure's all mine, Agatha," Seamus said. He rubbed the cat behind her ears and stood up. "I'm sure there's a fascinating story here."

"You know I've been wanting a cat. I just wasn't sure we could handle the responsibility. And I didn't want a custody battle if we broke up."

She suspected as soon as it was out of her mouth that it might have been too harsh, but Seamus just laughed. The return of his sense of humor was a little disorienting, Rose thought. It was going to take some getting used to.

Seamus eyed her outfit, an unflattering navy blue suit appropriate for gunfire. "I take it lunch is canceled?"

"There's a break on our serial gal. It turns out she's got a partner, and we've finally got enough to nail them. There's a team gathering in the Richmond right now to kick her door down."

"And I suppose you'll have to be right up there with the big boys." Rose shrugged. Seamus said, "Let Joshua go in first, okay?"

"It's my turn, actually. I don't think this gal's got a gun, anyway. Her boyfriend seems to favor knives." Rose hesitated. "Seamus, listen—"

"No, it's okay," he said. "There's plenty of time for that. A lifetime, I swear. You don't need to get anything said right now, Rosie. Just go do your job and try not to die in the line of duty today, and we'll talk when you come home to me."

"Do you remember our little prework ritual? Years ago, when I was on patrol on the graveyard shift in Hunter's Point, and you were so scared I'd get myself killed?"

Seamus's eyes softened and crinkled at the corners. The smile wrinkles were starting to set there, Rose noticed. It was incredibly endearing. He was going to be such an attractive older man.

"Yeah," he said.

"You'd make my lunch every day and hand it to me in a brown paper bag at the door, and you'd say—"

" 'Get on out there, kid, and win one for the Gipper.' And you'd say—"

" 'Fuck the Gipper. I'm coming home alive.' "

Their eyes met; they moved at the same moment and came into each other's arms. Rose pressed her face against her husband's chest and breathed him in. The PsiberSystems T-shirt smelled like tuna fish. It was very comforting, somehow.

"I guess I've been a pretty shitty white knight for you, at that," Seamus said after a moment, tentatively. He hesitated, and Rose sensed his smile. "It really *is* hell, though, competing with all these guys with .45s. Maybe I should buy a fucking gun myself and blow some poor slob away, just to get up to speed."

Rose pressed herself harder against him. "Seamus, I never thought less of you because you didn't kill anybody for me. It's easy, in a weird way, shooting the bad guys. What's really hard is loving somebody. It's living with the terror of losing the one you love."

She could feel the intensity of her husband's listening in the sudden stillness of his body. Rose leaned back and looked him in the face. "The thing is, sweetie, when all is said and done, you *are* my white knight. Because you give me back to myself, every day of my life. Because you're willing to live with the uncertainty and the weirdness. Because you have the courage to let me do what I have to do, no matter how much that scares you. *That's* what I need from a man. Just that. I never wanted some asshole on a big white horse."

Seamus's eyes filled. Rose put her head against his chest again. She could feel his body shaking, and a teardrop fell and landed on her nose.

They stood motionless, with the cat nosing around their ankles, until Rose's pager went off again. As she reached to silence it, Seamus snuffled and released her.

"I'm afraid I didn't get a lunch made for you," he said.

She smiled. "That's okay. I'm on the multiple-murder diet anyway. I'm sick of looking like a cow when I flip off the TV helicopters."

Her husband chuckled bravely. Their eyes met, and Rose lifted her face to meet his kiss, then turned to go.

Seamus bent to pick up the cat. "Get on out there and win one for the Gipper, Rosie," he said, as she reached the door.

Rose paused and gave him a smile.

"Fuck the Gipper," she said. "I'm coming home alive."

21

THE PICKUP TRUCK'S SPEEDOMETER nosed up over eighty, then eighty-five. The traffic climbing the grade back to San Francisco on 280 was the usual midmorning clutter, madmen on cell phones weaving their Mercedeses in and out, impervious housewives in SUVs, like tank drivers with to-do lists, and the occasional Buick in the fast lane doing fifty-seven. Jimmy found the holes in the traffic effortlessly, leaning on the seams between the other vehicles to force his way through—nothing personal, ma'am, drive it or park it—and opening the throttle up when the road ahead of him cleared briefly. Still accelerating, ninety, ninety-five, glimpsing the pale faces, startled and scared, in the windows flashing past. There wasn't really a hurry, there was time for everything important, as there always was; and all she'd be doing when he came in, whenever he came in, was sitting there in her little world, cold and spiky with contempt, like barbed wire, strung with a hundred reasons he was the world's worst man. But Jimmy could feel the flame inside him, burning clean and bright, hungering for fuel, and the speed was a kind of heat.

He loved this feeling. It felt great, strong and clear. "Bulletproof," his father used to call it: eight beers and a shot or three of Jim Beam and Daddy was bulletproof. In the end, Terrance Pesh had tested the proposition one too many times and bled to death on a bar floor with half a dozen .44 slugs in him. Not bulletproof at all, surprise, surprise. Like those Indians, Jimmy thought, the ghost dancers, who'd littered the ground at Wounded Knee in the shredded, bloody vests they'd believed would stop the cavalry's carbines. No one was bulletproof. But a man had to live as if he were, or he wasn't worth shit.

He gunned past an Oldsmobile, broke right two lanes, and went by a tractor trailer on the blind side, ignoring the horn as he cut back in front. Fuck 'em, Jimmy thought. Fuck 'em all. Today is a good day to die, was the other thing his father had always said. Some kind of thing from 'Nam. It had never made that much sense, coming from a man who thought he was bulletproof.

Mark stood unmoving for a long time, looking down at the dead pit bull. Not your usual fairy-tale rescue, Helen thought: The white knight wasn't supposed to find the dragon's watchdog slain in advance and the princess spattered with blood. It made for a tricky happily-ever-after, at best.

She sat on the couch with the gun in her lap, watching his face go through stunned disbelief, a transparent *What the fuck have I gotten myself into?* then dawning horror and, as the horror deepened, fear. The fear scared her, too. But it was beautiful, in its way. Because he didn't just turn and bolt. Maybe *that* was love, to be afraid of the same things, together. Jimmy had never been afraid of anything in his life.

Finally, after what seemed like an eternity, something like surrender settled on Mark's features. Something like resolve. He took a deep breath and let out a long controlled sigh, as if it were the amen of a prayer, then raised his eyes and met Helen's glance across the living room.

"You came," she said softly.

"Of course I came," he said. "I love you." He looked back down at Bubbles's bloody corpse, took another breath, and said, "Did *you*—?"

"Yeah."

"Jesus."

She put the gun down and stood up uncertainly. "There's still time to run."

He raised his eyes to hers again and actually smiled. Ruefully, gently, the smile she had adored from the moment she met him, the smile that seemed to have taken in everything broken and sick in her and forgiven it in advance. Embraced it, even, as you would embrace a weeping child, touching the tears away with a fingertip, turning the salt pain to mercy. "It was too late for me to run, from the first time I saw your face."

"It was too late for *me* to run, by the time I was twelve years old," Helen said. "I just never knew it until I met you."

He moved toward her at last, stepping around the pooled blood on the entryway floor and crossing the living room to take her in his arms. Helen buried her face in his chest. He still smelled like vanilla, she realized, breathing him in. She wondered if he would always smell like vanilla. *That* would be happily-ever-after.

"Have you . . . packed?" Mark asked, into her hair.

She pulled her head back and looked at him sharply. It

had never occurred to her to pack anything. There was nothing in her life worth carrying away, and nowhere to carry it to. "Wouldn't that be running, too?"

"It's not running to go home," Mark said.

Helen blinked, her eyes filling; she turned her face back into his body. *My God, my God, my God,* she thought, as if there were a God. *Thank you for this man.* It actually felt, for a moment at least, like everything was going to be all right. Mark had gotten there first. That was only the first of the necessary miracles. But maybe that was how love happened, beyond all expectation, beyond all reasonable hope, one miracle at a time. She wondered if he knew how to use a gun.

Rose parked in front of a corner store on Balboa just down from Forty-seventh. She was the first one there; the boys and their toys would be another fifteen minutes at least, coming from downtown, if they'd even managed to get themselves on the road yet. She sat listening to the cooling engine tick, feeling the edge coming on. That jitter, that nauseating little buzz that came in the wait before the action. The neighborhood was dead calm beneath the blanket of summer fog, a dank, gray midday torpor that only made the tension worse.

Jack had lived for moments like this, had always met the rising adrenaline eagerly, like an addict. He'd been a beat too ready—no, it wasn't even a beat, not even half a beat—to put his ass on the line, and it had always scared Rose a little. To call it trigger-happy was too much. It wasn't recklessness; it was something more subtle, and you could even make a case that it was just a ballsy cop's bravado. But she knew it was more than that. There had been something in Jack that had needed something to happen. Rose had never known a better detective; Jack had been a cop's cop, a consummate professional, and she'd learned just about everything she knew from him. For years she would have said that there wasn't a better man to have your back when the heat turned up. But she'd slowly and painfully come to realize that it wasn't so. Jack hadn't been happy enough with reality, in the end; he'd had to spice it just a little, to put his own pinch of danger into a situation. It skewed his reading of a situation almost indiscernibly, made him see the volatile elements just out of proportion and made him push them when he could have cooled them out. It wasn't something that showed in its pure form very often; but it showed when the stakes were life and death, in those weird, measureless moments when the guns were drawn and time seemed to move like a big slow balloon.

A garbage truck bulled past, startling her out of her reverie. Rose glanced at her watch, then pulled out her cell phone and punched Joshua's number on the speed-dial. As she'd suspected, they hadn't left the Hall of Justice yet.

"Fratello's in the crapper," he told her.

"So you guys could be another couple of hours."

"Five minutes. I swear. We're out of here in five minutes, with or without him."

"Well, I'm here."

"Don't do anything stupid."

"You know me, partner."

She could almost hear his smile. "That's why I said it."

"I'll see you soon, then. I'm in front of the corner store, on Balboa."

"Okay."

"Oh, and, Josh—"

"Yeah?"

"Could you bring the cat litter?"

"What?"

"There's a cat box and a bag of kitty litter in the coffee room. I forgot to bring it home with me when I brought Agatha."

"You're kidding, right?" She said nothing. "Oh, Rosie,

for Christ's sake. Where the hell am I going to put it? In the trunk with the shotguns?"

"That would be fine."

There was a moment's silence, and then Joshua sighed. "They told me it would be like this, working with a woman."

"You're da bomb, partner."

"Bite me," Joshua said fondly, before hollering, away from the mouthpiece, "Somebody go stick their head in the can and tell Fratello if he's not out of there in three minutes he can take the fucking train!"

"See you soon," Rose said.

"Sit tight, Rosie. I'm serious. There is no fucking hurry whatsoever on this thing."

"Yeah, yeah." She wanted to say something about Seamus and found that she couldn't. She realized that she was afraid of Joshua's reaction to the first decent conversation she'd had with her husband in months. As if saving her marriage were a kind of infidelity.

"What?" Joshua said, sensing her hesitation.

"Nothing," Rose said. "I'll see you soon, partner." She clicked off, feeling weirdly guilty, and sat restlessly for a moment, then got out of the car and went into the corner store, where she bought three cans of cat food, a little pink fuzzy cat toy on a string, and a cup of coffee. At the counter, on an impulse, she bought a box of Marlboro Lights as well.

Back on the sidewalk, she put the cat food in the car, set the coffee on the hood, and tore the cellophane off the cigarettes. Just one, she thought, pulling a Marlboro out and lighting up. Maybe two, just to pass the time until the rest of the team showed up. She knew she had to quit. She'd quit later, if she wasn't dead.

Jimmy hit the fog just past Daly City and slowed to eighty-five. He hated the fog; he always had, especially coming back into it from the real world where the summer sun shone. The near-perpetual coastal gray was like a circle of hell, the place where they sent sinners who had loved life's warmth too much, a dim realm where everything happened in a dank, dispirited slow motion and things made no noise when they fell. It felt like punishment, every time; it felt like Helen's moods.

He got off the freeway, skirted the zoo, and made his way north along the Great Highway toward Richmond. Despite the damping fog, the flame still burned in him, hot and clean and heartening. It had been great, finally telling that foreman to shove it. He hadn't even hit the guy, he'd counted to ten, as Helen always said he should.

She would like that. She'd laugh and say, "Good boy." Like he was a dog, like he'd plunged into a swamp after a duck she'd brought down and scrambled back out filthy and soaked with the bird in his teeth and laid it at her feet. "Good boy, Jimmy."

It was stupid, but he lived for that shit. Maybe he was nuts, but he just felt right, heading home. As he turned up Lincoln and then into the park at Forty-first, Jimmy even caught himself humming: "*She's once, twice, three times a lady . . .*"

Real cornball shit; what a sucker he was. But he loved that woman.

Helen packed underwear, her best panties and bras, all the stuff she'd never worn for anyone but herself. Most of her wardrobe was suitable only for a serial killer stalking men in bars, and she left it in the closet. When it came to normal life, she really didn't have a thing to wear. Maybe she'd shop at Kmart or something soon, with Mark in sheepish tow like a suburban husband, and she'd buy herself a bunch of Jaclyn Smith crap in soft pastels. Maybe she really would just settle into being an American girlfriend and cook a lot of pasta and watch TV. And maybe the moon would fall and the tides would fail to rise. Maybe it really was a fairy tale and somebody was going to wave a wand soon and make it all right.

She threw in a pair of her cheapest jeans and her toothbrush. It all fit into a Nordstrom's bag, with room left over for the gun. Mark stood by and watched, bemused, as she zipped the sack up.

"That's it?" he asked. He seemed more frightened by how little she was taking than he had by the slaughtered dog in the entryway.

"I'm thinking fresh start," Helen said.

The rest of the team finally showed up, Joshua alone in the lead car, Dick Burke and his asshole partner, Fratello, in a second vehicle, and Phil Russo and Dominic Alvarez right behind them. Everyone but Alvarez fired up a before-gunfire cigarette the second they hit the sidewalk; Dommie was trying to quit. Joshua gave Rose a disapproving look as she lit up another Marlboro, but held his tongue. He was still wearing the same rumpled clothes he'd worn the day before and looked haggard and grim, in need of sleep. They were all wearing their vests already, everyone bulky and awkward and a little self-conscious, like high school football players wearing their jerseys to class on game day. Rose took a vest of her own out of the trunk as they gathered around the hood of Burke's car to go over the plan. Joshua had brought the cat box, she noted, and the bag of kitty litter. She could have kissed him for that.

"Nice look, Dick," she told Burke, as she joined the rest of them. With his face swathed in bandages, he looked like a wombat with a nose guard.

"Fuck you, Rosie," he said, without heat. He had his game face on, like everyone else; they were all on the same team now.

"No hard feelings?" she said, not meaning it for a second.

Burke smiled, in the same spirit. "None whatsoever."

"The back doors on these Sunset places are hell to cover," Joshua said, ignoring the byplay, all business. He'd spread a block map out on the hood, with Rainey's house circled in red. "We'll have to come in through the house on the far side of the block to get back there at all, and every dog in the fucking neighborhood will be barking the second we start to move. Dommie, you'll cover that. Just badge the neighbor and go in through their place, and set up by their back door. You'll have to radio once you're in position. When we go, you move to cover the backyard."

"I'll bet they've got a fence with those little spikes on top," Dommie Alvarez griped. He was only five-eight, and it was easy to picture him getting hung up. "I hate those fucking spikes."

"Life is hard," Joshua agreed. "And watch out for dogs. Everyone got the memo on that right? If a Doberman or something comes after you, identify yourself as a police officer on official business and ask it to kindly step aside."

"And then shoot it," Fratello said, and they all laughed.

"Fratello, you've got the ram, on the front door. Rose and I will go in first, with Russo and Fratello following. Dick, you stay out front, in case they try to jump out the fucking window or something."

"I should be going in with Fratello," Burke said, offended.

"I'm afraid you'll give them a heart attack, with that nose thing," Joshua said. "We want to take these people alive." He looked around. "Any questions?"

"Any idea what kind of firepower these two pack?" Russo asked. He was a tall, pallid man, a bit undertakerish, with an acne-scarred horse face and a jaw like a cargo barge. He'd once kicked in the door on a suspect wanted for grand theft auto and had the guy open up on him with an

M-16, and he always asked about the suspects' armament now.

"Not much evidence of guns in their MO, but who knows?" Joshua said. "Rosie?"

Rose shrugged. "They are not nice people," she said. "Who knows?"

They were silent for a moment, contemplating that.

"I had a car thief once who carried a fucking M-16," Russo offered at last.

"We know, Russ," Joshua said.

Jimmy noted the Honda Accord parked in front of the house, but didn't give it a second thought. He set the truck's brake and went around to the passenger side to carefully slide the aquarium out. Jimmy didn't know what kind of fish that little blue thing Helen had brought home was, but the guy at the pet store had assured him that a twenty-gallon tank would be more than adequate for any kind of fish. The guy had tried to sell him the acrylic version, which was more expensive, but Jimmy had decided to stick with good old-fashioned glass. Things that didn't break made him nervous. The guy had also been pushing all kinds of pricey filtration systems, air pumps, heaters, and lights, but none of that made any sense to Jimmy. It seemed like twenty gallons of good water was enough for any damned fish.

He wrapped his arms around the tank and made his way slowly up the sidewalk. The front door wasn't locked, which was weird. He kicked it open and smelled the blood at once.

"Oh, Christ," he said.

Helen heard the front door open and waited. If it was the cops, there would be a rush of heavy footsteps and shouting. But there was only silence, which meant Jimmy.

Mark hadn't even heard it, which showed how innocent he really was. He should have been on red alert; he should have been jumping every time the house creaked, every time a car door slammed outside. But he was absurdly relaxed, standing there holding the fishbowl with the Blue Devil swimming around in it, asking her if she really wanted to leave her jewelry box behind, making sure she packed her tampons and perfume. He thought he was dealing with nothing more than a disgruntled, mildly abusive boyfriend who wasn't due home for several hours. He was unprepared for evil and fundamentally naïve. The pit bull with its brains blown out had given him pause, but not essentially damaged his sense that the world was a decent place and that love made it go around. Helen had been hoping to break him in slowly, if at all, to the full extent of what he had gotten himself into. It had even, briefly, seemed possible to her to just get into his car and go be Mrs. Mark, to wake from this nightmare life, splash some water on her face and set a pot of coffee brewing, and start clean. But it looked like she had run out of room to maneuver. She opened the Nordstrom's bag and took out the gun.

"Do you know how to use one of these?" she asked.

Mark smiled. "Why? Is there another dog?"

Rose sat beside Joshua in the lead car, parked beside a fire hydrant at the end of Rainey's block, waiting for Alvarez to check in by radio when he was set. Burke, Fratello, and Russo were in the car behind them, cigarette smoke coming out of three windows, but Joshua had taken the most recent Marlboro out of Rose's hand as soon as she tried to light up, and she hadn't argued with him. She realized that she actually treasured the frank intimacy of his silent insistence on the baby's interests, treasured him moving against her self-destructiveness with the tender authority of a lover.

The radio crackled and they both glanced up, but it was

just some random noise. Joshua took a cigarette out and put it between his lips unlit.

"I'll go in first," he said.

"It's my turn, Josh."

"Oh, come on Rosie, don't be greedy. I'll let you drive for the next week." She said nothing. "Scissors, paper, stone?"

"It's my turn, Josh," Rose insisted, and her partner wavered, then turned away and scowled out the window. She'd seen that same sullenness in Jack, near the end, the protectiveness beginning to turn stony. Things had gone way too far. She knew she had to tell him about Seamus, but she still couldn't make herself do it.

Jimmy took the stairs slowly, still carrying the aquarium as if it were a shield, as if it were a bulletproof glass box with his heart in it. The bedroom door was open; they hadn't even bothered to close it. He stepped into the doorway expecting to find them naked and entwined, which would have made it easy, but they were both standing beside the unmade bed, fully clothed, with Helen's packed bag. The guy was nothing, a nothing in jeans and a crew-neck shirt, with dishwater blond hair in a preppy cut, all crisp edges, and insipid blue eyes, wide now with fear. He was ordinary, as they all were ordinary. Helen believed that ordinary was what she really wanted, someone harmless, mild, and safe, someone useless, right up until the moment she realized that she didn't.

The nothing was clutching a fishbowl with that ridiculous little fish in it. Jimmy met his bland blue gaze and gestured toward the fishbowl with the aquarium, his biceps flexing with the movement, the snake tattoo flaring. "Looks like mine's bigger."

The nothing shifted uneasily. "I don't want any trouble, man."

"I reckon it's a little too late for that," Jimmy said. He set the aquarium down and turned to Helen, who was leveling a gun at him. Jimmy recognized the Vietnam-era Colt .45, the one he'd bought with a fake ID in Norfolk, the one they'd never found after he shot her father with it. She'd taken it out of his hand that night as he'd stood over Parker Rainey and told him she'd get rid of it, and he'd always thought she had. They'd both agreed it was dangerous to have a gun in the house, and Helen had always been too twitchy to use one anyway. But she was holding the .45 steady now, cop style, with both hands, as if she'd been practicing.

Well, she had been, of course: she'd just practiced on Bubbles.

"I don't know what that dog ever did to you, that you had to go and do a thing like that," Jimmy said. "That was just plain mean."

"Just turn around and walk away, Jimmy," Helen said. "It's over now. It's finished."

"Is it? Damn, that was easy. Who knew it would be that easy?"

"Don't make me shoot you, too. You know I'll do it."

Jimmy met her eyes, her sea-green eyes, and shrugged.

"It's as good a day to die as any, I reckon," he said. He started toward her, as amazed as he'd ever been by how beautiful she was, and wondering if his daddy had ever really believed he was bulletproof.

She'd thought it would be just like shooting Bubbles, but it wasn't. Helen hesitated before she pulled the trigger, and had time to feel the unexpected sting of tears, and to wonder if that was love, or some twisted sense of indebtedness, or just plain lack of guts, before she squeezed it. She squeezed as hard as she had for Bubbles, aiming for the chest this time because she was afraid she'd miss the head, and bracing herself for the boom. But the trigger didn't budge. She'd put the safety on when Mark showed up. She'd actually felt safe, like a fool, for the first time in her life.

As she groped with her thumb for the little knob, Jimmy took the gun out her hand.

"Where did you hide it?" he asked, in a tone of perfectly normal domestic curiosity, as if he were asking what she'd made for dinner.

"With the cleaning supplies. Behind the Murphy's Oil Soap."

"Smart," Jimmy conceded, hefting the .45 and clicking off the safety.

Helen looked at Mark. His eyes were enormous, the pupils dilated until there was almost no blue visible. He'd seen her finger whiten on the trigger, she knew, and she waited for him to flinch, to deny her now, to turn away from what she was.

"I love you," she told him.

Mark met her gaze briefly, then shook his head, almost apologetically. It was too much for him, she saw. She felt the searing disappointment, and the old familiar rage. But it *was* too much. She could see that now. It had always been too much.

Jimmy was still standing there with the gun, not pointing it anywhere in particular, but not putting it away either. Mark hesitated, then reached for Helen. He took her arm with his free hand and eased her up against him, the way he had when they had danced in the bar, moving her, guiding them around Jimmy, toward the door. Helen held her breath as they walked away, but Jimmy didn't shoot them in the back, the way he'd shot her father. He just stood there watching them, looking dangerous and amused.

At the door, Mark released her and paused, to let her go through first.

"You got nowhere to go, Helen," Jimmy said quietly.

"There ain't nowhere out of where we've been. You know that."

Helen hesitated. She could see the stairs through the open door. Maybe she had nowhere to go, maybe she had somewhere. She really didn't know.

"She's got somewhere to go," Mark said. "She's going home. With me."

"She's already home, friend," Jimmy said. His arm came up, quick and easy, the way Helen had seen it when he was shooting cans in the woods. He fired once and the fishbowl exploded in Mark's hand. Helen screamed and Jimmy shifted the gun and fired again, still as casually as if he were picking off cans, shattering the aquarium at their feet.

Mark met Helen's eyes, amazingly calm, trying to comfort her with his look. He still didn't believe it, she saw. He thought Jimmy was just throwing a macho fit, a last temper tantrum. He would never understand a man who could kill someone, not in a million years. But she could see Jimmy's eyes, and she knew her man; and as his arm came up and he aimed again, Helen stepped in front of Mark. Because Jimmy was right, of course. There was nowhere else to go.

The bleat on the radio was unintelligible, but there was no mistaking the note of panic in Dommie Alvarez's voice. Joshua and Rose both snapped forward in their seats; Joshua, getting to the mike first, pushed the button.

"Say again, Dommie," he said. "Slow and easy, man. We're not reading you. Over."

"Shots fired, for Christ's sake! *Shots fired!*"

"Jesus," Rose exclaimed, and reached for her door handle. Joshua dove across the front seat to grab her sleeve and stop her.

"*Who* is shooting?" he bellowed into the radio.

"How the fuck do I know?!"

"Are they shooting at *you?*"

"No, fuck no, it's *inside!* Inside the fucking house! Two—*shit*, there's another one!—make it three shots, repeat, three shots, from inside the house, upstairs."

"Josh, let's *go,* for Christ's sake!" Rose snapped.

He glared at her, but didn't let go of her arm. "Hold your position and cover the back," he told Alvarez. "We're going in. Do you copy? *We are going into the house.* Over."

"Copy that. I'll hold here. Watch your head, man, whatever's going off in there sounds like a fucking howitzer."

Joshua let go of Rose and she flung herself against the door and was out onto the sidewalk, pulling her 9mm from the shoulder holster as she went. Burke, Fratello, and Russo were scrambling out of the car behind them, Burke and Russo both carrying shotguns, Fratello with his service revolver drawn. Joshua grabbed a shotgun as he got out of the driver's side of the lead car, and all five of them sprinted toward the house.

"Same plan, on the wing," Joshua hollered as they ran. "Rose and me in first, Fratello and Russo next. Dick, keep the sidewalk covered, and call for some fucking backup. Dommie says the shots are from upstairs, people, we're going *upstairs—*"

*Are those her ribs through which the sun
Did peer, as through a grate?*

The surprise was that there was no pain. No pain, no confusion, and, finally, no fear. Helen marveled at how quiet it had gotten. And how beautiful. It was so easy, so perfectly simple. It was like love, like an explosion in your chest, one deft blow to the heart, shattering everything to make everything clear.

She'd fallen back into Mark's embrace and he'd never even let her hit the floor. He'd caught her, held her, and laid her on the unmade bed. Her mother would have loved the irony of that: the one time in her life she hadn't made the bed and she was going to die in it. But how sweet it was, superior to every irony, the unforeseen benediction of everything somehow being just right at last.

She knew that this was what Cora had felt, when her mother's eyes turned peaceful at the end: free. Free of the vacuum cleaner's roar, of the squeak of the rag on surfaces that could never be clean enough, free of the dead marriage and the living hell of sustaining the lie through sheer relentless effort, free at last of the ongoing griefs and the compromises and the daily defeats. It was as simple, in the end, as dying in the arms of someone who loved you. All the detritus and debris of a wasted life vanished into a perfect mercy.

Helen smiled and tried to tell Mark, who shushed her gently.

And is that Woman all her crew?

Jimmy was still standing there with the gun dangling at his side, stricken, like a kid who'd just hit a baseball through a church window. She wanted to tell him it was all right. No hard feelings. She did love him, Helen realized. From this quiet lucid place, it turned out that she loved everyone. She could see she always had. It had just gotten all fucked up somehow. But they'd done the best they could.

She tried to say that to Jimmy, to give him the comfort of that, but the words weren't coming out, just the warm, salty blood. Like Jesus, she thought. No words necessary. My blood is my love. For those with ears to hear.

Is that a Death? and are there two?
Is Death that Woman's Mate?

"It's going to be all right," Mark told her. "Just hang on. The ambulance will be here soon."

Her eyes came back to his blue, blue eyes, those pure, cool eyes the color of a glacial vein. Her father's eyes. Had she told him, that she'd finally seen the love in her father's eyes, in him? While they were dancing, Helen thought. She must have told him while they were dancing.

"I love you," she said, though the words weren't happening anymore, just the deepening silence that was so much, so much more beautiful, and she would have reached to touch his cheek.

Rose got to the front door half a step ahead of Joshua and paused for a beat to let him take his position. When he was set on the other side of the door, the shotgun at port arms, she met his eyes and he nodded, *Go,* and she kicked the door open and went in, past the dead dog, glancing quickly left and right and starting straight up the stairs. Joshua was right behind her and behind him Fratello and Russo peeled away to either side to make sure the downstairs was clear.

From near the top she could see the open bedroom door and the blood on the floor. She hit the landing and it was two steps into the doorway and she came in hard with her gun level, hollering, "Police! Freeze! Don't fucking *move!*" and wishing the baby was far enough along to be saved if she died here and there were three of them, like one of those pop-up exercises at the training academy, the shoot–don't-shoots, but only one of them had a gun and Rose covered him and said again, loud and hard and clear, "Don't fucking move."

Joshua filled the doorway behind her, the shotgun at ready, and she eased to the left to let him in. The floor was slick with blood and water, and crunchy with shattered glass. It was Rainey on the bed, and she looked gone. The guy holding her was harmless, his face streaked with tears, a civilian.

"Drop the gun," Rose told the one with the .45, and as he didn't move, *"Drop the fucking gun."* She could feel Joshua beside her like a sapling bent to the ground, ready to snap back up, and she said, "Hold your fire, Joshua. Nobody else needs to die here."

The guy met her eyes, a quiet, mournful look, ashen with sadness and resignation, but uncrazed and even lucid, and Rose thought they were through it. But he still didn't drop the .45 and she said again, more calmly, "Just put the gun down, mister. Just put it down. It's over."

"Not just yet," he said, almost regretfully, in a soft drawl, and he brought the gun up toward them, moving precisely and very, very slowly, with infinite care, as if he had all the time in the world, and there was nothing left to do but what he wanted done.

22

LIEUTENANT ALEXANDRA THANH ARRIVED in a commandeered police cruiser with the sirens screaming, within ten minutes of the shooting. She had left the Hall of Justice when the first "Shots fired" came over the radio. She took charge of the scene with her usual placid precision, overseeing the emergency medical personnel as. they pronounced both Helen Rainey and James Pesh dead at the scene, setting up a line to keep the media at bay, having someone call Animal Control to deal with the body of the dog, personally taking the first statements from the entry team, and making sure that Rose and Joshua surrendered their weapons in meticulous order for the inevitable shooting board review. The two of them had fired simultaneously and both guns had delivered what would have been fatal wounds, but Sandi Thanh assured them it was a slam-dunk righteous shoot. The suspect had been armed, had just killed someone else, and was aiming his weapon at them with obvious intent to use it. They even had a witness whose only regret was that he hadn't shot Jimmy Pesh himself ten minutes earlier and who said that he thought Rose and Joshua had held off firing a little too long, if anything. The first thing Mark Price had done when the action stopped was paw through the shards of the fishbowl by the door and pick up the Blue Devil fish. He'd cut himself retrieving it and was clutching the glass it swam in now with bandaged hands.

After Sandi Thanh had accepted Rose's gun in its shoulder holster and taken her statement, the two women stood for a moment in the kitchen, where Sandi was staging her paperwork on the table.

"Hell of a day," Thanh said, more conversationally.

Rose gave her a small smile. "I've had better."

"Can you believe it, I left my purse at the office. I don't suppose you've got an extra tampon with you?"

Rose hesitated, then said, "Actually, I'm in the middle of missing my third period in a row."

"Ah!" Thanh said. "I'd . . . wondered."

Rose laughed. "Oh, come on."

"No, really. The trash can in the women's room has been suspiciously clear. And the way you hit Dick Burke? That's hormones, baby."

"That's Dick Burke being a horse's ass."

"That, too," Thanh allowed. "We all know that. But it's not like people punch him every day."

Rose conceded the point with a shrug.

"So, um—congratulations?"

"Yeah," Rose said. "Thanks."

"Seamus must be thrilled," Thanh said, still tentative.

Rose hesitated, then said, "It took him a while. But he seems to be working up to it."

Thanh studied her for a moment, her dark eyes quiet. "Let's talk soon about how we're going to work it, with you taking leave."

"It's not a big deal," Rose said.

"The hell it's not," Thanh said. One of the guys from the coroner's team was approaching, probably wanting to know whether they could move the bodies out yet. Thanh held up one slim hand to hold him off for a moment, leaned closer, and said, "Go home now, Rosie. Get some rest. I'll deal with the paperwork and the brass, for the moment."

"Okay. Thanks, Sandi."

"And don't say anything to the media out there, for God's sake. Refer them to my office for any statements. I mean it, Rosie, not a word."

"Actually, I was thinking of just flipping them off again."

Thanh gave her a quick look to make sure she was kidding, then smiled. Rose smiled back and turned to go. But the lieutenant touched her arm to stop her and said quietly, "It was a righteous shoot, Rose. There was nothing else you could do."

"I'll keep telling myself that," Rose said.

Thanh held her eyes, a warm firm look, and turned away to deal with the coroner's guys.

Rose took the opportunity to slip away to the bathroom and throw up. It was hard to sort out morning sickness from her sense of futile carnage. She could not forget the look in Jimmy Pesh's eyes, just before he'd brought his gun up.

When she came out of the bathroom, a young uniform cop was standing nearby, trying to look casual.

"Are you all right, ma'am?" he asked.

"Did Lieutenant Thanh tell you to check on me?"

He hesitated, then nodded.

"Tell the lieutenant I'm fine," Rose said.

She kept her head down on the way out through the bloody entryway, where Perry was painstakingly photographing the dead pit bull in situ, and found Joshua on the porch trying to light a cigarette. His hands were shaking so badly he couldn't do it. Rose took the lighter from him and cupped her hand around his cigarette to touch the flame to it. Her own hands were shaking, too, but not as much.

"Sandi sent me home," he said.

"Me too."

"You want a ride?"

"I've got my car around the corner."

"Oh, yeah, right."

They stood quietly for a moment, looking at the media people milling beyond the yellow caution tape the uniforms had strung across the sidewalk. The street was crowded with illegally parked TV vans, and the neighbors had all come out to watch the show.

"You fucked me up, with that story about Jack Brady shooting too soon because he'd fallen for you," Joshua said at last. "I held off about half a second in there, watching that guy's gun start to come up, thinking maybe I was misreading it, that maybe I—"

"Don't say it, Josh."

"—just loved you too much. That maybe I'd lost perspective too."

Rose was silent, trying to formulate a response and failing, and failing again, until finally it seemed that her silence itself was a response, and Joshua blinked and looked down at his shoes, then took a drag off the cigarette and blew the smoke toward the media vans.

"I should call Seamus," Rose said at last, almost apologetically. "This must be all over the TV by now."

Their eyes met.

"Yeah," Joshua said. "I guess you should."

"He'll be worried sick."

"Of course he will."

"Walk me to my car?" Rose asked; and, mock-coaxing, as he hesitated, "I could use some help with the kitty litter."

Joshua gave her a grudging smile. "That fucking kitty litter." He took a last drag off the cigarette and ground it out beneath his heel. "Yeah, let's get out of here."

They went down the steps to the sidewalk, ducked under the tape together, and waded through the cameras and microphones, shaking their heads as they went. The last reporter gave up on them halfway down the block, and they walked on in silence until they reached the department-issue car at the end of the street. Joshua opened the trunk, took out the cat box and the bag of litter, and set it on the sidewalk for her.

"Thanks, partner," Rose said. "I can take it from here. I'm just up the block there."

"No problem," Joshua said.

She bent to pick up the cat box and litter and they stood for a moment in silence, neither quite willing to say goodbye. Down the block, amid a flurry of firing flashbulbs and cameramen scrambling for position, the animal-control team came out of the house, carrying the dog's body covered with a yellow tarp on a jury-rigged stretcher.

"What a fucking circus," Joshua said sadly.

"Yeah." Rose hesitated. "It was a righteous shoot, Josh. We fired at the same time."

"Yeah," he said. "Both of us, half a second late."